Ten Nobodies

(and their somebodies)

Other novels by Martin Drapkin:

Poor Tom

The Cat Tender

Now and at the Hour

Ten Nobodies

(and their somebodies)

Martin Drapkin

Three Towers Press
Milwaukee, Wisconsin

Published by Three Towers Press,
An imprint of HenschelHAUS Publishing, Inc.
Milwaukee, Wisconsin
www.HenschelHAUSbooks.com

ISBN: 978159598-981-9
LCCN: 2023951305

Printed in the United States of America

Table of Contents

Foreword

GROWING UP in boring Milwaukee, my favorite times were visiting my Aunt Sylvie and cousin Solly in New York City and then, after Solly graduated from Erasmus Hall High School, in Miami Beach. I was a few years older than Solly and always considered him a basic nothinghead; he'd never done anything to speak of, never went to college, and had no ambition that I could see. I figured he'd end up as boring and as much of a nobody as I. But I was wrong.

I remember that when he first moved to Miami Beach, Solly pissed and moaned about leaving Brooklyn, grousing that his mom had *shlepped* him to Florida just because she wanted to land herself a rich husband. But I guess her dreams didn't work out too well, and she wound up working as a waitress at Wolfie's, a well-known Jewish deli—"pink palace of overstuffed sandwiches," as Solly put it. Solly worked there, too, for a while, as a busboy. It was there that he met the man who, he said, had a big influence on him—Meyer Lansky, the famous yid gangster. Solly went on and on about Lansky: how the old man hired him to be his research assistant to look up, at the public library, answers to trivia questions for him and his brother, Jake, and their alter kocker brunch buddies at Wolfie's. He told me how obsessed those guys were with *The Godfather Part II*. "That old man," Solly said, shaking his head. "Tough? Oh, my God! A *mensch*, he was. And he showed me how to be."

The surprising thing was how far Solly went, and quickly. Just a few years after they moved to Miami Beach I visited him and he took me to the Eden Roc, one of those huge hoity-toity hotels on Collins Avenue, where he worked. I never learned exactly what he did, but he dressed well, favoring pastel silk shirts and Italian-leather shoes, and spent a lot of time on the veranda out back, overlooking the beach, with a small group of older guys, mostly Jewish but not all, who smoked fat, black cigars and drank banana daiquiris and played gin rummy. When it was windy, they held the cards down on the corners of the table with rubber bands. Solly kibitzed around with these guys, and it was clear they liked him. By then Aunt Sylvie had stopped working at Wolfie's and was hitched to some short, bald Jewish guy with thick black-rimmed glasses. She sported a gold ring with the biggest rock I've ever seen. I felt sorry for her new husband, though; Aunt Sylvie had a temper and a mouth on her—*vey iz mir!*—and tongue-lashed that poor bald bastard on a regular basis.

Solly's success was apparently due to his relationship with Mr. Lansky, as he always called him, and with Jake too. That's what he said. How, I don't know.

So that got me to thinking about nobodies like Solly working for or otherwise serving famous or well-known people like Lansky. I started doing some research and was quite fortunate to uncover the narratives that appear herein. All of these muckety-mucks that the nobodies worked for or served interest me one way or another—Shakespeare, of course; the great Lewis Carroll, whose latter days young Mimsy brightened a bit; Gertrude Stein and Alice B. Toklas, fascinating women, for whom the slim-hipped Antoinette worked for one fateful evening; poor fragile Marilyn Monroe, seeing her sometime foster mother, Jean, for the first time in twenty years; Davy Crockett, certainly, ever since the old Walt Disney TV series with Fess Parker; and that long-haired pretty boy Custer and his silly but famous "last stand" at the Little Bighorn. I got a kick out of Buffalo Hump Woman's story about her and the general "making the beast with two backs." I'd known a little about Anne Bonny, the fierce but insomniac pirate, but learned a lot more from Mose's story of his brief but tempestuous time with her aboard the ship *Revenge*. And corpulent William Howard Taft, who never wanted to be president but, according to his outsized press aide, Louie, did it to please his ambitious wife, Nellie. And certainly the great Vince Lombardi. Growing up in Wisconsin in the 1960s, I was, of course, a huge Green Bay Packers fan. I'd heard that Lombardi loved Paul Hornung and Max McGee, two of his famous players, but until seeing Percy's story I had no idea about the coach's supposed pathological envy of their erotic adventures and successes.

Solly read the stories that I'd uncovered and asked if I wanted his about meeting Mr. Lansky at Wolfie's.

"Oh, *absolutely*," I said.

A Muse to William Shakespeare

I SERVED AS A SEXTON at Holy Trinity, a little country church in Stratford-upon-Avon in England, for many years. Later, I also served as a sort of muse, as 'twere, for the poet and actor Will Shakespeare. I was an aging, corpulent, white-haired widower when first I met Shakespeare. My wife, Beatrice, had died in the horrid plague of 1592 and after that it was just Jack, my three-legged hound, and me.

Beatrice was buried in the little cemetery behind the church. I'd dug every grave there for the last fifty-two years, but not hers. That I couldn't do. Since her death, Jack and I'd made our way to the grave-yard most evenings, usually about an hour before sunset. It was our favorite time of day, and had been Beatrice's. We'd sit quietly on a small patch of grass, the two of us, enjoying the evening breeze and listening to the birds chattering, gossiping. Well, I listened. Jack paid the birds little heed; fat and old like me, he was worn-out, had little energy, and was in any case single-mindedly focused on just two things: begging for cheese parings or pieces of bread which he would then practically inhale, and watching for me to nod off for a second so that he could stick his ugly snout into my sack and steal such treasures himself.

I met Shakespeare in mid-April, 1595. It was a lovely spring evening in the churchyard, balmy and bright, and we were just finishing our usual supper of cheese, bread and, for me, wine. I was particularly missing Beatrice; the pesky omnipresent sparrows—like Jack, ever hoping for a morsel or two of bread—had always amused her so. "Oh, Horatio, I could watch them for hours," she'd said more than once. "They have such energy!" She was buried less than a score of yards from where we sat, and Jack and I found her spirit presence comforting. Well, I did anyway. As for Jack, I couldn't say; he only occasionally displayed emotion, but I believe he missed her. Although Beatrice had gotten him as a puppy, his left foreleg hopelessly shattered by a misplaced snare, and had cared for him and doted on him—constantly

1

petting and kissing him and scratching him behind the ears and calling him "my darling boy" and "my beautiful prince" and giving him treat upon treat from the table until he swelled up into the disgusting tub of blubber that he now was—he'd been indifferent to her, never seemingly grateful for her care and kindness, expecting solicitation as his due. Yet after Beatrice's death, he'd gone into a month-long funk, barely eating and now and again whining and thrashing about in his sleep. I, too, had reacted poorly to her passing.

After we'd eaten and I'd finished most of my flagon of wine, I leaned back against a big chestnut tree and took from my sack a long bone I'd retrieved earlier that day from the edge of the graveyard. "Tell me, Jack," I said, holding it close to his snout and letting him sniff, "who do you suppose this belonged to? Mayhap a great buyer of land, with his statutes, his recognizances, his fines, his double vouchers, his recoveries? *Ha!* Will his vouchers vouch him no more of his purchases than the ... " Just then Jack raised his hoary head, sniffed the air, and growled loudly. "Peace, ye fat guts," I scolded. "How now, wool-sack, what mutter you?"

I heard high-pitched laughter and turned to see a balding, middle-aged man with bright blue eyes holding the hands of two blond children, a boy and a girl, both of whom looked to be about ten years of age. "Sirrah," the man called out, "how doth the dog offend thee for you to chastise him so?"

"Who, he?" I answered, rubbing the top of Jack's head. "Why, sir, the cur's very existence offends me heartily. Indeed, wherein is he good, but to taste cheese and eat it? Wherein industrious, but in larceny? Wherein slothful, but in everything? Wherein worthy, but in nothing? Nay, sir, he is but a scurvy companion. And yet, 'a will do for one such as I."

The man laughed again. "Why," he said, "'tis a worthy reply. My name, sir, is Will Shakespeare, and these my twins, the fruit of my loins, Hamnet and Judith."

"Horatio, sir, and your humble servant. And this tripoded knave is Jack. Where are thy manners, Jack? Canst not welcome our guests?" At that, my dog, inexplicably showing more energy than he had in the last three years, leaped up and hobbled over to the boy and rubbed against him and licked his hand and gazed up at his face adoringly. The child, giggling, let go his father's hand and bent down to embrace Jack. He hugged him around the neck and then scratched him behind his ears exactly—*exactly!*—as Beatrice had done so often over the years. Jack loved it; his big brown eyes warmed and softened, and I swear that he smiled. He leaned against the young man, and even licked his cheeks.

"Father," Hamnet said, "he loves me! Can we not keep him?"

"Nay," Will answered, "for he belongeth to this good gentleman. Is't not so, sirrah?"

"Not so, m'lord. The mongrel belongs to none but his maker, whosoe'er that might be. 'Tis true he follows me day and night, roguish pestilence as he is, but that was ever his wont. I own him not, nor he me."

"Why, then," the man said, "if he is not yours then mayhap we will take him to abide with us. My son seems to favor the old fellow."

"Nay, sir, 'twill not do. Though the ill-bred ruffian vexes me daily, yet we are strangely attached, he and I." I paused. "Would not the young lady like to greet poor Jack as well?"

The man bent down to look into his daughter's eyes. "Judith," he said, very gently. "Would you like to make friends with Jack? He seems to like Hamnet. I think he'd like you too. Come, child, exchange greetings with the fellow."

Judith looked at her father and then at Jack, who was still submitting most willingly to Hamnet's caresses. Her lower lip began quivering and she started to sob. She put her arm around her father's neck and buried her face into his shoulder.

"Judith," Will said, "pray tell, what's the matter?"

"Oh, father!" she answered, sniffling. "He hath but three legs! Oh, the poor creature. I feel so *sorry* for him!"

Just then the creature in question hopped over to Judith and rubbed his head against her side and then licked her hand. At first she seemed scared, and backed away. Then she smiled, just a bit, and allowed Jack to slurp at her fingers.

"You see," her father said, "he's a friendly fellow indeed. His legs will serve, though they be fewer than most. Tush, child, tush. Hamnet, would you and your sister play with Sir Jack by the wood for a time whilst I converse with this good gentleman? With, of course, your permission, sir."

3

Sitting next to me, Will picked up the bone that Jack and I had been discussing. He studied it intensely for perhaps half a minute, from top to bottom. "So," he said, "this is what is left, you say, of a great buyer of land, a man of great note. Indeed, to this end shall we all come, mighty or lowly. Is't not so?"

I offered him some bread and cheese, which he accepted, and a cup of wine. "I suppose," I said, shrugging my shoulders. "'Tis our fate. Your grand lady and your paltry gravedigger, the same lonely ground awaits both. It awaits you, too, sir, some day, and Jack and me as well. But I hope not too soon for any of us." I took the bone from him and considered it. "Yea, sir, this might well be the arm of a great buyer of land, or mayhap that of a renowned lawyer. *Ha!* Where be his quiddities and quillities now, his cases, his tenures, and his tricks? Why does he suffer a fat and insignificant knave such as I to wave about his limb so disrespectfully and not tell me of his action of battery? Or perchance 'tis the appendage of a painted-faced harlot who has served the citizens of the township for many a good year and now, weary and back aching, has gone to her well-deserved long sleep." I paused, rubbed the bone against my cheek and kissed the end of it. "Goodnight, sweet princess, and flights of angels serenade thee in thy rest."

Will's eyes brightened and he laughed again, a high-pitched laugh more like a silly adolescent girl's than a grown man's. He slapped his knee twice, hard. "Oh, that's good!" he squealed. "'Goodnight, sweet princess ... ' I love that! 'Where be his quiddities and quillities now?' Why, sir, thou art a fair philosopher indeed. But tell me truly, Horatio, whose is't?"

"Nay, sir, I know not." I paused to belch, and not softly; since Beatrice's passing, my digestive system—never very good—had ceased functioning at all well, and I'd become a great emitter of noxious gases both north and south. Same with Jack. Thank God nobody lived with us; no one could. "Oh, excuse me, good sir. 'Tis a travesty to grow old. Now, as to your query. Marry, sir, this could e'en be the forearm of great Julius Caesar, could it not? Imperious Caesar, dead and turning to clay, whereupon we might well make good use of him, perchance to stop a beer barrel or to patch a wall t' expel the winter's flaw. Why, sir, to such base uses may we all return. Ha!"

Will laughed again. "I' good faith, Horatio, I like well your wit. 'Imperious Caesar,' indeed. Yet why may *not* imagination trace the noble dust of Caesar until he find it stopping a bunghole? But tell me, sir, how long hast thou been a gravemaker?"

"Why, I have been sexton here, man and boy, for more than fifty years."

"Ah. Death to you is then no stranger. But teach me of thy trade. How long will a man lie i' the earth ere he rot?"

"Faith, sir, if he be not rotten before he dies, as many are these days, he will last you some eight or nine years. A tanner will last you nine, for, sir, his hide is so tanned with his trade that he will keep out water longer. And your water, sir, is the great decayer of your vile dead body."

Shakespeare nodded and seemed lost in thought for a few minutes. I heard his children by the wood, playing with my dog, giggling. It had been a long while since I'd heard the laughter of children. It was a pleasant sound—that and the birds in the nearby bushes and trees.

"Death!" Will said. "That dark spirit. A sure physician he is, sir. A sure physician, indeed."

"Tut, man. All that lives must die, passing through nature to eternity. 'Tis no great matter. Why, we owe God a death; pay thy debt this year, and thou wilt be quit for the next. Is't not so? The ripeness, sir, is all … But no more of that, and 't please you. May we not consider happier thoughts on this soft evening?"

Shakespeare nodded and smiled briefly, bravely, but continued to stare glumly at the bone. He turned it over and over and again studied it intensely, his brow furrowed and his blue eyes squinted. As for me, I felt tired from all this unaccustomed talking; except for Jack, I spent most of my time alone and, though I missed Beatrice horribly, had grown content with the limited company.

Just then Jack and the children returned. I could tell that my dog was tired too, but happy. His new friends had worn him out. He plopped down beside me, panting loudly, while the twins rested quietly next to their father. Judith laid her head in Will's lap. "How, now, my sweet creature of bombast?" I greeted Jack, rubbing his head and scratching behind his ears, endeavoring to approximate Hamnet's technique. "Why, you are as fat as butter, and all your breath is ta'en away. Jack, thou art too much cloyed with fat meat. Amend thy ways, and soon, else wilt thou explode and litter the churchyard with thy surfeited and disgusting guts."

As was his wont, Jack paid me little heed. He glanced toward Hamnet and Judith, happily, and then closed his eyes and soon was snoring.

"Father," Hamnet said, tugging at Will's sleeve, "why does that man insult his dog so? Will he not hurt poor Jack's feelings?"

Will smiled. "Nay, my son," he said. "The good gentleman is not serious. He but jests; it is a sort of game. Is't not so?"

"'Tis somewhat true, young man," I replied. "I joke with the fellow, but also do what I must to keep him humble. An' I did not, his self-opinion would be so inflated that there would be no abiding him."

"Well," Will said, giggling, "thou knowest best. In faith, sirrah, thou hast a pretty wit and a scathing tongue. Why, I heretofore considered myself a master of invective, but I see now that I am but an apprentice. I shall store up thy golden words and use them anon, thief as I am. But, sir, twilight approaches and we must take our leave of you."

I stretched and yawned. "You cannot, sir," I grunted, waving my hand dismissively, "take from me anything I would more willingly part withal."

He grinned and extended his hand, which I grasped and shook. "Well," he said, "this has been most interesting. I hope that we shall meet again, sage professor, so that I may learn from you further. Farewell, Master Jack. Sir, adieu. Children, say goodbye."

I DID NOT SEE Shakespeare again for more than a year. I was told by one of the parishioners that he spent most of his time in London, where he worked with a renowned acting company. That was the first I learned of his profession. And when next I saw him, it was not on the happiest of occasions.

It was in late August of 1596, a blistering hot Tuesday afternoon, and Jack and I were taking a midday nap when one of the deacons rapped on my cottage door and told me to prepare a grave for a child's burial next morning. "What child?" I asked. When he mentioned the name, Jack—and I swear on my dead wife's head this is true—who the previous moment had been sound asleep and snoring like a sow, snapped awake and commenced whimpering and shaking as if ague-struck. Nor could I do anything to calm him for the better part of an hour, when finally he curled himself into a pathetic ball in the far corner of the room, near the woodpile, his face to the wall, and lay unmoving.

In my years as sexton at Stratford, I'd buried many children. Indeed, what with disease and pestilence rampant, I wager that as many as one in four of the queen's subjects never reached adolescence. But this passing struck me harder than any. Though I'd met Hamnet only that once, he'd touched my heart. Jack's too, apparently.

At the funeral and burial next morning, I saw Shakespeare but didn't speak to him. He and his family were, of course, awash in their grief. Poor Judith was inconsolable—sobbing and trembling, wringing her little hands, and saying over and over, "Oh, Hamnet, my sweet brother, thou'lt come no more. Never! *Never!*" At one point, as everyone recited the "Our Father," Will looked toward me, our eyes locked, and we nodded to each other.

That night, I considered getting drunk. It had been four years since I'd so contemplated, but now I felt like it. The last time I'd felt similarly was shortly after Beatrice's death. That was the worst time of my life; I'd coped well enough with her illness and helped her with her dying the best I could, but then after a month or so alone, thinking of her hourly, I nearly fell apart. At night I'd lie abed, tossing about, finally falling asleep but then popping awake in the wee hours and unable to get back to sleep. It was all I could do to get out of bed each morning, and some mornings I couldn't even do that. Oh, I went through the motions of living my little life, doing my work, but it was a major effort. My world was for a time gray, colorless, devoid of pleasure or seasoning; the little things that had given me pleasure—even the sparrows flittering in the trees—now were strange as a barely-recallable dream. I'd found my only solace in wine—it was how I could escape temporarily from the heaviness of my self—but feared letting myself overindulge. After a few months my deep gloom lifted of its own accord, somehow, and after that I was myself again and had been, more or less, since—except for a day or a few days now and again when the black mood would envelop me yet again.

"'Tis a rotten world we live in," I told Jack. "A world filled with thorns and vipers."

Then I saw Will two days after his son's burial. Jack and I had as usual made our way to the churchyard at day's end, and were about to enjoy our customary evening repast. But before we did, I strolled over to poor Hamnet's grave to pay my respects and was surprised to see Shakespeare there already. He was squatting at the very edge, his face in his hands, rocking back and forth slowly. Not wishing to intrude on his grief, I started to walk away but Jack, insensitive lout, hobbled right to him and butted his head against Will's left arm. Startled, he jumped up. "A thousand pardons, sir," I said. "The cur knows not his manners. He ... "

"Nay," Will interrupted, "I am glad to see thee. You too, Sir Jack."

"Good my lord, how does your honor for this many a day?" As soon as I said it, I knew it was a foolish question; how, after all, should he be?

He looked at the ground, at the flat stone marking the grave. "Why," he said, "well. I am well. That is ... I am ... I am ... " At that his chin began to tremble a bit and then his whole body began to shake and he started to sob, huge wracking spasms overwhelming him. "Oh, GOD!" he cried out. "My God! How couldst thou *do* this to me? Oh *Hamnet!* HAMNET!"

I put my hands on his shoulders and held him to me. "There," I said. "There now. Go ahead. To weep is to make less the depth of grief." He allowed himself to lean against my bulk, his head on my shoulder, and vented his sorrow for perhaps three minutes. I suspected that this was the first time he'd cried over his son, such was the extent of his catharsis. He'd probably felt the need to be stoic for others. I was glad to be there for him, recalling how alone I'd been with my grief over Beatrice. At last Shakespeare's sobs began to subside a bit, and he grew quieter. "Oh," he finally said, catching his breath, "I am embarrassed. 'Tis not meet to loose these water drops upon my man's cheeks."

"Oh, tut! Man or woman, thou art human. Come, let's sit and talk. You must give sorrow words, sir. The grief that does not speak whispers to the o'er-fraught heart, and bids it break."

He pushed himself from me and flung his arms skyward. *"Words?"* he bellowed. "WORDS? What words? What words can there be? What words might there ever be? There are *no* words for what is in my heart! I know not any words that might sooth my heart which, yes, is 'o'er-fraught.' Of *course* it is, thou great fool!" By now his face was red, he was practically screaming, and he was starting to thump on my chest with his fist. "What do YOU know of grief?" he went on, yelling directly into my face. "Who are you to … ARGH! Oh, God!" He collapsed to the ground in a heap and grasped his left leg at mid-calf. "Oh, the miscreant cur!" he screamed. "*Ouch!* Damned hound from hell!"

"Why, man, what is the matter?" I asked. "Hast thou been stricken with a thunderbolt?" He looked up at me from the ground, almost doubled over, still holding his leg, his sparse hair messed and his face tear-streaked. I felt like laughing, he looked so ridiculous, but contained myself.

"Nay," he finally answered. "Thy accursed mongrel hath bitten me, the vile slave. O, I am in pain and bleed apace. *Zounds!* Is't not enough that my poor child lies breathless in the unfeeling ground, but now I am assaulted by this limb-lacking demi-wolf and made to bleed o'er the same blessed earth in which he is sepulchered? Oh, *why* God? WHY?"

I could control myself no longer, and laughed aloud. I picked Shakespeare up, perhaps not gently, and stood him on his feet and brushed the dust off of his sleeves. "Why," I said, "cease thy pitiful wailing and assume the part of a man. Thou art not bleeding. I see no blood. Thy hose is not even pierced. Doubtless, the hound thought you were hurting me and thus served as my true and valiant protector. Is't not so, Jack?" But he had retreated several yards to the edge of the graveyard and was lying prone on the grass with his head resting on his one folded forepaw, eyeing Shakespeare suspiciously.

"Come," I said, leading Will to my customary patch of grass near the trees. "Let us eat." We sat beneath the big chestnut tree and I offered him bread and cheese, which he gladly accepted and washed down with loud swallows of wine. I ate and drank too. Neither of us said anything for a while and it was, as always, pleasant to listen to the birds in the trees. Three sparrows, seeing us eat, descended to the ground several feet from where we sat and waited for their accustomed handout, cocking their tiny brownish heads obliquely from side to side. I threw them pieces of bread and within moments a half dozen of their kin swooped down and awaited their due as well. Then more did, and soon nearly two dozen hyper sparrows had gathered. I threw out morsels enough for all, which they either devoured on the spot or held in their beaks and flew away with to eat in peace nearby. Shakespeare followed my lead, and chuckled at the birds' antics as he tossed them pieces of his bread. He'd calmed and Jack, sensing that, moved closer. He plopped down directly between Will and me and stared pleadingly at each of us in turn. I fed him cheese and bread, which, as usual, he chomped into his jaws and swallowed whole.

"May I?" Will asked. I nodded. "Sir Jack," he went on, offering three small morsels of cheese, one at a time, "you deserve this not, but I forgive you right readily."

"Thy forgiveness, sir, carries no weight with him," I said. "He is a stranger to contrition, dull and muddy-mettled rascal as he is."

"*What?* You insult the fellow again? Was it not two minutes ago you praised him for defending you?"

"Nay," I answered. "He but acted upon instinct. He is a coward, sir, a fat coward who is affrighted of his own shadow. A *plague* of all cowards, I say! He is a base coward and, worse, is old and fat. Dost hear me, Jack? What art thou but a bolting hutch of beastliness, a swollen parcel of dropsies, a stuffed cloakbag of guts, a roasted Manningtree ox with pudding in thy belly? *Ha!*"

Shakespeare smiled a bit, his eyes brightened, and he even chuckled. "Fat?" he said. "Why, no offense, sir, but I have watched you stuffing the mutt's mouth with bread and cheese and if, therefore, he is fat, why, 'tis thee who is to blame. And old? Why, 'tis no sin to be old. You yourself, sir, have seen younger days. Yea, and, begging your pardon, thinner ones."

I nodded. "'Tis true, m'lord. That I am old, my white hairs do witness it—the more's the pity. And, indeed, I have all the characters of age: a moist eye, a dry hand, a yellow cheek, a white beard, a decreasing leg, an increasing belly; my voice is broken, my wind short, my chin double, and my wit single. I am as a candle, the better part burnt out—a wassail candle, all tallow. Yet 'tis no matter. We could be well-content, Jack and I, to entertain the lag-end of our lives with quiet hours."

Will looked across the graveyard, to the west where the sun was starting to set. He smiled, almost imperceptibly, but said nothing. Between us, Jack was asleep.

"And," I went on, "as for having seen thinner days, why there, sir, you speak truly again. When I was about thy years, Will, I was not an eagle's talon in the waist; I could have crept into any alderman's thumb-ring. A *plague* of sighing and grief! It blows a man up like a bladder."

He laughed aloud: his healthy, high-pitched laugh at last, just as I remembered from the year before and which I'd been seeking to raise. "Sighing and grief?" he said. "About what, sir?"

I reached down to rub Jack's head. He opened one eye, stared at me for a moment, and then went back to sleep. I told Shakespeare about Beatrice. I'd not spoken to anyone before about how I'd felt, what I'd gone through after her passing. It felt good to talk. I told him of my melancholia, what it had been like: how weary I'd felt; how I'd lost my mirth and forgone all custom of exercises; how stale and flat the world seemed to me for a time. "Indeed, sir," I said, "it went so heavily with my disposition that this goodly frame, the earth, seemed to me but a sterile promontory. This brave o'erhanging firmament, this majestical roof fretted with golden fire, you see, why it appeared to me nothing but a foul and pestilent congregation of vapors. Men delighted me not, nor women neither. A dark cloud, sir, hovered about me day and night."

"How didst thou pass through it?"

"Through it?" I thought back to that time, to how I'd coped with my grief. How did I survive? I almost hadn't. There'd been a time when I'd very much wanted to put a period to life's sentence, when the weight of the world and myself in it was too much. I felt ashamed to tell Shakespeare of it, but we'd gone this far together and I trusted him. "In truth, Will," I said, "there was a period when I contemplated crossing over to that ... that undiscovered country, from whose bourn no traveler returns. Indeed, sir, there was a time during my melancholy when I was, well, obsessed with making my quietus with a bare bodkin. Life, being weary of these worldly bars, never lacks power to dismiss itself. And I tell you, during practically every moment of every day then I craved— *craved*, mind you—the sweet, soothing comfort of oblivion, of simply being no more a part of this dreary, empty world. Oh, how I wished this sullied flesh to melt, thaw, and resolve itself into a dew. 'Twas a consummation for which I devoutly wished, to simply ... to merely ... *be* no more. That was in my mind when I went to sleep and again the moment I awoke, and on and off the day through."

"Yet here thou art. How so?"

I looked at Jack sleeping, his mouth opened slightly, and remembered that time. "I' good faith, sir, I know not," I answered. "The days passed. There were times when the black mood was hard upon me and I craved an end but simply had not the energy to direct the bodkin. I got from one day to the next, God knoweth how for I do not. Then one day I awoke and the ill thoughts that had plagued my mind were still there but not as poignant. The next day was better, and then the next, and in time my old self, or at least its remnants, had resurfaced."

Will looked at me, studying my face, but said nothing. "There was something else," I said. "This life I had ... have ... I was not happy, but it was at least familiar. But the dread of something after death—what, I knew not but feared learning. For who knows what dreams may come when we have shuffled off this mortal coil? Was that cowardly? Well, ... "

Shakespeare looked pensive. He had a way of sinking deeply into himself, into his thoughts, seemingly oblivious to whatever else was going on. The skin on his forehead wrinkled, and his eyes seemed focused on something in the distance. At such times, his eyes turned from their usual light-blue to a steely gray. "I see," he finally said. "'That undiscovered country, from whose bourn no traveler returns.' Indeed."

"And then," I said, tapping the crown of Jack's skull with my forefinger, "there was *this* unworthy but needy beast, waiting for his dinner, loath to be orphaned." I didn't say so to Shakespeare, but I recalled, too, feeling that to have left Jack betimes would have been a betrayal of my Beatrice. During even the bleakest hours of my bleakest nights I would now and again hear, somewhere in my poor head, her sweet voice calling him: "Oh, Jack, you are my *prince*! My beautiful, beautiful prince!" He was hardly beautiful and as unprincelike as a dog could be, but my wife had loved him, perhaps as the child she'd never had.

"Enough of that," I said. "Let us talk of thy departed pretty one. In sooth, though I met thy Hamnet only the once, methought 'a was a fine, spirited lad."

"Yea," Will said. "A spirited lad. And now he is but a spirit indeed." He paused, and stared out toward the graveyard. "Words, you say. 'Give sorrow words,' you say. Why, one might loose a rhapsody of words, but 'twould be bootless. He's dead, Horatio. Dead and gone!"

"From this earth he's gone. But now he must needs live in your memory alone. Thy heart must be his sepulcher, for from thy heart his image ne'er shall go. With that must thou be content, my friend."

He nodded, and his eyes moistened. *"Content?* Oh, Horatio!" he practically whispered. "Grief, I tell you, fills the room up of my absent child, lies in his bed, walks up and down with me, puts on his pretty looks, repeats his words, remembers me of all his gracious parts, and stuffs out his vacant garments with his form. O, the memory is green, Horatio!"

"Keep it e'er so. Here, come with me." I reached into my sack and took out some things I'd brought from home for the evening. Then we walked back, the three of us, to Hamnet's grave. The sun was almost down now, and the birds had quieted. A nice breeze was blowing across the cemetery, bringing relief from the August heat. We stood next to the grave. "There's rosemary," I said, placing a bit of that shrub at the base of the stone. "That's for remembrance. And there's pansies, that's for thoughts."

Will looked as though he was about to say something, but, before he could, Jack leaned his hindquarters against the stone and deposited his own personal offering, directly on top of mine. "FIE!" Shakespeare cried out, shaking both fists at him. "What are you *doing?* O shameless cur!"

I laughed out loud; God forgive me, I couldn't help myself. And to compound my sin, I then loosed a horrible noisy fart due to the jiggling of my gut. "Oh," I said, "excuse me, sir, but … I just … I only … " And then I totally lost control and had a laughing fit the likes of which I hadn't had since Beatrice and I'd been newlyweds and I'd accidentally set the privy on fire with her mother in it. My mother-in-law was fine, but the absurdity of the scene caused me to go over the edge. Beatrice hadn't spoken to me for a day after that.

Shakespeare gave me a sour look, his face taut and eyes cold. When he saw that I wasn't able to stop laughing, his face loosened a bit and he even chuckled. Just a little. Then he started laughing too, and soon he was guffawing as much as me and his eyes began to water. Then we were both sitting on the ground a few feet from the boy's grave chortling uncontrollably like fools, both of us, as though drunk. Soon Will was crying a bit and laughing at the same time and then he was just crying, fat wet tears rolling down his cheeks, and then he was quiet. Jack hobbled to him and looked into his face, quizzically, and Shakespeare reached over to him and patted the back of his neck. "Oh, tell me truly, Sir Jack," he said. "What should such fellows as we do crawling between heaven and earth?"

"*Ha!*" I said. "Coddle him not. Is he not the veriest varlet who ever chewed with a tooth? Jack, you stale old mouse-eaten dry cheese! Why, thou wouldst eat thy dead vomit up, and howl'st to find it!"

Shakespeare grinned, and I cleaned up the mess. Jack, for some private reason, took offense at this and growled at me, baring his fangs to show his decrepit gums and the few paltry teeth left in his aged head. "Peace, good pint-pot!" I intoned, wagging a finger at him.

"Yea," Will added, mimicking my scolding gesture. "Peace, good tickle-brain."

I stroked Jack's head and scratched behind his ears. "Nay, sir," I said. "Let be. For let Hercules himself do what he may, the cat will mew and dog have his day."

IT WAS MORE than another year ere I saw Shakespeare again. It was a cold gray day in late November, 1597, with early winter's damp cold seeping through my considerable flesh to chill my aging bones. I'd spent the day patching cracks in the northwest corner of the church to expel the winter's flaw and pulling weeds that had snaked around some of the gravestones, including Beatrice's. Of all the graves in our little cemetery, I of course gave hers the greatest care. Hamnet's too.

And Jack's.

My dog had died of old age three weeks before—peacefully, in his sleep—and I'd buried him beneath our favorite tree. He didn't really have a gravestone, just a pile of carefully selected white stones. Each evening, I sat with my back against the chestnut tree and ate my supper of bread and cheese and talked to Jack, telling him of the tedious details of my tedious days. Each evening I straightened the stones marking his resting place so that they looked just right. Sitting in the place where my dog and I had spent so many pleasant hours, I felt Jack's spirit presence, found it comforting.

I didn't intend to, but fell asleep after eating. Though not wont to dream, I dreamt nevertheless—an empowering fantasy in which I was somehow hovering in the air above the shire and could fly from place to place as an act of will, my bulk no longer a hindrance. Awakening, unsure where I was, it occurred to me that I must have expired myself, for standing before me was a lovely angel—a young one, with long golden hair and bright blue eyes. *Well*, I thought, *at least I'd outlived Jack and had cared for him as best I could, for which Beatrice—whom I'd now hopefully see again—would thank me.* Then the angel spoke. "Oh, father," she said, "his eyes flutter. He lives." I recognized her voice; alas, she was no angel, but Judith Shakespeare.

As I came more awake and my eyes focused more clearly, I saw Judith's father standing a few paces behind her. "Sirrah," he said, "how is't with thee? We feared you dead."

"Nay," I answered, rubbing my eyes. "I merely slept, which is death's counterfeit. The sleeping and the dead are but as pictures, 'tis true. Yet I am sorry I frighted thee, child. I am glad to see you both well."

"And we thee. Dost feel refreshed after thy slumber?"

I yawned and stretched my arms above my head. "Indeed. Sleep, sir, is nature's soft nurse. It knits up the raveled sleeve of care, is sore labor's bath, our chief nourisher in life's feast. Sleep, gentle sleep, is the balm of hurt minds."

Shakespeare looked around the churchyard. "I see," he said after a moment. "Thou says't truly. 'The balm of hurt minds.' But where is Sir Jack?"

"Here," I answered, patting the little pile of white stones. "Jack sleeps here, and his slumber is no counterfeit."

"What?" Judith cried out. "Thy dog is *dead?*"

"Yea, young lady. He lived a goodly long while, and now, after life's fitful fever, he sleeps well."

"Oh, the poor fellow!" she whimpered. Her eyes moistened and she began to weep softly. I studied her and noticed how much she'd grown in just the past year: she was taller, rounder, prettier—now straddling that fragile and worrisome precipice between girlhood and young womanhood.

Will walked over, knelt down, and placed his hand on the stones. "Alas, Sir Jack!" he said quietly. "Adieu. I shall note you fondly in my book of memory." He turned to me and touched my shoulder. "I am sorry for thy loss. 'A was a commendable fellow."

"'A was a goodly companion, take him for all in all. I shall not look upon his like again. But how hast it been with thee since last we met?"

Shakespeare stared out toward the graveyard, which looked unusually forlorn in the gray late-November twilight. "Well," he sighed, "death, as the Psalmist saith, is certain to all; all shall die. And 'tis said the ripest fruit first falls. So 'tis said. Yet these maxims offer but cold comfort, Horatio. Thou woulds't not think how ill all's about my heart, e'en now."

I nodded, and handed him a goblet of wine. "Upon the rack of this tough world are we all stretched. We all, man and beast, must somehow endure our going hence, even as we did our coming hither. We must endure. You will endure. But let us raise a cup to our departed ones. Here, sir." We lifted our wine, looked at each other, and drank. I poured us each another, and we downed them as well. I looked around to see where Judith was, but she'd disappeared into the wood.

Will held his goblet close to his face, and twirled it so that the small amount of wine remaining swirled from side to side. "Tell me," he said, "hath the doleful dumps oppressed thy mind since Sir Jack journeyed over to that undiscovered country?"

"'Doleful dumps.' That's good." I shrugged. "Yea, sir, the black mood hath at times paid its unwelcome visitation, mostly at night. I sorely miss my Jack, but at least he lived out his allotted term. I have told my sorrows to the stones. For now, though, I breathe and, i' good faith, am glad of the chance. When our brief light has set, there's the kingdom of perpetual night. I would fain not enter that kingdom until its gates gape wide—thrice wider for me, I suppose, than for another—and I am summoned."

Shakespeare took another long swallow of wine, and looked thoughtful. Then he smiled to himself and turned his head away. "Yea," he finally said, "and now thou hast not thy Jack to berate. Well, tell me, Horatio, where wilt thou find another such to cudgel with thy paltry wit?"

I looked at him, but his face was still turned from me. "How say'st thou? 'Paltry wit'?"

"Ay," he said, raising his voice. "'Twere my words. Have you not ears? Why, thy wit's as thick as Tewkesbury mustard, though not as plentiful."

"I see," I replied. I looked at him, saw him trying to hide his face from me, and took his bait. "And what of thee? Why, 'tis whispered throughout the shire that thou, great poet, hast not so much brain as ear-wax. Thy pia mater, 'tis well known, is not worth the ninth part of a sparrow. *Ha!* Why, I would the fountain of your mind were clear, that I might water an ass at it. Oh, to be so pester'd with a popinjay!"

"Why, thou clay-brained guts, thou knotty-pated fool, thou obscene greasy tallow catch! Why, you said true: the gates of the kingdom must open thrice wider—*more!*—for thee than another. Tell me, Horatio, when was the last time thou sawest thine own knee?"

"*What?* Oh, you starveling, you eel-skin, you dried neat's-tongue, you stock-fish! O for breath to utter what is like thee! Why, you tinker's yard, you sheath, you bow-case, you vile standing tuck! What *wind* blew you hither? Oh, mad mustachioed purple-hued maltworm!"

Will laughed aloud, and slapped his knee twice. "Why," he said, "why ... that is ... then ... "

"Ha! Is thy purse empty already? Oh, *cudgel* thy brains no more, for your dull ass will not mend his pace with beating. Look, Jack," I said, turning to the white stones beside me and pointing toward Shakespeare. "He's winding up the watch of his wit; by and by it will strike. Why, thou crusty batch of nature. '*Sblood!* Why, Jack, he is as tedious as a tired horse, a railing wife, worse than a smoky house. What, you poor, base, rascally ... " Just then my exertions quite outdid me and I inadvertently loosed a loud, disgusting and prolonged flatulence, perhaps the loudest and most disgusting in a long and unsheltered life.

"*What!*" Shakespeare cried, screwing up his face in horror. "Dost thy other mouth call me? O horrible! This is the rankest compound of villanous smell that ever offended nostril!"

I took another swallow of wine. "Ah," I said softly. "A thousand pardons, sir. 'Tis the infirmity of age. An aged man is but a paltry thing."

"Ay. A paltry thing indeed. *Phew!* Canst not control thyself?"

I smiled weakly and shrugged, but said nothing. Will and I were silent for a time. I was glad of his presence. I felt better than I had in the last three weeks. I'd endure.

Just then Judith returned from the wood, holding something—I couldn't tell what—in both hands. As she got closer, I could see that she was crying again. I liked the child very much, and she was certainly comely and would someday be a great beauty, but, my God!, what a weeper. Every time one saw her, tears were dribbling down that pretty face for one reason or another. "Oh, father," she sobbed. "Look! He's dead! I saw him on the ground, barely moving, and picked him up so you could save him. But, *oh*, he's dead and gone." Shakespeare and I looked at what she was holding, and I took the little bird from her. It looked tiny and forlorn in my meaty paws.

I nudged Shakespeare. "Thou see'st," I said. "There's a special providence in the fall of a sparrow. If it be now, 'tis not to come; if it be not to come, it will be now; if it be not now, yet it will come. The readiness is all. Since no one of us—man, beast, or bird—knows aught of what he leaves, what is't to leave betimes? Is't not so?"

He furrowed his brow and stared into the distance, absorbed yet again with his thoughts. After a few moments, I wondered if he'd forgotten that Judith and I were there. "'A special providence,'" he finally said. "'The readiness'? Yet I wonder. How ready can one be who must perforce leave this world betimes? Was my poor son ready? Thy Beatrice? Nay! 'What is't to leave betimes?' Why, 'tis a tragedy."

I nodded. "And that's true too," I said, yawning. "A tragedy. Oh, pardon me, sir. I shall consider thy wise words anon. But not now. For now, sir, my poor weary brain is o'er-taxed and the spectre of sleep hangs heavy on my penthouse lid. I must take my leave of you."

Shakespeare stood and, with a dramatic flourish, bowed formally. "You *cannot*, sir," he intoned in a deep mock-stentorian voice, "take from me anything I would more willingly part withal."

I chuckled and so did Will and we agreed to meet at the churchyard the following summer, on the anniversary of Hamnet's burial, to sup and imbibe and remember and trade barbs. "Sharpen thy wits, old man," Shakespeare said. "And sleep well. I pray thou'lt enjoy pleasant dreams."

"I humbly thank you, sir." I looked at young Judith and at her father and at the pile of white stones marking my dog's grave and then out toward the dark cemetery. "We are," I said, "such stuff as dreams are made on."

Shakespeare nodded. "Thou say'st true," he said. Then he paused, and nodded. "And," he went on, "our little lives are rounded with a sleep."

A Masseur and Bedtime Reader
for Anne Bonny

I SERVED FOR A BRIEF but tempestuous time as a masseur and bed-time reader to Anne Bonny, the quick-tempered and fierce but nervous and insomniac pirate who served—literally—under that pathetic drunk-ard Captain John "Calico Jack" Rackham during the last days of his misbegotten Caribbean buccaneering career. I was a short but muscular and bald-by-choice mulatto with one brown eye and one yellow-specked blue eye—an accident of birth that caused many to view me superstitiously, a circumstance upon which I endeavored to capitalize when necessary.

I first met Anne on New Year's Day of 1720 when Calico Jack brought her to the Three Horsemen Tavern in Nassau, New Providence, to rest from the rigors of her pregnancy. She was some eight months along, haggard and anemic, but—to me—lovely and desirable nonethe-less: a half-foot taller than I and big-boned, silky auburn hair, lovely clear hazel eyes, and a large face with well-defined features—in the main, I suppose, a rather masculine face. She was dressed in men's clothing—long, loose-fitting brown pantaloons; a purple vest over a dirty ruffled green shirt; and a scarlet kerchief binding her beautiful hair. One might have thought her a man except for the unmistakable swell of her belly beneath the green shirt and the more subtle swell of her breasts. She said nothing when Rackham escorted her into the main room of the tavern and eased her into a rough wooden chair at a table near the door and then sat beside her. He immediately commenced pounding his fist on the table. "Rum!" he bellowed. "RUM! And *now!*"

I disliked Calico Jack from that moment, and my dislike intensified from then until the hour nearly three months later when I had the pleas-ure of seeing him and most of the rest of his worthless crew of alcoholic brigands—"gen'lemen o' fortune," as they referred to themselves—swinging stiffly in the wind at Gallows Point in Port Royal, Jamaica, their fortune expended. That was also the last time I saw my beloved Anne Bonny, and, thankfully, the last time, too, that I saw that wretched slut Mary Read.

I'd worked at the Three Horsemen for two years, since running away from the sugar plantation southwest of Puerto Plata on Hispaniola where I'd been born a score and ten years earlier. I'd had to leave. The mistress had become increasingly demanding and out-of-control, summoning me at any and all hours to massage her plump white body from head to toe and then perform the deed of darkness with her. Oh, she'd taught me to read in exchange for my favors and had given me a book of my choice from their library each Christmas during the ten years I'd been her masseur and stud, and she was certainly an enthusiastic lover, but that was also the problem: she was *too* enthusiastic—thrashing about more and more violently, moaning louder and louder, constantly ordering me to try new positions, and sobbing and calling me a nigger and a dog when she failed to achieve satisfaction. She even took to pulling my hair during moments of passion, which is why I started shaving my head every day. When she began raking my bald pate with her nails and twisting off bits of skin, I began oiling the top of my head so that her grip would have less purchase during lovemaking. I eventually tired of meeting the mistress's requirements and, perhaps more to the point, feared that her husband would find us out. Like most of his ilk, that man was decidedly intolerant of certain behaviors on the part of his chattel and generously employed the whip and hanging rope.

When I brought Rackham his rum, he glared at me. "Next time, nigger," he growled, "be quicker when I call for spirits. D'ye understand me?"

I turned my head so that I was peering down at him with just my blue eye and concentrated so that the eye bulged out and even vibrated a bit, causing the yellow specks to appear to twirl around, kaleidoscope-like. That was my technique. I'm sure that Calico Jack expected the usual scraping and shuffling and the customary mumbled "Yarsuh, I'se pow'ful sorry, suh." Instead, I held my gaze for perhaps twenty seconds and then quietly but firmly replied, in a low, even tone of voice. "I understand you," I said. "I understand you *very* well." Calico Jack peered up at me suspiciously, unsure of my intent, but said nothing.

I went to the bar to make a special drink for Anne: extra strong cocoa with just a thimbleful of rum, a touch of cayenne, a dash of salt, and a large spoonful of Digby's Sympathetic Powder.

When I returned, Anne looked worse. She took a few sips of her cocoa and then put her face in her hands and moaned pitifully. "Oh, *God!*" she murmured. "I feel horrible. Oh, Jack, what'm I to do?"

Rackham looked at her derisively. "Do?" he sneered. "*Do?* Why, ye flamin' cow, ye'll rest with this damned infant and later ye'll come back to the *Revenge* with me, where ye belong. In the meantime, this darky here'll be bringin' yer meals." He paused and stared at me. "And ye be respectful, nigger. D'ye hear me? If I l'arn otherwise, I'll skin ye alive and dangle yer miserable black ass from the yardarm."

I ignored him and instead helped Anne upstairs to her room. She lay on the bed and turned her face to the wall and began shivering and even sobbing a bit. I covered her with a blanket and brought an extra pillow and eased it under her head, and then helped her remove the scarlet kerchief so that her hair spilled free. "You just relax, ma'am," I told her. "I'm Mose and I'm going to help take care of you. You're safe here. Everything'll be fine."

But it wasn't. That evening, after Rackham had finally stumbled out of the Three Horsemen to return to his ship, his belly full of rum, Anne delivered. She'd turned paler yet and couldn't get warm and just shivered and moaned, and I'd stayed with her constantly, rubbing her shoulders now and again to help her relax, and had covered her with another blanket, and had gently rinsed her face with a wet cloth, and then, when it was finally clear that something was dreadfully wrong, had Pierre, the owner of the tavern, summon Doctor Bell.

But before he arrived almost two hours later, barely sober, Anne Bonny's baby had commenced its brief sojourn in this earthly paradise. She'd turned over on her back and screamed and clutched my hand and begged, "*Help* me, Mose. For God's sake, help me! Oh, please, *please!*" And I'd called downstairs for Big Beulah, Pierre's wife, and together we removed Anne's pantaloons and mopped her brow and urged her to push and let her grasp our hands tightly while she spread her thick white thighs wider than I would have imagined possible, and groaned and screamed, again and again, until finally a red, squalling, shriveled … thing squeezed out of her, a boy, and it gasped for breath for a few moments and cried briefly and then was quiet, though still breathing. Beulah held up the baby and cleared his mouth with her finger and wrapped him in a blue shirt that had been hanging on a peg near the door. She placed him on Anne's chest and let her hold him for a few minutes, then picked him up and clutched him to her considerable bosom. "It ain't over, darlin'," she said to Anne. "Push again." Anne did and shortly thereafter a bloody slab-of-liver-like mass oozed out of her, while I—not knowing what it was, never having imagined such a thing—tightly controlled my urge to retch all over the new mother. Beulah handed the baby to me and then disposed of the bloody mass in a nearby chamberpot. Taking the child from my arms and heading for the door, she said, "I'll see to the little darlin' … *if* he survives."

Anne Bonny was nineteen years old when we met. She told me so about an hour after she'd given birth. She'd closed her eyes and slept lightly for forty-five minutes and then awakened and remembered what had happened and began to weep. That was the moment I fell in love with her, for despite her distress she was beautiful: her hazel eyes wet, her sweat-soaked and plastered-down auburn hair framing her large face, and her left hand wriggling nervously in both of mine. I thought to calm her by getting her to talk, and, haltingly, she told me her story.

She'd come to South Carolina from Ireland as a bastard child with her father and his mistress, Anne's mother. She said she'd been married young to "a rapscallion named James Bonny," who'd decided to make his way in the world by becoming a spy and informer for Nassau Governor Woodes Rogers. Disgusted with Bonny, she began hanging around the pirates who frequented New Providence and it was there she met and fell in love with Calico Jack, "a fellow Irisher," who was gallant and exciting and who wooed her with jewelry and other finery. He'd tried to buy Anne from Bonny, an accepted form of divorce, but her husband had declined the offer and asked Rogers to have her whipped as an adultress, so Anne ran off with Rackham and had been sailing with him on the *Revenge* for a year or so since, capturing merchant ships when they could and trying to avoid Captain Thomas Barnett, the well-known former pirate turned pirate hunter. "Jack has his faults," she said, "but at least he loves me. He really does! He told me so once, Mose."

I nodded. "Love is good," I said. "Just try to relax, ma'am. Here, let me rub your neck a bit. It'll make you feel better."

She was quiet then for a time until Big Beulah and Dr. Bell came in, looking glum. "I'm sorry, darlin'," Beulah said quietly. "The little one didn't make it."

"He was *too* little," the doctor added, slurring his words. "Too damned puny, as you might say. Couldn't fight hard enough." He paused, and belched. "It ain't that uncommon, ya know."

I expected Anne to start weeping again, but her reaction surprised me. "DAMN yer eyes, ya bloody drunk!" she screamed. "Ye're an incompetent imbiber just like all the rest of 'em. Had ye been here when ye shoulda been, my baby'd be alive now. Now git OUT! Leave us alone, now, before I bash yer besotted face in. D'ye *heed* me?" I was afraid that, weak as she was, she'd jump out of her bed and throttle Bell. But she merely glared at him, her chin trembling, and he, startled, backed out of the room and exited the premises without a word further.

"Well," Beulah said, staring at Anne, "ye're a spirit'd one, ta be sure. I'll check on ya later, darlin'. You rest now. Mose will stay here with you."

After she left, Anne asked me to rub her neck and shoulders again. I did, but it didn't stop her shaking. She started to sob again and then her floodgates opened and she bawled and bawled, her big body heaving, her head resting back against my chest. I put my arms around her from behind and held her to me. "It'll be all right, ma'am," I said, as quietly and soothingly as I could. "This is a terrible thing that happened, but you're young. You'll get past it. Now go ahead and cry. You deserve it." After a considerable while she quieted. "Try to sleep now," I whispered. "You need to rest, ma'am."

She shook her head. "I can't. I never could. I lie awake half the night, night after night. And stop calling me '*ma'am*,' fer God's sake. My name's Anne."

"Anne," I repeated. "Anne. Yes." Then I had an idea. I went to my shack out back of the tavern and got one of my books and returned to her room. "Now you just close your eyes and try to relax," I said. I helped position another pillow under her head and pulled the blanket to her chin and smoothed it around her. Then I sat on a stool beside her and read to her, a sonnet by Mr. Shakespeare:

When forty winters shall besiege thy brow,
And dig deep trenches in thy beauty's field,
Thy youth's proud livery, so gazed on now,
Will be a tattered weed, of small worth held:
Then being asked where all thy beauty lies,
Where all the treasure of thy lusty days,
To say, within thine own deep-sunken eyes,
Were an all-eating shame and thriftless praise.
How much more praise deserved thy beauty's use,
If thou couldst answer, 'This fair child of mine
Shall sum my count and make my old excuse,'
Proving his beauty by succession thine!
*   This were to be made new when thou art old,*
*   And see thy blood warm when thou feel'st it cold.*

When I'd finished, I wasn't sure I'd chosen the most appropriate selection but I glanced at Anne and saw that she was asleep. I, too, was now exhausted and closed my eyes, and stayed right next to her all night.

Anne remained at the Three Horsemen for a week. I spent as much time with her as I could during the day, bringing her meals and again coming upstairs to see her when things got slow in the tavern, and then was with her every evening. For the first three nights, at her request, I rubbed her neck and shoulders as I had that first day. Then, on the fourth night, she asked me to rub her back as well. Before I could say anything, she took off her shirt and lay prone on the bed and turned her head to look at me, directly, just for a moment, smiling mysteriously, and then turned back to bury her face in the pillow. I wasn't at all sure what to do; in a way, it seemed too reminiscent of that plantation mistress. But Anne was not she, so I rubbed the top of my head to oil up my hands and commenced massaging her back. I started with long strokes up and then down the length of her spine and then did flat-handed lateral crossover strokes, starting at her neck and progressing down to the small of her back and then back up to her neck, and finished with shorter, gentler strokes outward from her spine along each rib. As I massaged her back, Anne moaned softly. "Umm, that feels *good*, Mose," she murmured. "Ye truly know what ye're about." I finished with a relaxing stroke in which I moved one open hand down the length of her spine from her neck, slowly and lightly, and when that hand reached the small of her back immediately commenced the same downward stroke with the other hand, and simultaneously returned the first hand to the nape of her neck to start the stroke again.

And then, later each evening, I read sonnets to relax her. Once she'd fallen asleep, I liked to just sit quietly and watch her for a few minutes before I went back to my little shack. Anne's face! Nothing I'd seen was more lovely. I particularly liked to look at her lips while she slept—the bowed curve of the upper lip with just a sprinkling of fine light hair above it, her lips slightly separated while she breathed evenly. Even her gentle snoring was dear to me.

That week was blissful: to be near Anne Bonny, to be alone with her each evening, to comfort her to her rest night after night.

Then Rackham returned.

It was mid-afternoon on a Saturday and Anne was upstairs napping while I was sweeping up downstairs, getting ready for the late afternoon rush. Calico Jack and two of his crew members sauntered in and sat at the same table as before and again he immediately demanded rum. "And be quick about it, nigger!" he added. "I ain't a patient man, and I ain't in a good mood." I wasn't disposed to jump at his command, and so continued sweeping.

After a minute, one of his men—a squat, bowlegged miscreant whose breath smelled like carrion, a nasty bully named Fenwick whom I subsequently learned was Rackham's quartermaster—stood up and stuck his ugly squished-in face close to mine. "The Cap'n gave you an order, blackie," he snarled. "Maybe ye're deef too, huh?" I turned my head and gave him my wonted stare with my blue eye, making it bulge out and vibrate. His face turned pale and he lowered his eyes and walked away without saying more.

When I eventually brought them their rum, Rackham glared at me. "The lady," he said. "How be she?"

"She lost the baby," I replied tersely. "Other than that, the lady is … perfect. She's perfect."

"'*Perfect*,' is it?" he sneered derisively. "What da ye know 'bout her, nigger? She's a red whore, and ye may lay to that. Lost the baby, did she? Well, so be it. What might we do with a shittin' infant on board anyway? Gen'lemen o' fortune can't be troubled with such, by the powers. Where is she, anyway?"

"Upstairs."

"Well," he said, "I reckon she can come with us, back to the *Revenge*. Go fetch her and her things, darky, and be quick about it. We need ta be catchin' the tide."

"JACK!" We all looked to the top of the stairs, where Anne stood, dressed in the long purple sleeping robe Big Beulah'd given her, looking furious. "*Jack!*" she yelled. "*Belay* that talk! 'Red whore,' am I? Why, I've half a mind to settle yer hash here an' now, exceptin' I'm a lady and wouldn't desecrate this establishmen' with yer cowardly blood!" She paused and pointed toward me and again addressed Rackham. "And understan' this, ya lubber: I ain't goin' nowheres without Mose. He comes aboard, or I don't."

"Why, dearest," Calico Jack said, looking sheepish, "how wunnerful ye're lookin'. Lost the wee one, did ye? Well, it's a bloody shame, that is. I can't tell ye how sorry I am, as it were." He paused and glanced toward Fenwick and then back at Anne. "But dearest, ye know we can't be bringin' this here darky on the *Revenge*. Fo'c'sle hands wouldn't be likin' that."

Anne descended the stairs very slowly, never once losing eye contact with Rackham. When her face was a few inches from his she stopped and just stared for perhaps a minute directly into his face. Then she addressed him softly and deliberately. "Heed me, Cap'n Rackham. I ain't *askin'* ye, I'm *tellin'* ye. This man comes with me, or ye've seen the last of me. De ye fancy sleepin' alone, I should wonder? Now, what say ye?"

MY LIFE aboard the ship *Revenge* was a combination of sweetest heaven and direst hell. The hell was being amongst my shipmates—a pathetic mixture of lowlife murderers and thieves from the colonies and islands who'd as lief slice a throat as spit, mutineers from colonial and European merchant ships, and deserters from the harsh and punitive British Royal Navy man-o'-war vessels that ruled the Atlantic and Caribbean. Only a few could read or write, most were compulsive gamblers, and all had visions of fabulous wealth to be gained from their pirating—visions that rarely, if ever, materialized. They all drank—

mostly rum, and brandy when available—as often and in such quantities as Calico Jack and Fenwick would allow, and their most desired form of recreation seemed to be to drink themselves into oblivion whenever possible. Yet stumbling drunk as they may have been the night before, next day the pirates would be scurrying about in the rigging—high in the air, nimble as monkeys—and only once did one tumble screaming onto the deck.

Many of the buccaneers harbored diseases, ranging from chronic coughs and colds to malaria and dysentery, and little wonder, for their living conditions were abominable. Ordinary crew members lived in a below-decks section of the ship called the forecastle—fo'c'sle, for short—which was always wet, gloomy, lit only by lanterns, and in which the stink of omnipresent tobacco smoke and the fetid odors of dozens of cramped-together and unwashed men were pervasive. The air quality was little improved by the smells of bilge water and rotting meat from the ship's hold which wafted over to the fo'c'sle. Rats, cockroaches and other vermin bred in the bilge and scurried about freely.

The heaven was being with Anne Bonny. She'd somehow made clear to Rackham that I was her personal manservant and to be regarded as such, and I was thus exempt from living in that horrid fo'c'sle with the stinking crew members or performing any sailorly duties, and was given my own little corner of a storage bin below decks where I slung my hammock and hung a ship's lantern so I could read my books. The pirates naturally resented my privileged status, but I cared not; I desired to have as little to do with them as possible. Happily, that was easy because Fenwick had spread the word that I was a spook or a demon, maybe a male witch, somehow unnatural, and the crew avoided me. Oh, occasionally, one might approach and test me: "Get outta my way, ya nigger runt, afore I ram a marlinspike so far up your black ass the end of it'll tickle yer dusky throat." I never answered, just stared at him directly and did my thing with my blue eye until my would-be tormentor blanched and swallowed hard and slunk away.

Anne and Rackham shared a cabin in the stern, far and away the best living quarters on the ship, and slept together every night. But I got to be with her the rest of the time, during her hot-tempered days and—most wonderfully—during her nervous evenings, while Calico Jack drank and gambled and it could be just the two of us.

During the days, she practiced with her cutlass and boarding ax. I sat on a puncheon beneath the mainmast and watched, and it was a sight to behold: Anne held her cutlass, a frightening yard-long thing with a slightly curved blade, in her right hand and the ax in her left and went through her movements—parrying, thrusting, slashing—all the while screaming and cursing like a madwoman. "EE-YAH!" she'd yell while swinging her blade in a frightening arc from right to left, an arc guaranteed to separate any future foe from his head. "Have at it, ya goddamned bloody lubbers. *I'll* show 'em the color of their insides, by the powers!" It was a side of her I'd not seen, and I wondered what she'd be like in a real fight.

Sometimes she practiced her cutlass moves with one of the sailors, a handsome smooth-faced young man named Mark Read. He looked more like a choir boy than a brigand, with huge long-lashed deep blue eyes that seemingly took up a quarter of his face, but was every bit as fierce as Anne when wielding edged weapons; the two of them swung their blades at each other in mock fury, their faces tight and determined, yelling like savages, cursing and threatening. Read had a high-pitched voice, almost womanlike.

Anne surprised me one morning. She was taking a break from her weapons practice with Read when she noticed one of the pirates, a scurvy-ridden and chronically coughing maggot named George Hitchcock, tamping his pipe. She watched calmly while he lit it and drew and then sat down with his back against a jollyboat and closed his eyes and smoked and sipped rum from a tin cup. Without warning, she trotted over and kicked him in the ribs. "Ya damned *blockhead!*" she screamed. "Jesus, Mary and Joseph! I've told ye before—I've told *all* ye damned imbibers—ye're to put caps on them pipes afore ye smoke. Do ye want to start a fire aboard this 'ere ship? I see ye do that ag'in, George, and I'll settle yer hash once and fer all. *Certain* I will!" Then she kicked his left leg hard, just below the knee, causing him to scream in agony.

When not practicing with her weapons, Anne spent much of each day with Mark Read. The two of them sat huddled together like conspirators in a shaded area near the windlass, giggling and talking in low tones, like schoolgirls, their shoulders touching. I noticed that Rackham watched them during such times and didn't look pleased.

As I say, the evenings were our time together. Every night, shortly after sunset, Calico Jack and Fenwick and Lessard, the boatswain, or "bos'un" as he was known, and two or three other no-accounts commenced their wonted drinking and gambling sessions—mostly a penny-pitching game known as chuck-farthing—usually on the quarterdeck or in Fenwick's cabin if the weather was bad, and Anne retired to her cabin and summoned me. "Rub my shoulders, will ye, Mose?" she'd say. "Do me gentle, and my neck, too." I would, slowly as always, pressing firmly and kneading especially carefully with the fleshy part of my palm where her muscles were most tense, for by now I knew Anne Bonny's big pale body very well. Sometimes she was just quiet, but most often she'd commence shaking after a few minutes and maybe sobbing a bit too. "What is it, Anne?" I'd ask quietly. "What is it to-night, my lady?"

Most commonly, it was the baby. "I can't git over it, Mose," she said more than once, sniffling. "I just can't get past it. Oh, Mose, I wanted that little one so badly." Or, it was her worry about a fire aboard the *Revenge*; that was her fear, and she obsessed about it daily. "Them *lunkheads*," she'd say, pounding her fist against the mattress, "ye'd think they'd l'arn. My God, Mose! Can ye imagine what'd it be like, the ship to be burnin'? What'd happen to us? Oh, lordy!" Other times it was violent storms; the thunder crackling and lightning sheeting across the sea frightened her horribly. And sometimes it was nothing specific; she just buried her face in her hands and trembled. At such times, I bundled her red blanket around her tightly and securely and held her very closely to me from behind, sometimes for as long as fifteen minutes, until she stopped shaking and calmed a bit. Finally, I'd always read to her. "Shall we have this one?" I'd ask gently, holding up my book of sonnets. She'd nod, usually without looking; it didn't matter to her, she claimed to like them all equally. But I knew her favorite, and read it often:

When, in disgrace with fortune and men's eyes,
I all alone beweep my outcast state
And trouble deaf heaven with my bootless cries
And look upon myself and curse my fate,
Wishing me like to one more rich in hope,

30

Featured like him, like him with friends possess'd,
Desiring this man's art and that man's scope,
With what I most enjoy contented least;
Yet in these thoughts myself almost despising,
Haply I think on thee, and then my state,
Like to the lark at break of day arising
From sullen earth, sings hymns at heaven's gate;
    For thy sweet love remember'd such wealth brings
    That then I scorn to change my state with kings.

By time I'd finished, her eyes would be closed. She wasn't always asleep, but was finally relaxed enough to sleep and would be able to—if not sooner, then later. "Rest now, my lady," I'd say soothingly. "Everything's well."

At times, she wanted me to massage her back as well before I read to her. She never asked directly, just took off her shirt and lay prone on the bunk and—usually—turned her head from me. But once in a while she turned to look directly into my eyes and held her gaze for a moment or two. I'd oil up my hands from the top of my head—I'd kept on doing that just out of habit—and do her back gladly, using the strokes and pressures I knew she liked best: knuckles of my index and middle fingers pressed hard against the sides of her spine and progressing ever so slowly downward from her neck to the small of her back and then back up; the flat criss-cross strokes using the entire palm, stopping my hands at the outer curve of her ribs for just a moment to press inward with my palms; and always ending by pressing firmly with the fleshy part of both palms against her most tense muscles, those just above and below her lovely shoulder blades. Always she moaned lowly when I pressed there and said, "Oh, God, Mose, that is *so* bloody good!" and sometimes I'd catch a brief glimpse of her turned-away face—smiling, I think, just a bit. Her little sounds, that subtle smile, the sight and feel of her warm flesh: it was more wonderful than I'd imagined possible and, more, it was … arousing.

I always left before Rackham got back, to return to my tiny berth in the storage bin where I'd lie in my hammock and conjure up the image of Anne Bonny's face, her neck, her big smooth white back. I remembered, too, our week together at the Three Horsemen—the best days of my life. Often, I wouldn't be able to sleep until close to dawn.

Calico Jack resented my being with Anne every evening. I knew that. He would have killed me, I'm sure, except that he knew Anne wouldn't tolerate it. I was under her protection, and she was fierce as to that. More than once, I overheard them arguing about it. Their last such fight was toward the end, nearly three months after I'd come aboard, the evening before the pirates took a Dutch merchant frigate they'd been trailing for several days. I'd left a few minutes earlier but was taking the night air, thinking of Anne before retiring, and Rackham stumbled in drunk and immediately started in on her. "Why d'ye insist on humiliatin' me with that spooky nigger?" he practically shouted. "WHY? Fer all I know, he's put a spell on me. Ye know what I mean."

"Why, ya chuckleheaded *lubber!*" she shouted. "The only spell anyone's put on you is to make you stupider than ye already are. 'Humiliating' ye, is it? Ye humiliate yerself, imbibin' night after night with them scum and then ye come back here to me stinkin' of rum and more often than not ye're, well, *worthless* to me. Ye know exactly what I mean."

I heard him sniffle, and there was a pause. "But dearest," he practically whispered, "ya know that I care fer ye. Ain't I showed ye that?"

Anne said something then, quietly, but I couldn't hear what, and then I heard soft groans and labored breathing and heard Anne moan, "Oh, *Jack!*" and then it was quiet. I went back to my bin then and was awake, uneasy, the rest of the night.

The next day, I had my answer as to how Anne Bonny would be in a real fight. Around mid-morning, the buccaneers closed on and boarded the Dutch frigate they'd been following. I got to watch from the deck. The boarding itself was a frightening enough spectacle: the pirates tossing grappling hooks onto the other ship and drawing it to the *Revenge* and fastening the ships together; and then leaping onto the frigate, yelling obscenities and waving their cutlasses and axes and pistols and even a few pikes; and some of the sailors on the other ship resisting, fighting back, but most not—just throwing their hands in the air or sitting passively on the deck, resigned to death or whatever other fate awaited them.

Anne was the fiercest of the boarders, and watching her was most frightening. She was the first to leap onto the merchant ship, swinging her cutlass in her right hand and her ax in her left, her hair tightly bound by the same scarlet kerchief as the day I'd met her, and shouting louder than anyone. "EEY-YAH! *Down*, ye bastards, or I'll show ye the color of yer cowardly insides! *Certain* I will!" One of the Dutch sailors foolishly opted to take her on and was immediately rewarded with a cutlass slash that opened his chest from breastbone to navel. He screamed horribly and dropped to his knees, staring at his bleeding front, his white shirt now crimson-soaked, and looked up at Anne, surprised, his eyes glazing over, and she kicked the side of his head harder even than she'd kicked George Hitchcock. The poor man slumped to his side, curled in a fetal position, his arms crossed protectively against his chest, and his body convulsed for perhaps ten seconds and then he was still. Anne looked at him for a moment to be sure he was done. "Well, ya swab," she exclaimed loudly, "I reckon I settled *yer* hash!"

Mark Read was almost as ferocious. He was right beside Anne during the brief fight and screamed as loudly as she, in that high-pitched voice, and wielded a cutlass and a big pistol. Shortly after Anne had dispatched the Dutch sailor, I saw Read, his face red and furious, come up behind a tall, bearded, confused-looking man and put the pistol against the back of his head and blow a huge ugly hole in it. He and Anne stayed side-by-side throughout and then when it was over looked into each other's eyes, Anne taller and looking down at her friend, and Mark put his hand on Anne's shoulder and murmured something. I couldn't hear what. I noticed Calico Jack, standing maybe twenty feet from me on the quarterdeck, watching them.

That evening, the pirates celebrated their minor victory. Fenwick authorized rum all around, and by an hour after sunset practically every hand was slobbering and stumbling about and some were singing "Fifteen Men" and others dancing a hornpipe. Rackham, Fenwick and Lessard were as deep in their cups as any and led a chuck-farthing session near the mizzenmast.

Anne was in her cabin, away from the imbibing. I stayed close, observing the debauchery from afar, awaiting her summons. But more than another hour passed and no summons came, so after a time I started to worry about her and decided to peek through the tiny window to be sure she was well, and was ... *surprised* at what I saw. Anne Bonny was naked on the bunk, her big creamy thighs quivering, and lying beside her was another naked woman, one with smallish milky white breasts and sumptuous buttocks. They were locked in an embrace and kissing, tongues entwined. At first I couldn't see the other woman's face, but after a minute they turned so that Anne was on the bottom, on her back, and the other was stretched out on top of her, her eyes closed and her face contorted with pleasure, rubbing the length of her small, lithe body against Anne. It was Read.

I slinked back to my bin and huddled into my hammock and pulled both my blankets closely around me, but it wasn't enough. I couldn't stop shivering. I just lay there until after dawn, when finally I dozed for a short while. Then I stayed in bed the rest of the day, no longer shaking yet not able to keep the images of the fight and its aftermath from flooding my mind. I considered staying in that hammock for the next few days, not seeing anyone, when of a sudden there was a loud, frightened scream: "*Oh, God!* FIRE! Oh, Jesus Mary and Joseph! What'm I ta *do*, lord? Please! Someone *help* me, fer God's sake!, Oh, Jack! Mose! *Someone*, fer bloody Christ's sake, PLEASE!"

I leaped up and ran to the quarterdeck, where Anne was squatting, pale and quivering, holding her big face in both hands. About six feet from her, a pile of rags was burning; it was but a small conflagration, of minor consequence. I threw a bucket of water on it and there was an end to the emergency. I went over to Anne, knelt, and put my arms around her and drew her close to me. "There," I murmured. "*There* now. You're safe. No fire, my lady. Everything's ... " But before I could finish I felt a sharp blow against the small of my back, and was momentarily stunned. I turned around, painfully, and saw Rackham looking down at me, his upper lip curled, grasping a handspike. Fenwick stood just behind him, and Read a few yards beyond. "Get yer filthy black hands off her, nigger," Calico Jack snarled, "unless ye mean to feel the length of my dirk in yer belly."

"That's right," Fenwick said. "Let's keelhaul him and be rid of his bewitchery."

I started to glare at each of them with my blue eye, making it bulge, despite the pain in my back. But Rackham hit me again with the handspike and I winced, involuntarily shutting both eyes.

"Let's burn 'im, the damned witch!" Lessard exclaimed. "Let's lash the damned nigger to the mast and burn 'im alive."

"JACK!" We all turned around to see Anne advancing, her face flushed and furious and her hands balled into quivering fists. She pushed Rackham to one side, causing him to stumble, and grabbed Lessard by his shirt collar and practically lifted him off the deck. "Belay talk of BURNIN', ya damned *cockroach!*" she screamed. "And if I hear any more of keelhaulin' or dirks or witches or *any* of the rest of yer damned blarney, from any of ye lubbers, hell'll be comin' to breakfast 'board this here vessel, and ye can lay to that!" She looked into my eyes and held her gaze for just a moment and then glanced back at Read, who was still standing where she'd been, small and smooth-faced, her expression betraying nothing. The image of her silky naked body atop Anne's flooded my mind and I felt pangs of both jealousy and hatred.

That evening, just after sunset, Rackham ordered the *Revenge* to be sheltered in a lovely inlet called Dry Harbor Bay on the coast of Jamaica, and again ordered rum and brandy for all hands. I watched as he and Fenwick and Lessard carried four puncheons and a half-dozen bottles down to the fo'c'sle, and didn't see them return.

I could have used some of that rum. My lower back ached horribly and I had trouble getting a full breath. I tried to rest in my hammock but couldn't get comfortable, no matter what position I tried. I couldn't lie still and couldn't read. *Read!* In my agony, I obsessed about Anne and her lover—whatever her real name was, the miserable slut—and wondered whether they were together.

Finally, I had to know and slipped over to her cabin and peered through the window. Anne was alone in the bunk, curled into a fetal position, sobbing quietly. I watched her for perhaps five minutes, longingly. From somewhere below decks I heard drunken laughter and heard someone yell, "Give me that bottle, ya blasted limey!" Then I could contain myself no longer and tapped on the window. Anne, startled, saw me, jumped up, and opened the door. As soon as I entered she put her arms around me and drew me to her and held me and rubbed her cheek against the top of my oily head. "Oh, Mose," she whimpered. "Thanks fer today. I was ... I was ... that fire ... it ... oh, *God!*"

"Shh," I whispered. "You're safe now. Everything's fine." I put my arms around her thick waist and held her too, for just a sweet moment, my face against her breasts. "Anne," I whispered, "shall I rub your shoulders?" She nodded and pulled her shirt over her head and lay prone on the bunk, still trembling just a bit, saying nothing, and I massaged her tense shoulders, slowly, working particularly on a knot at the conjunction of her right shoulder and lower neck, and then oiled my hands and did her back, concentrating on the hard-muscled areas around both shoulder blades, and using the lateral crossover strokes with the flats of my palms that I knew she liked, down the length of her spine and back up again, my own back aching from the exertion, and breathing hard, but my pain more than compensated for by the wonder of yet again touching Anne's flesh. She moaned each time I pressed hardest. "Oh, *good*, Mose!" was all she said, just once, and then after a time asked if I'd read to her. I chose this time, one of my favorites:

> *Being your slave, what should I do but tend*
> *Upon the hours and times of your desire?*
> *I have no precious time at all to spend,*
> *Nor services to do till you require.*
> *Nor dare I chide the world-without-end hour*
> *Whilst I, my sovereign, watch the clock for you,*
> *Nor think the bitterness of absence sour*
> *When you have bid your servant once adieu.*
> *Nor dare I question with my jealous thought*
> *Where you may be, or your affairs suppose,*
> *But, like a sad slave, stay and think of nought*
> *Save where you are how happy you make those.*
> > *So true a fool is love that in your will,*
> > *Though you do anything, he thinks no ill.*

When I'd finished, Anne was asleep, snoring softly. I covered her with her red blanket and stroked her auburn hair and nuzzled the back of her neck and whispered, "Rest well, my love," and left to go back to my bin.

But before I did, I paused for a bit and sat wedged between two coils of rope to catch my breath and calm myself. A few minutes afterward, I saw Read tiptoe over and look through the window of Anne's cabin and then open the door quietly and enter. Through the doorway, I saw her touch Anne's shoulder and then saw Anne stand up to embrace the other woman and kiss her lips and stroke the back of her hair and heard her murmur, "Oh, Mary! Mary Read, my Mary Read! Oh, thy *sweet* love remembered! Come, Mary. Oh, *haply* I think on thee." Then the door closed.

I walked back to my berth and sunk, defeated, into my hammock. Part of me wanted to jump overboard and be blessedly sepulchered in the dark water, while another part wished to set the goddamned *Revenge* on fire and send all hands—particularly Mary Read—to a fiery hell. Either would do.

I lay there in that tortured wise until just before dawn, vacillating between thoughts of suicide and homicide, when I was startled out of my self-absorption by a half dozen booming explosions, cannon shots, and felt the *Revenge* being hit amidships, larboard side, knocking me from my bunk and causing my lantern to crash to the floor. That was followed by loud yelling, and I knew we'd been boarded. I ran to the deck and saw Anne and Read, both now dressed in their usual men's clothing, their faces fierce, screaming and cursing, fighting back-to-back with a group of four men in dark-blue uniforms, and prevailing. "C'MON, ya cowardly lubbers," I heard Anne shout as she swung her cutlass in that wonted frightening arc, keeping two men at bay. "Let's see what ye've got, ya damned *blackguards. We'll* show ye the color of yer insides, fer bloody Jesus's sake!" After they'd scattered that group, Anne scurried over to the hatch leading to the fo'c'sle where Calico Jack and Fenwick and the rest of the crew apparently still were and shouted down at them. "JACK!" she yelled. "It's Barnett. 'E's *boarded* us, by the powers. Ain't ye comin' out?"

There was a long pause. Then I heard Rackham, his voice slow and words slurred. "Well, darlin', we're all somewhat unable at the moment, as it were. We've had a bit too much rum ta do much good, as ye might say. Tell Barnett that poor gen'lemen o' fortune surrenders and begs for mercy as honest seamen what maybe went astray a bit, though never meant no harm."

"WHAT?" Anne screamed back. "Why, ya miserable lily-livered *cowards!* Ya damned imbibin' sonsabitches! Jack, if I had yer lubber throat in my hands I'd throttle ye ta doomsday! Certain I would, damn yer eyes! *Men*, ye call yerselves! HA! Powder monkeys and swabs, more like. Well, *I* ain't surrendering." Then she pulled a pistol from her belt and pointed it down toward where the crew cowered and discharged it. A moment later Mary Read dashed over, her face blackened and bloody, and she, too, delivered one shot. "Well, Jack," Anne shouted, "I reckon I've settled yer hash once and fer all. If not, I'll do it when I can."

Then the two women, still screaming and cursing, were overpowered by a dozen blue-coated sailors and the *Revenge* was taken.

THE *EN MASSE* TRIAL of the pirates in Port Royal was quick and the verdict and sentence even quicker: guilty, death by hanging. One escaped such fate, claiming that he'd been captured by the horrid pirates and threatened with torture and death unless he joined the crew and signed ship's articles, and the naïve Admiralty Court commissioners believed him. Mary Read tried to worm out of the noose by appearing in court wearing a pretty light-blue dress that perfectly complemented and accentuated the blue in her big eyes, her short brown hair clean and shining and framing her little face, and altogether looking small and feminine and helpless. Her story was that she'd lived every moment in dread fear of being raped and brutalized if she revealed her true gender, and thus had dressed as a man and had tried to appear fierce though, really, she was just a gentle soul who wanted nothing more than to escape the buccaneers and return to England, to dear Devon, to see her poor aging parents once again. She even produced tears at will, sniffling into a pink handkerchief when she described how terribly afraid she was each day of Captain Rackham and, especially, the brutal quartermaster Fenwick.

As for Calico Jack, to his credit he never sniveled. When asked if he had any final words before sentence was passed, he glared at each of the commissioners in turn and said, "What I done I done, and all o' ye can go to Davy Jones for all I care. Swing and sun-dry or not, it's all one ta me." More to his credit, he did what he could to save Anne. He asserted with a straight face that she'd been an indentured servant in New Providence who'd been obliged to turn to prostitution when her miserable husband abandoned her and that he, Jack, had taken pity on her and brought her aboard the *Revenge* as ship's cook. "I thought she weren't a true lady when first I met 'er," Rackham exclaimed with a straight face. "But really, ya know, she's just a tender flower and never could abide some o' the mean things we done."

But the commissioners would have none of it for either woman, knowing that they'd been the fiercest fighters when the *Revenge* had been taken, and condemned both to the same fate as the rest of the crew. Mary Read said nothing when sentence was passed, but Anne fell to her knees and trembled and wept and turned to the Chief Commissioner and cupped both hands over her stomach. "Yer lordship," she said softly, "I pleads my belly. Do what ye will with me, but 'til then at least spare my little one."

Calico Jack glared at her. "*What?*" he shouted. "Why, ya red whore! Who's the damned father, I should wonder? Is it that bewitchin' nigger? I reckon it ain't that other whore, though not from want of tryin', as it were."

She just stared at him, her eyes cold. "It's *you*, Jack," she finally said, sternly. "It's you, damn yer eyes. And maybe if ye'd acted like a man back in Dry Harbor, we wouldn't be here now and ye wouldn't be about to hang like a dog."

After conferring, the commissioners agreed to delay Anne's execution until after the birth of her baby. "But not *one* minute longer!" the Chief intoned.

It was Fenwick who saved me—inadvertently, to be sure. After the commissioners had passed sentence on everyone else they turned to me, their brows furrowed. The ugly little quartermaster, noticing that, pointed a stubby finger at me. "Him too!" he exclaimed. "That damned nigger's a witch, by God! He laid a spell on this 'ere crew and made us lazy and careless. *Drunkards!* Barnett, he never woulda caught us except for that goddamned spook. If we swing, then, by the powers, he oughta too." The Chief Commissioner asked Fenwick directly if I'd ever fought alongside the others or made my mark on ship's articles. "Well, no," the idiot answered, "he never. He never done nothin' 'cept put spells on poor helpless seamen and moon over that there cow."

That night, I wanted to see Anne. She and Read were shackled together in a small wooden shack just above the beach. There was just one guard, a hulking blond country boy named Billy, and I bribed him, just after midnight, with a small silver goblet that Anne had given me, one of the prizes from the Dutch frigate. "One hour," he said, smiling nicely. "That's all I can give you."

But it was no good. Anne seemed glad enough to see me and hugged me with her one unshackled arm and wept immediately. "Oh, Mose," she whimpered, "what's ta become of us? What're we ta do?"

"It'll be fine," I whispered. "I'll be with you all the time. I'll take care of you."

She shook her long auburn hair. "My Mary!" she cried. "Oh, Mose, tomorrow they hang my Mary! What're we ta do? Oh, *Mary!*"

Mary Read said nothing. She just stood there, fastened to Anne Bonny by one arm and a leg, still wearing the blue dress she'd worn in court, impassive, staring at me with those goddamned big blue eyes. She never even blinked—just stared with those huge eyes, just looking at me, almost looking *through* me.

It was no good. I had Anne sit on the bunk and tried to rub her neck and shoulders, and was glad to touch her again, but Mary was right there, silent and never taking her eyes from me. Anne was glad enough for the attention and relaxed a bit under my touch, though never stopping her crying and trembling, but it wasn't the same and I didn't know what to say to her, and felt too self-conscious to read to her, and after a while I couldn't go on.

Then something came over me. Just then I simply had enough of Anne's whimpering and Mary's staring and the two of them together. I loved Anne Bonny and always would, but enough. I stood, gently touched Anne's cheek, looked into her wet hazel eyes, and left the shack without another word.

They hanged the pirates in groups of three just after dawn at Gallows Point, a lovely spit of land north of the harbor and beach. Calico Jack went quietly, looking out to sea just once and then staring straight ahead as they tightened the noose around his neck. Fenwick, though, struggled and cursed and spat at his executioners until the last, and squirmed horribly while dangling at the end of the rope until finally he strangled and was still. As for Lessard, he wasn't in good shape, having been hit in the side of his chest by one of the pistol balls fired into the fo'c'sle by Anne and Read. He seemed in so much pain from his wound that death was perhaps a relief; he was sickly pale and sweating and hunched over to his left and said nothing when his time came, and didn't struggle at all as he dangled.

I watched and waited for Mary Read to be hanged. But after they'd finally done for the buccaneers and still she hadn't been brought out, I asked one of the nearby soldiers if he knew when she'd be executed. "That little bitch in the blue dress?" he sneered. "Gone! She and that other pig slit poor Billy's throat sometime before dawn and got his key. They stole ole Willy Dipple's fishin' boat and took off fer God-knows-where, the damned whores. I imagine Barnett'll catch 'em, but if not then good riddance, says I."

Later that morning, I walked alone along the main street in Port Royal and then down some of the side streets. Black folks, many wearing brightly colored clothes, sold mangoes and bananas and fish. Black women with their big protruding buttocks strolled slowly, many carrying babies in slings across their chests, talking to each other, animated. Some nodded to me. Then I walked back to the beach and took off my shirt to let the sun warm my still-aching back. To the north, I could see the last batch of pirates left hanging, their bodies swaying stiffly in the nice breeze, their hands tied behind their backs. I thought George Hitchcock was one, though they were too far away to be sure. I decided I'd let my hair grow back. I was tired of oiling my damned head every day, and, really, there was no reason for that now; I was finished with massages.

I liked Jamaica. It would be good to sit on the beach and read my books, to eat fresh fruit and fish, to warm my back. The beach was sparkling white, and that was the only whiteness I hoped to see for a while. Certain it was.

A Spiritual Advisor to Davy Crockett

I SERVED AS A SPIRITUAL advisor for a fondly remembered time to Davy Crockett, the so-called "congressman from the canebrake." I was by then a thin, balding, white-bearded, frail-appearing, watery-blue-eyed hypocrite known by all just as *Parson* due to my long-time posture as a devout Methodist minister. I say *posture* because I was in fact the most cynical of atheists, and had certainly never been ordained; it was all an act, my piety and warmth and caring, the sole aim of which was to further my true calling: the seduction of my female parishioners, many the wives of senators and representatives in Washington City.

I first met Davy in 1834 at the behest of a certain Whig senator and was with him from then until the eve of his violent demise, though not mine, at the sad and unnecessary massacre at the Alamo in San Antonio on March 6, 1836. If truth be known, I was largely responsible for our being at that miserable crumbling mission in the first place, having advised Davy during the election of 1835 to tell his constituents that, if they chose not to re-elect him, they could go to hell and he would go to Texas.

That responsibility was particularly weighing on me during the twelfth day of the Alamo siege, a cold and drizzly Saturday morning during which the unwonted sense of gloom I'd been feeling for several days seemed at odds with the joyous behavior of Davy and about a dozen men gathered near the south wall, close to the main gate. Some of the boys had carried out Colonel Jim Bowie on his sickbed, but I don't see how he could have enjoyed much: his face was shockingly pale, he was simultaneously sweating and shivering, and now and again his eyes rolled back in delirium. The renowned knife fighter had typhus and I figured him to last another day, maybe two at most. Davy'd gotten a fiddle somewhere and he and Scotty McGregor, playing an ancient bagpipe, were making the welkin ring. It was a musical contest, if you could call it that, apparently to see who could most closely approximate the sound of a panther giving birth, breech delivery, and Davy was winning. The boys were whooping it up, slapping each other on the back and good-naturedly insulting the musicians. "By God, Davy," one bellowed, "you oughter see if you can play for old Santy Anny. By Henry, I wager he'll up 'n *surrender* on the spot!" And other such droll carryings-on.

Crockett lapped it up. He was in his element: the much-admired center of attention in a straightforward world of men much like himself—hunters, backwoodsmen, adventurers—and done now with the tangled intrigues of Washington City and the cynical politicians who had, with my unwitting help, so exploited him during the last few years; and done with the enmity he'd earned as an opponent of the powerful regime of his onetime political ally and long-ago military leader in the Creek Indian war, President Andrew Jackson. Here at the Alamo it was a man's world and Davy was a man's man.

There were only a handful of women in the mission, mostly Mexicans and one Anglo, the nineteen-year-old wife of Lt. Almeron Dickinson. Her presence seemingly went unnoticed by most of the men, but not by me—a perverted lecher for whom married females were a prize vigorously to be sought, even in a perilous situation like ours. In the two weeks we'd been in the mission, I'd done what I could to ingratiate myself to Susanna Dickinson. She had an eighteen-month-old baby, Angelina, and I'd cooed over the child and kissed her and offered to pray for her. I almost disgusted myself since, in truth, I couldn't stand children, particularly babies, but I figured that slobbering over the kid would somehow help me bed the mother. However, Susanna never warmed to me as I'd hoped she would, and also I'd not found the chance to be alone with her long enough to win her over.

Under other circumstances, seeing old Davy enjoying himself and entertaining the men might have been more joyous. He was a man you couldn't help liking. But, as I say, my heart at the moment was not light. As it turned out, one of my recent acquaintances, a Frenchman named Louis Rose, standing beside me watching the festivities, had similar thoughts. "Tell me, Parson," Louis said, "do you think our friends here know what a tight anchor we are in? Because, *mon ami*, I am not sure they do."

I nodded. Louis's characterization of our plight was an understatement. There were only about two hundred of us in the mission and maybe four thousand Mexicans out there, many of them battle-hardened professional soldiers, according to Colonel Travis. They had bayonets—big scary knives they could attach to their muskets and rifles—and we didn't. Their artillery pounded away at the thick stone walls day and night, each cannon ball crumbling our meager defenses a bit more, jangling our nerves, and rumor had it that their biggest guns hadn't even arrived yet. We couldn't get out without being hacked to pieces by cavalry, and each day the likelihood of help arriving seemed dimmer. General Houston was reportedly somewhere to the north trying to put together an army and Colonel Fannin was ninety miles away at Goliad with a few hundred men, but even if they did come it didn't seem likely that they could get through the constricting ring of Mexican army that surrounded us. Any day now, I thought, Santa Anna will decide to stop farting around and will send his soldiers pouring over our walls. It would be bloody and over quickly.

"Point well taken, Louis," I replied. "Not exactly an enviable position."

"I have seen *le carnage,* mon ami, as a young conscript fighting with Napoleon, on our retreat from Moscow: the frozen corpses in the snow, the limbs askew at all angles, the eyes and mouths open wide in final horror, the blood quickly congealed, turned black. No honor or glory, my friend. I wonder, Parson, how many of our compatriots have seen the same."

I nodded again. Louis's pessimism was on-target. It wasn't only the increasing desperateness of our situation that worried and depressed me, but the general living conditions: bad food and little of it—mostly old beef and dried corn—and, worse, no coffee; alkaline drinking water; the pervasive odors of unwashed men, common toilet facilities and constant smoke and gunpowder; and the jarring booming of the Mexican cannons and our pitiful return fire. And on top of all that, there was the distressing lack of suitable female companionship. For a man who'd been used to finer things, life at the Alamo was not pleasant.

I don't know if Davy shared my sentiments. If so, he didn't seem too troubled. In fact, he seemed to be having a pretty good time—playing his fiddle, telling stories, impressing the boys with his marksmanship by picking off Mexican soldados who thought they were out of rifle range. He was a big celebrity among the raw frontier hicks: an actual United States congressman, and not just any old representative but one whose adventures and escapades—wildly exaggerated, to be sure—had been a major focus of national attention through books and articles and even a play, *Lion of the West*, all of which had made him larger than life on the one hand and a sort of national buffoon on the other.

Watching Davy, I thought back to the beginning of our time together and to my work for him. My weakness for the feminine fandango was behind the genesis of my relationship with Congressman Crockett, and ultimately for our journey to San Antonio. As it happened, the wife of a powerful Whig senator from Pennsylvania, a Mrs. Elizabeth McKean, had blabbed to her pot-bellied husband about the weekly trysts she and I had enjoyed for several months, usually on the sofa in my church office following Wednesday Bible discussion luncheons. The couple had apparently had yet another in a series of episodes of marital discord over a continuing theme—the amount of time he spent smoking expensive Spanish cigars and consorting with fellow solons at Washington watering holes—and she'd weepingly confessed to him about her afternoons of forbidden passion, claiming to have been driven to the arms of her caring minister, contrary to her high sense of moral values, because of being left alone so very much, horribly ignored. The senator approached me the next day and presented an interesting ultimatum: either agree to accompany Crockett on his upcoming Whig-sponsored tour of the Northeast as his spiritual advisor or be exposed for the womanizing hypocrite that he now knew me to be. I immediately opted for the former, not wishing to jeopardize my access to the intimate favors of my fairer-sexed congregants.

I'd heard about Davy, of course, but had never met him. He'd arrived in Washington a few years back straight from the canebrakes of Tennessee where he'd been a mediocre state legislator, homespun and barely literate, but handsome, charming and glib. He'd come as far as he had not because of his interest in or grasp of national politics—rudimentary at best—but because he was a great storyteller and simply charmed people on the hustings. He was a Democrat, but allied with the anti-Jacksonian branch of the party. He and Old Hickory, once Davy's political mentor, had had some serious fallings-out over such issues as the national bank and land use policy and Jackson's miserable treatment of the Indians, forcing the Cherokees and a few other peaceful tribes to

45

leave their homelands and move westward to less-hospitable environs, and Davy'd not been shy about publicly expressing his disagreements. In fact, Crockett's rantings against the president had made clear that he was a Whig in all but name, and the Whigs were doing all they could to capitalize on that schism for their own purposes.

It was a Friday afternoon when Senator McKean approached me. I was in my office at the church, writing my sermon for Sunday—a tedious bit of fluff about how Moses's travails in leading the people of Israel to the Promised Land teaches us about the value of perseverance. It was nonsense, of course, but I hoped it would have the desired effect—heating up the ladies in the audience—due not to the contents but to my sincere and personal delivery. My modus operandi was to make direct eye contact with a particular female whom I coveted and maintain that contact, my china-blue eyes oozing caring and warmth and understanding, while I uttered my silly platitudes seemingly to her alone. "And so," I'd say, "as we face life's trials and difficulties, alone and vulnerable as we all are in this harsh world, we must take courage from the example of brave Moses, a man who ... " Blah, blah, blah. It worked most of the time. After the service, she—the object of my desire—would approach as I stood outside the church entrance and say, "Oh, I was so deeply affected by your sermon today—'alone and vulnerable as we all are in this harsh world'—ah, that is so true." I'd take one of her small hands in both of mine, squeeze gently, and again stare deeply into her eyes. "Yes," I'd say, "but is it not also true that to get through this hard life we must cling to each other desperately? Do we not, my dear, need to comfort and encourage one another?" Usually, that would do it. Or if I sensed that wasn't quite enough, I'd unclasp one of my hands and subtly rub the inside of her wrist with just the pads of my index and middle fingers. If she wore long sleeves, I'd push the sleeve up just a bit and then rub. That move rarely failed, and within the week—most often the next afternoon—she'd be on my sofa, the two of us clinging to each other desperately.

Fortunately, the senator wasn't privy to my larger motives. When I told him I was working on my sermon, he merely grunted, unimpressed, set forth my two options, and, after I quickly agreed to his terms, explained my assignment. The idea was that I'd stand near Davy during his appearances in the northern cities so as to convey the idea that he was a serious guy, a spiritual man, not just some clever backwoods bumpkin. The Whigs were—if one could believe it—building up Crockett for a run at the presidency on their ticket in 1836, figuring that his rustic charm and verbosity could effectively counter the brilliant but stiff Jackson-selected Democratic candidate, Vice President Van Buren, and they knew he'd need a more elevated image to be credible. I wouldn't have to say much, just look pious—my specialty—and once in a while mumble a prayer or invocation or such. I could do that. I could even make my eyes moisten or cloud up at will to convey the impression that I was so very affected and moved by what I was feeling or hearing. It was a role perfectly suited to a phony such as myself, and I was impressed that the senator saw through me so quickly and accurately.

I was to meet Crockett on Monday of the next week in Philadelphia, where he was to give an Independence Day speech before a gathering of the local Young Whigs group. I arrived in the city about an hour before the event and had just a few minutes to meet the congressman. I was prepared for a loudmouthed buffoon, a clown, a braggart. But I was surprised. Instead of the grizzled half-horse-half-alligator-and-a-mite-touched-with-snapping-turtle cartoon figure I'd been expecting, before me was an average-looking middle-aged man, a bit taller than most, clean-shaven, dark-haired, with a long narrow nose and somewhat feminine lips. He was wearing not a greasy fringed deerskin hunting outfit, as I'd imagined, but a conventional brown broadcloth coat and fashionable gray pantaloons. "David Crockett, sir," he said, politely extending a hand. "Proud to make your acquaintance. I look forward to our journey together."

"The honor, sir, is mine," I replied, slightly taken aback but liking the man immediately.

Soon it was time for my invocation. "Please give those gathered here today your blessing, kind Sir," I implored, rolling my eyes heavenward and grasping an oversized leatherbound Bible to my breast with both hands. "And please help us to do our best in the face of harsh oppression!" This last was intended to show that I was their ally, but it was disingenuous; I cared not a fig about Jackson or Van Buren or Democrats or Whigs or the national bank or westward expansion or any of it.

Then Davy stood up and gave his speech, and it was a ripsnorter: on the one hand full of sneers at the administration—"Old King Andy ... " and "the tyranny of one-man rule ... "— and on the other hand just what the country had come to expect from him as a colorful comic figure. "Now they's been times," he said, "when I've been so disenfrangled with Ole' Hickory and that passel of varmints who pant after him, including that puffed-up she-wolf Martin Van Buren, that I purely have wished I was back in the green hills of Tennessee with my good dogs, Blue and ole Elmer, trailin' after bears and coons and such. Say, I recall the time I had a coon cornered in a old oak and he looks down at me and he says, 'Davy, is that you?' he says, and I says back at him, 'Well, it most surely is.' Then he nods his head and says, 'Well, don't bother shooting. I'm a-comin' down, Davy. I *surrender!*'"

After he'd finished, to thunderous applause, the fuzz-faced leader of the Young Whigs thanked Davy effusively, praised him as "a man destined to carry the bright shining torch of democracy ever forward to the shining sea," and presented him with a beautiful fifty-caliber percussion cap rifle custom-made in Lancaster, Pennsylvania, with an engraved alligator on the trigger guard and a silver plate in the stock on which was another engraving, of a possum and a deer, and with a small gilded arrow inlaid onto the barrel, near the muzzle. Crockett fondled the weapon as if it were a precious child and for a moment seemed near tears. "Oh, *my!*" he finally exclaimed. "This here surely is the most awesome rifle gun I ever have seed. With a gun like this, a man could put a rifle ball through the moon. I reckon I'll call her Pretty Betsey, and I promise you folks that I'll use her always in defense of our poor country." Again, big applause. Afterward, we were invited to join about a dozen or so of the Young Whigs at Stoodley's Tavern on Broad Street for an Independence Day drink—"or two or ten," in the words of the fuzz-faced young man. "Well," Davy responded, "I've been persuaded."

In no time he had the table at Stoodley's in an uproar, describing how he'd captured and tamed a huge black bear near his home in Obion, Tennessee, named him Deathhug, and taught him to sit at the dinner table with the family. "Within a week, dagnab if he weren't teaching the children their manners. If one of them slurped milk, ole Deathhug he'd lean over and put his big hairy face about an inch from that child's nose, his horrible bear breath oppressive, and just glare! Pretty quick, that boy'd straighten up and do right. 'Okay, Mister Deathhug, sir,' he'd say, sipping his milk perfectly. 'Is *this* better?'"

After his second rum Davy started in again on Jackson, employing some of the same phrases he'd used in his speech—the "Old King Andy" line and "this political Judas, Martin Van Buren" and "one man rule ... now, folks, that just ain't right!"—and within a short time I learned something about Congressman Crockett: when it came to politics, he was a bore. I'd known him just a short time but already I felt I knew all there was to know about his relatively simple-minded viewpoints and beliefs, and during the nearly two years that I was with him I learned little more; there was little more to learn. He was sincere in his beliefs, to be sure, but a tedious bore in regard to them nonetheless

Davy and I had breakfast together the next morning before boarding the *New Philadelphia* to sail to Camden City, New Jersey, where we were to take the Camden and Amboy Railroad to South Amboy, on our way to New York. When we were alone, he was a different person—more genuine and, I believe, more himself—than when in public; he seemed less a rube and more a rather ordinary, soft-spoken man. We ate buttered rolls and drank coffee and talked politics a bit, not much, but when it was just the two of us he was nowhere near as strident. He quietly read a newspaper while sipping his coffee, and I had to stifle a chuckle while watching him; his facial expression was intent and his brow furrowed and usually his lips moved as he struggled to make sense of the words on the page. I soon realized that the public Davy Crockett—the rabid anti-Jacksonian and colorful semi-grammatical frontier caricature—was mostly a persona in which he'd become enmeshed because it was what people expected of him and he knew he had to deliver. The private David who sat across from me at the breakfast table was perhaps less interesting but more human.

In the train, Crockett asked me what I thought of his "speechifying," as he called it. The question caught me off guard, but it was something I'd thought about. "Well," I answered, "there might be some ways you could spice it up a bit. For example, I notice you always say 'Old King Andy.' But that sounds almost affectionate. Why not try 'King Andrew the First'? Wouldn't that have more bite?"

His face brightened like a little boy's who'd just received a shiny new toy for Christmas. "That's great, Parson!" he exclaimed. "I'll do 'er. Say, how 'bout givin' me some more idears that I might could use?"

That was an intriguing proposition and as we clacked along toward South Amboy I thought it over and came up with some suggestions. By the time we arrived, I'd written them down and handed them to the congressman. "Let's see," he said, holding the paper at arm's length and knitting his brow. "Oh, this is good: '... a greater tyrant than Cromwell, Caesar, or Bonaparte.' Now Bonaparte I know, but who are these other two? Well, never mind. This is *terrific*, Parson. You ain't only a man of faith, which I do so admire, but a man of learnin' too."

That evening, he used almost all the ideas I'd given him, mixing them in with his own tired phraseology. "Now you men know," he intoned, "how I feel about the many injustices heaped on us all by King Andrew the First, as I call him. I do consider him a greater tyrant than Cromwell, Caesar, or Bonaparte. Him and that imp of egotism Martin Van Buren—well, their tyrannical abuses are legion. And we all know who the king has chosen to sit on his exalted throne when he's fixed to step down. Oh, yes! His Eminence hath, from on high, already anointed his successor and who are we poor commoners to dare question his majestic judgment? Now, men, I know that I ain't all that popular amongst the folks back home, many of 'em, for what I been sayin', but I reckon I'd rather be politically dead than hypocritically immortalized." I'd anticipated that that line would get a big reaction, but not so. Few of my lines did. Mostly, the men in the audience merely stared at Crockett, puzzled, not quite sure what to make of him, as though they'd just witnessed a familiar and beloved hound suddenly get up from his nap in front of the fireplace to put on a silk robe, sit in a rocking chair, smoke a pipe, and read *Paradise Lost.*

When, however, Davy, just before ending, launched into one of his familiar homespun yarns—a good-natured piece about his legendary three-day fight with Mike Fink—the usual grins and guffaws ensued. And when he finished the speech with his trademark slogan—"Be always sure you're right, then go ahead!"—the audience applauded politely, though not, I thought, with quite the same enthusiasm as before.

I knew at once that Davy and I'd made a serious error in judgment: it was not high-sounding literate phrases or learned allusions that the people wanted from Davy Crockett, but, instead, the frontier pablum for which he was famous. I understood clearly that the Whigs were looking not for a serious politico in him, but, rather, an entertainer, an American folk hero—despite what they may have said to the contrary.

Davy, however, didn't quite see it that way. "Parson," he said to me at breakfast the next morning, "I want to thank you. With your help, I feel like a new man. I never had much education, you know, but now I calc'late that folks'll figure I do. This is gonna work out real fine."

But it didn't. Crockett continued to deliver the same basic speech in each city, using more of my lofty phrases and fewer of his own each time, and the reaction was always similar. Yet he was oblivious—so swept up with the high tone of his *speechifying* that he noticed nothing else. At one point I tried to persuade him to go back to being himself, to drop my ideas, but he'd have none of it. "Oh, no," he said, "you don't understand. For the first time in my life, Parson, folks are really takin' me serious. I owe you more than I can ever repay." After that, I gave up.

By the end of the two weeks, I sensed that the Whigs were starting to feel disenchanted with their adopted champion. It was almost palpable.

That aside, Davy Crockett's Northeast tour was one of the best times of my life. All I had to do was say my silly little benedictions and other platitudes and then just look pious and interested. That was okay. But the finest times were always later, at the taverns and parties, where Davy could just be himself, telling his stories and being the center of attention. I never had to say much, could just watch and soak up the fun, enjoy the male camaraderie. Now this was a new experience. I'd so spent my life thinking about women, obsessed with them, pursuing them, that men had held little interest. The only men I'd known were my boring, stiff parishioners. So this was a new world for me, and I liked it: the simple fun, the open laughter, the good-natured insults, the constant crudity, even the omnipresent cigars. As fond as I was of the feminine fandango, it was good to take a reprieve.

But that reprieve was short-lived. Soon after our return to Washington, I saw Elizabeth McKean again. Intimately. I didn't intend to,

51

but she approached me one afternoon in my office and apologized for confessing and started sobbing and soon we were naked together on my sofa, slippery bodies entangled. We continued to see each other after that, but were careful—*very* careful—not to arouse her fat husband's suspicion. We didn't adhere to a regular schedule and even did it now and again in places other than the church. I was worried sick about being found out, and at one point considered trying to break off with her, giving some lame excuse. But before I could think of what to say, I found that I couldn't tolerate not seeing her, in fact looked forward desperately to seeing her. Worse, I started needing her emotionally. I believe that I fell in love with her, although not having experienced that particular emotion previously I couldn't accurately identify it. Yet I thought about her all the time. I found myself conjuring the image of her oval face—her beautiful green eyes looking up warmly at me when first we embraced each time we met, and remembering how she looked following coitus: her face a bit flushed; her light brown hair askew, falling about her thin shoulders; her lovely breasts heaving as she sought to catch her breath; her small hand rubbing the back of her white neck. I constantly recalled little things she'd said, and couldn't wait to see her the next time. These feelings were not just new for me, but uncomfortable—so much so that I temporarily lost interest in other women; whereas on Sundays my endeavor had ever been seduction and conquest, now I was uninterested. I still delivered my sermons with my wonted phony warmth, but now my doing so was aimed not at charming someone out of her clothes but due merely to long habit. I wanted to say something to Elizabeth, to tell her how I felt, but didn't know what to say.

A good thing that happened during this time, though, was that Davy joined my congregation. As he explained, he'd been impressed during our time together with my faith and devotion, and felt the need to "get closer to my creator." He also said that he missed me, particularly our quiet breakfasts together. He wondered, in fact, if we could continue meeting for breakfast once or twice a week. "Seems like everyone wants somethin' from me, Parson, but not you. With you, I can just be myself and not have to put on a face." I quickly agreed, and we became even closer friends. We not only breakfasted together, but I occasionally accompanied him to political events or, more commonly, to social gatherings. These were repeats of the Northeast tour—good times among Davy and his male admirers—and I cherished those hours.

As the 1835 congressional election approached, things weren't going so well for Crockett. The Whigs had ceased courting him, and it was clear that they'd dropped the idea of running him against Van Buren next year. That didn't seem to bother Davy much, for he was putting his energy into running again for his seat. He'd been getting a lot of flack from his constituents and the Democratic press about his constant harping against Jackson, and re-election was by no means a given. That worried him, but he was unwilling to let up on the president because, as he told me, "Like I've said, I'd rather be politically dead than hypocritically immortalized. You gave me that idea, Parson, and I reckon I believe it with all my heart."

As the campaign progressed and the level of criticism of Crockett grew, he asked me for some "idears I might could use." I thought about that. There'd been more and more stories in the papers about the brouhaha in Texas, where a bunch of colonist rabble-rousers were stirring up trouble and making noise about breaking away from Mexico and where huge chunks of cheap land were available. So one morning, over poached eggs and toast and coffee, I suggested the you-can-go-to-hell-and-I'll-go-to-Texas line. Davy loved it, and used it immediately—over and over and over, after his fashion. Unfortunately, all it did was to irritate his constituents even more, and he lost.

By the time of the election, I'd become more and more enamored of Elizabeth, in spite of myself; I simply couldn't get the woman out of my mind. Finally, I had to tell her how I felt. But her reaction was not what I expected. It was a Wednesday afternoon following the Bible discussion luncheon, and we were at last alone and naked and about to commence the deed of darkness yet again. "Elizabeth," I murmured, "I must tell you something. I ... I ... I *love* you. I've never loved anyone, but I love you. I think I do, my darling ... I want you to know that."

She stared at me, her lovely green eyes cold. "*No!*" she hissed. "I don't want you to love me! That's *it!* It's over!" She jumped up, dressed, and started to leave. "And let me tell you something ELSE, Mister Holy Holy," she practically screamed. "I *knew* this would happen. All I ever wanted from you was a goddamn tumble, something forbidden. I KNEW this would happen sooner or later! Damn you to hell anyway! I *never* want to see you again!" And then she was out the door, forever.

I was devastated. For more than a week afterward I could barely eat or sleep. I thought about her constantly, longed for her. One evening, alone, I cried real tears for the first time in nearly half a century. I didn't want to see anyone, including Davy.

He, however, reached out. After not hearing from me for more than a week, he showed up at the church one Friday morning and, over coffee in my office, asked what was wrong. I couldn't tell him the truth, of course, so just said I'd been feeling out of sorts. Davy nodded. "Me, too," he said. "I reckon I don't know what to do with myself next. I've had a bellyful of Washington City, I can tell you that." He paused for a minute and stared out the window. I was glad he was there with me; his simple masculine presence was reassuring, comforting. "One thing I've been thinkin' 'bout, Parson, is Texas. A fella can get himself a lot of land there, maybe make a new start. I told the folks back home I'd go there if they didn't want me back in that Congress job. I weren't serious, but now I calc'late that ain't such a bad idea. I know a few others who've been talkin' 'bout it too."

I looked around my office, stared at the couch where I'd enjoyed Elizabeth and so many others. "Davy," I said, "if you go to Texas, I'd like to go with you."

That was how we got to the Alamo, where now we were in dire peril.

ABOUT AN HOUR before sunset, the Mexican cannons suddenly stopped. It was still drizzling and getting colder. With the quiet, I thought I'd take a nap when Major Evans loudly announced that Colonel Travis wanted everyone to gather in the courtyard, near the long barracks.

With Bowie sick, Travis was the big boo-hoo. He was a twenty-six-year-old firebrand lawyer originally from Alabama who never smiled and always stood so straight that I wondered if he had a steel rod up his ass. I'd been told—though I didn't know if it was accurate—that it'd been his asinine idea for us to be penned up defending this broken-down mission against twenty-to-one odds, he having defied Houston's orders to blow the place to hell and fight elsewhere. He was a humorless fanatic, and I disliked him intensely.

"Men," Travis said when we'd all gathered, "I have bad news. Jim Bonham has just returned from Goliad. We can expect no help from Colonel Fannin. He started out, but his wagons broke down and he had to turn back. Failing reinforcements, the Alamo cannot hold. Our scouts report that the Mexicans are even now building scaling ladders, and we can expect a total assault at any time. Men, we cannot hope to prevail but we can make Santa Anna's victory expensive for him. We can kill them as they charge our position, kill them as they scale our walls, kill them as they put the bayonet to us. Oh, we'll all die, no question about that, but in so doing we can help save the glorious life of Texas ... However, I want no man to stay against his will." He paused and, with a silly dramatic flourish, pulled his sword from its sheath and with it drew a long line in the mud. "Those who will stay and die with me, cross over this line."

At first, no one moved. Then Tapley Holland, a good-looking kid barely out of his teens and dumb as a log, exclaimed, "Well, boys, what the *hell!*" and leaped over the line. Then, one by one, a few more did. Then whole groups did. Davy and I looked at each other, then he shrugged his shoulders and crossed. Finally, it was just Louis Rose and me. I didn't relish the thought of dying, but neither did I want to be singled out. "Louis," I said, "I guess this hellhole's as good a place as any."

"Not for me, mon ami," he said. "I didn't survive Russia to die in this desert." I nodded but crossed the line to stand next to Davy Crockett, and Louis was alone. Looking directly into my eyes, he crossed himself and then closed his eyes and silently mouthed the words to what I assume was a prayer.

"Thank you, men," Travis said. "Parson, how about saying a few words?"

I looked around at the two hundred or so men standing beside me, those with whom I was going to perish. I looked at Travis for just a moment, afraid to let him see my eyes. I stepped forward, turned around and took off my hat, feeling the cool rain on my bald head. The men bowed their heads and some took off their hats as well. "Well, kind

Sir," I intoned, "we're here to do our duty, the best we can. Give us a little encouragement, if you please. And have mercy on our souls."

"*Amen!*" Davy boomed. Then everyone echoed.

Afterward, I needed to be alone and went into the chapel, which was empty except for the few rooms where the women were housed and one storage area. *Goddamn you, Travis*, I thought. *Goddamn you and your silly heroics and goddamn your line in the dirt. Why didn't you just do as you were told instead of setting these poor bastards up for slaughter, like cattle. "Kill them as they scale our walls ... kill them as they put the bayonet to us." Kill, kill, kill! Now you're going to kill me and the best friend I've ever had. Goddamn you to hell now and forever, you long-winded jackanapes, you miserable smooth-faced rod-up-your-ass sonofabitch!*

I was so worked up I could feel my face burning. My hands were shaking. I needed some relief.

Nearby, I heard soft moaning. It was Susanna Dickinson in the sacristy, sitting on a low stool, eyes closed, holding Angelina tightly against her and rocking the child gently. *This is my chance*, I thought. Entering the room quietly, I put my hand on her shoulder and squeezed just a bit. "My dear," I said, "I can only imagine what you are going through. What a harsh world we live in! Is there anything I can say or do to ease your terrible burden?"

"I doubt it," she answered. "Not unless you have more authority than I think you do."

I stared deeply into her eyes, and subtly rubbed her shoulder. I touched the back of her neck with the pads of my middle and index fingers. She didn't object, so I rubbed a bit harder. "Susanna," I whispered, "shall we pray together?"

She shook her head, but said nothing.

I tried another tack. "My heart goes out to you, my child. May I ... may I give you a hug?" I figured she'd stand and melt into my arms, but instead she rolled her eyes upward as in disbelief and shook her head. I said nothing more. Then, after a minute or so, she stood, almost reluctantly, put the baby in her crib, and faced me. She looked into my eyes, not warmly, and just stood there. I took the initiative and stepped toward her and put my arms around her and hugged her, pulling her close against me, feeling her breasts crushed against my thin chest. Her arms hung limply at her sides. I held her to me, not moving, and soon she seemed to relax just a bit and allowed her head to rest lightly against my chest. I moved my right hand up to sweetly stroke the hair on the back of her head and then allowed my left hand to drift ever so subtly down her back to the lovely swelling south of her waist. Immediately she stiffened and pushed me away, causing me to stumble backward three steps. "You ugly horny old goat!" she hissed. "Get the hell out of here! The *nerve!* Who the *hell* do you think you are?"

"My child," I stammered. "Please understand. I was only ... "

"I know what you were 'only.' I know you for who you are, you disgusting old fart! Now get the hell out of here and leave us alone. *Out!*" Then she practically pushed me from the room and slammed the door.

Later that evening, I was sitting with Davy and a few of his Tennessee friends at our assigned post on the south wall, in a stockaded area near the chapel. The Mexican guns were still quiet, and I think I knew why: they wanted us to let down our guard and lull us to rest so they could sneak up on us, probably before dawn. Some of the men were dozing, others were playing cards by the light of a torch, and one was just staring out into space. "Well, Parson," Davy said, "I'm powerful sorry I got you into this b'ar trap. It ain't exactly what I had in mind when we come down here."

I looked at him holding the beautiful rifle he'd been given by the Philadelphia Young Whigs. I remembered him speaking to them the first day I met him, charming them and then afterward entertaining the gathering at Stoodley's with his Deathhug story. I recalled us riding in the train on our way to New York and how excited he was about my silly suggestions for his "speechifying." I thought about our quiet breakfasts together, and how he'd once said he felt he could be himself with me. And now an end was near. "Not to worry, my friend," I said. "It's been a good time. The best."

He nodded. "Well," he said, "I reckon we'll give 'em what-fer when they come after us. They'll eat snakes before they get inside these walls, I'll g'arantee you that." He paused, yawned, and pulled a blanket around him. "I guess I'll get a little shut-eye. Will you excuse me, Parson?" Then he slumped against the wall and closed his eyes.

Finally, I was the only one awake. Sleep wasn't an option. "They'll eat snakes," Davy'd said. "Kill them as they put the bayonet to us," Travis had said. I found I was having trouble getting a full breath.

Then Louis, wearing a heavy overcoat and carrying a bundle tied in a rough gray blanket, tiptoed over to where I was sitting. "Mon ami," he said, "I've come to say goodbye. I am leaving now."

I grasped his hand. "Take care of yourself, brother," I whispered.

He looked around at Davy and the sleeping men. "Parson," he said, barely audibly, "come with me. There is no point staying. Soon they will sound the *deguello* and then will be *le carnage*. If we leave now, we can hide near the river in a place I know, and escape during the confusion of the battle or afterward."

"*Deguello?* What's that?"

"Nothing good, mon ami," Louis whispered. "It is the Spanish call for no quarter—take no prisoners, cut all their throats. It is from the Moors."

I looked over at Davy Crockett sleeping peacefully, his mouth slightly open. It had stopped raining, but the night was still damp and very cold. In the distance I could see the Mexican campfires—hundreds of them, maybe thousands. At the other end of the Alamo, near the north wall where Travis commanded a cannon post, someone was coughing uncontrollably. I imagined that the Dickinsons were, in the sacristy within the chapel, together for a final time. *Cut throats!* I thought. "Okay, Louis," I whispered. "I've been persuaded."

Within minutes we were a few hundred yards from the mission, hiding under a pile of wood near the river. Louis told me that his plan was to slowly make his way northeast to Nacogdoches, far from the fighting, to seek employment. He said he knew a couple there who owned a little dry goods store. "The wife is a great beauty," he whispered, "but she and the old man do not get along well. She is haughty and, I think, quite bored with him." He paused for a moment and looked around to be sure we were safe. "Do you want to come with me, Parson? Perhaps they could use a man of the cloth there."

"Sure, Louis," I answered after a moment. "Nacogdoches will do."

A Hairstylist to
General George Armstrong Custer

IN MY MIDDLE YEARS I was employed by General George Armstrong Custer, whom I and my Indian friends more commonly knew as Son of the Morning Star or sometimes just Long Hair. I was a short and only mildly plump Cheyenne named Buffalo Hump Woman, so-called because of a lifelong growth on my upper back, just below my neck, which resembled the hump of the animal upon which my people depended in so many ways until the whites—*wasichus*, as we called them—slaughtered most of them in their relentless effort to destroy our way of life and thus us.

I worked for Custer for almost eight years, from 1868 to 1876. That work ended on a hot Sunday in late June of the latter year when he and most of his command were rubbed out at the Greasy Grass, the pissant river that the wasichus called Little Bighorn, by my people and the Lakotas, led by that great visionary and my sometime lover, Sitting Bull. During those eight years, my main job was to cut and style the general's wavy blond hair. I was, I'm not ashamed to say, the best hair-stylist within two hundred miles of Fort Abraham Lincoln in Dakota Territory, having spent my adolescence among the Crows after being captured by them in a raid when I had but twelve winters. Whatever one might say about the Crows—and I say plenty about at least one of them—they were in their heyday absolute fanatics about hair and were highly regarded throughout the Northern Plains for their marvelous raven tresses that often hung to below their knees and for their skill in styling and decorating. I learned much from them about hair, a talent that served me well in later years.

My relationship with Son of the Morning Star was somewhat more complicated than merely that of employer and employee. I was also his lover for eight years as well as his mother-in-law, since in 1868 he'd unintentionally married my headstrong daughter, Young Grass That

59

Shoots in the Spring, shortly after his Seventh Cavalry had rubbed out her father and my first husband, Little Rock, at the Battle of Washita in Indian Territory. I was also grandmother to Yellow Swallow, my daughter's blond-haired son by Custer. In addition to all that, I was dearest of friends with and a great admirer of Custer's truly lovely real wife, Libbie.

I understandably had mixed feelings about Son of the Morning Star. In his role as a big war chief of the wasichu soldiers with whom my people and the Lakotas and a few lesser nations were at war, I of course did not hold him in high esteem. But I loved him dearly as a man. Of all my many lovers, Indian and white, he was the best—the tenderest and most considerate, though not the most well-endowed. There he was pitiful. But he knew how to please a woman and always took the time to do so. My, oh my! He certainly wasn't one of these silent, selfish bores like Sitting Bull, Gall, Little Rock, Bloody Knife, or Custer's brother Tom—renowned light-cavalry fighters all who did little more than shove your dress above your waist, mount immediately, grunt once or twice, dismount, and walk away with barely a civil remark, leaving you shivering and alone and unsatisfied. Not my Long Hair! What I think I liked best, and what I missed so much after that horrible June day in 1876, was how Custer would sing to my hump following our copulations, which he referred to as "making the beast with two backs." I'd be lying on my stomach, naked and relaxed and happy, and the general would straddle me from behind, gently rub my shoulders for a few minutes, and then press his thin lips softly against my poor protrusion and sing the words to his favorite tune, "Garry Owen," the Seventh Cavalry's regimental theme song. I never understood what the words meant, but I recall them so fondly from those delicious times:

> *Let Bacchus' sons be not dismayed*
> *But join with me each jovial blade;*
> *Come booze and sing and lend your aid*
> *To help me with the chorus.*

Instead of Spa we'll drink down ale,
And pay the reckoning on the nail;
No man for debt shall go to gaol
From Garry Owen in glory.

Afterward, we'd take turns brushing each other's long hair, slowly and gently, carefully undoing any tangles, both of us reveling in the sensuousness of our luxuriant tresses being so lovingly attended to. Often, our hair brushing excited us so much that we made the beast again and sometimes yet again. Finally, and always sadly for me, Son of the Morning Star would pull on his blue uniform trousers, kiss me gently, tell me, "Hump, you are the best," and leave my tiny shack outside the northern boundary of Fort Lincoln to return to his wife.

I'm sure that Libbie never knew. She was pure of heart but naive and worshipped her husband so completely that I doubt she could have conceived of the possibility that he would be unfaithful or in any wise less than perfect. Though, over the years I was with the Custers, I had occasion to speculate as to the shortcomings of adult males in general and of a few specifically, I never said anything remotely negative about her beloved Autie, as she called him. For one thing, I had no criticism of him other than as mentioned. For another, she wouldn't have tolerated any such observations.

Besides those precious stolen moments beneath the buffalo robes in that miserable shack I shared with my second husband, White Man Runs Him, my favorite times were the long afternoons in the parlor of the Custers' quarters at the fort. Naturally, their home was the finest abode in the facility and the social center for the Seventh Cavalry's upper echelon. Libbie often had the officers' wives to her house for cards or quilting or just to sit around and gossip, which they did incessantly and skillfully and with great enthusiasm. Sometimes, she or another of the wives played a piano that the Custers had rented from someplace called Saint Paul and they all sang songs, many of them "hymns," as Libbie called them, which meant that they had favorable things to say about the wasichu gods. Libbie considered me "one of the girls," as she put it, and allowed me to sit with her and the wives, albeit I generally stayed in the background and said little while listening much.

Occasionally I helped one or another of the wives with her quilting, a task at which I'd become quite accomplished since the Washita fight.

My favorite of the wives was Custer's sister, Maggie, who was married to Lieutenant Calhoun. She was quite the opposite of her sister-in-law. Whereas Libbie was soft-spoken and polite and ladylike in all ways, Maggie was loud and brash, sometimes vulgar. While Libbie would merely cover her mouth with a little pink hand and titter mildly if amused, Maggie would throw her big head back, open her mouth wide, and whinny like a horse while slapping her ample thighs with hamlike hands. Yet they loved one another and were best of friends and did all they could to help each other and the other women get through the tedium and discomfort of the dry, blistering, mosquito-plagued Dakota summers and the frigid, dark, and seemingly endless winters.

On a balmy afternoon in mid-May of that final year, General Custer, Libbie, Maggie and a half dozen officers' wives were gathered in the parlor, where I was cutting and styling the general's hair. I had my combs and a lovely pair of scissors that had been given to Libbie as a wedding present by her cousin Rebecca, as well as my special buffalo tail brush. An invention of the Crows, this consisted of a foot-long section from the very top of the beast's tail, which was stiff and thick and from which about half the hair and bristle had been scraped so that the remainder formed a brush of perfect texture—neither too hard nor too soft. It was also useful as a curling device; Son of the Morning Star favored a gentle inward curl of his blond locks at the bottom edge, on level with his shoulders, but subtle so that his men would not readily detect it had been done, and for this procedure the buffalo tail device was perfect. I had two of these brushes, one which I kept at the Custer home and the other at my miserable hovel for use during our post-copulatory groomings.

"Oh, Hump," Libbie said, "get a little more above the ears—just a bit, so that it doesn't stick out so from beneath his hat."

"*Hah!*" Maggie boomed. "Who's to notice? Those hapless hayseed bogtrotter soldiers? I doubt it. Any officers? Perhaps our moon-faced Major Marcus Reno, the Seventh Cavalry's king of fashion? Now *there's* a man who would appreciate a good haircut, huh? Or am I wrong?"

"There's a man who could *use* a good haircut," Custer added, "so as to better frame that inspiring round face, the physiognomy of a true leader of men—those trusting puppy eyes, that pathetic downward turn to his mouth, that ridiculous drooping mustache."

"Oh, Autie," Libbie said. "You must not be so disparaging. The Lord requires and expects us to be generous in our assessments of our fellow man. Major Reno is very nice. Of course, it would be nice if Maggie's husband were a major too, or at least a captain. Don't you agree, Mrs. Calhoun?"

"Hah!" Maggie again boomed. "A major! I love Jimmi to death, but the man has, shall we say, his limitations. Of course, I suppose if my fat-arsed idiot brother Tom can be a captain, Jimmi could too. Does the position require use of the brain, or can one get by on Celtic charm alone?"

"Well," said Long Hair, "as for that, I'm not sure any of my officers are too gifted with intelligence. Tom is no genius, and Jimmi's at best a cut above him."

"Just a cut," Maggie added. "No more, I warrant you that. Eh, Hump?"

I hesitated for a moment. "Well," I said, "Lieutenant Calhoun seems very capable. And Captain Custer, he is, well, a man like other men, I suppose. He is ... " I looked to Maggie while trying to think what to say, but she was no help.

Maggie—no one's fool—knew the general was bedding me. She never asked and of course I never said aught about it, but she knew nonetheless. She and I were sisters at heart and knew what men were like—shallow and self-centered little boys, really—but we liked and accepted them for who they were and what they could offer, primarily in matters of the flesh. As for me, I'd always craved being touched by a man, held by a man, loved by a man; the scent of him, the feel of him, his strength, his nearness—all these I longed for and had sought again and again since my first lover, Hates His Horses, had made a woman of me when I'd been a captive of the Crows and had but fifteen winters. Like so many others after him, Hates His Horses had been a disappointment as a companion—one I could talk with a bit, share a thought with, enjoy the company of after we'd done the deed. He was one with Sitting Bull, Tom Custer, both of my rotten husbands, and so many others:

abrupt and not at all gentle, using me for their relief and then goodbye. At first that bothered me, but eventually I realized that's just how most men are and came to expect little more of them than their warm arms around me for a few minutes, our bodies rubbing together, and now and again a moment of intense pleasure if one of them happened to take his time and possessed a bit of skill. Just a bit.

Nor, I think, did Maggie care about me and her brother. She herself was no angel and had, I'm sure, been making the beast with Captain Frederick Benteen for years. She'd hinted as much more than once and I'd seen the way he looked at her on the parade ground. Now there was a man I had little use for and, though I had great affection for Maggie Calhoun, could not comprehend her choice of Benteen as a lover. He was sullen, humorless and sour, to say nothing of unusually ugly: he had a huge head covered with dirty whitish hair that had never been cared for other than maybe to have a comb run through it once a week, his pockmarked nose was red and veined because he was a rummy, and he had the lifeless eyes of a serpent. His looks aside, I never understood how Maggie could lay with one who hated the Custers as much as Benteen did—not just the general but his brothers Tom and Boston, his brother-in-law Lieutenant Calhoun, and Custer's young nephew Armstrong Reed, all of whom were gathered at Fort Lincoln there at the end and none of whom survived the Greasy Grass fight, whereas that mean white-haired snake did. Benteen called them "that goddamned Custer clan" and never missed an opportunity to badmouth any of them— particularly my beloved Son of the Morning Star. I never knew what his grievances were and didn't care. But if Maggie could abide the man, who was I to criticize? After all, most of my choices in men had not been the best either.

My two husbands, for example. Little Rock was the worst man who ever lived—foul-mouthed, lazy, and vain to the core, though he had little to be vain about—and I was ever so grateful to whatever wasichu soldier rid me of him by putting a bullet into his worthless skull at the Washita battle in late November of 1868. Just the night before that event, I'd been contemplating doing him in myself by plunging a knife into his fat gut and claiming self-defense. Others in the village would have believed me; they'd often enough seen him abuse both me and Young Grass That Shoots in the Spring, both with his fists and his nasty tongue. He and Young Grass—a pair of big-mouthed hotheads—had more than once awakened the entire community with their late-night screaming matches. I feared that if I didn't kill him, she would.

As for White Man Runs Him, there, it turned out, was another bad choice. I'd first met him when I was with the Crows. He was a cousin to Hates His Horses and either my third or fourth lover. Time passes and these things blur. But I well remember how handsome he was. In a village of many men with magnificent locks, he was outstanding: his hair, oiled with bear grease, with the male Crows' signature short cut in front and a pompadour atop, hung to his ankles and was decorated simply but elegantly with perfectly spaced dots of white paint. As an adolescent, I, like all the girls, was awed by the sight of him strutting through the neighborhood. After being bought back by the Cheyennes for six ponies when I had nineteen winters, I forgot about White Man. Then I met him again a few days after the Washita fight, where he'd served as chief of Custer's Crow scouts. The Crows, of course, were the sworn enemies of the Cheyenne and Lakota nations and gladly served the wasichus by helping locate those foes in the various campaigns on the plains. He was as good-looking as ever and I soon became infatuated. I asked if he remembered me and he said he did, though I doubt he really did. I quickly ingratiated myself to him in the only way I knew and soon we were married. I was glad to have the status of being wife to one who was so handsome and who had such an esteemed position among the wasichus. But that aside, I quickly came to regret my marriage. White Man turned out to be just another Little Rock in that he was inconsiderate to the extreme and full of himself, particularly since Custer apparently put so much stock in his scouting abilities, and mean to boot.

Within less than a year following our union, he'd practically stopped talking to me at all except when he wanted carnal comfort and began spending almost all his time with his worthless Crow scout friends, Half Yellow Face and Goes Ahead. Except when performing their military duties, the three of them hid in a wooded ravine about a mile west of the fort where they drank rotgut supplied by the post sutler and no doubt made disparaging remarks about the wasichus. How often I imagined and wished the worst for my husband on one of his drunken outings: perhaps a flash flood to roar through the ravine and drown the besotted trio; possibly a confrontation with a hunting party of

Cheyennes who would wrap White Man's beautiful hair tightly around his miserable neck, causing his eyes to bulge, before staking him to the ground with arrows; maybe just an intoxicated stumble in which his magnificent head would strike a sharp-edged rock and split open. But, alas, none of my fantasies were realized and I remained encumbered.

The only worthwhile thing that White Man ever did for me was to tell Custer about my hairstyling skills. He did so at my request shortly after we became re-acquainted but, being self-centered as well as apathetic, never asked my reason. It was so that I could get to know the general, whom I'd seen just once at that point, and hopefully to impress him with my various gifts and talents. Long Hair called me in for a styling audition shortly thereafter, was apparently satisfied with my skill, and thus he and I commenced our relationship, workwise and otherwise.

Although I'd been lovers with Son of the Morning Star since shortly before marrying White Man Runs Him—in fact, it was two nights before our marriage that Custer and I first made the beast—my husband never suspected. Or if he did, he never let on. Nor did he give any indication that he knew about any of the other men I'd been with, Indian or white, including Long Hair's main scout, Bloody Knife, an Arikara, or *Ree* as they were commonly known, whose brain matter was later splattered over Major Reno at the Greasy Grass. I was with Bloody Knife just once, and that was enough; his breath made me gag and he sobbed like a child following our copulation, blubbering about how much he *hated* himself for working for the whites and how the Lakotas, of whom his father'd been one and with whom he'd once lived, despised him as a traitor, and on and on. He was a self-pitying weakling for whom I had no use, which is just what I told him when he asked if he could see me again.

Nor did White Man know about my trysts with two of the leaders of his foes, the Lakotas. Needless to say, I never told him how I'd done the deed with both Sitting Bull and Gall, the former in the morning and the latter in the evening of the same day, during an autumn hunting encampment of the Lakota and Cheyenne near the Tongue River, during which Sitting Bull had attempted to impress everyone by cutting the flesh on his arms fifty times and going into a near-trance and predicting that a great herd of buffalo would soon appear to get us all through the coming winter. As it turned out, he was right. I made the beast with the Bull just once again after that, two days later, but he said not one word to me during the whole encounter or thereafter, causing me to lose enthusiasm for the prospect of future lustful encounters with him.

My beloved Long Hair didn't know how much I hated my second husband. When he and I were together, I never mentioned White Man Runs Him and the general never inquired as to my opinion. In truth, he never sought my thoughts on any issue. However, he talked a great deal about himself and his many accomplishments and lofty ambitions, including his desire to be great chief of all the wasichus and live in a white house in some place called Washington. He was, I suppose, as self-centered as any other man I ever knew, but with him I didn't mind; I adored him purely and loved being with him when I could and the sound of his voice was ever golden to me, no matter what he said.

Maggie, though, knew how I felt about White Man. She'd studied him and his lowlife Crow friends, had overheard them talking nasty about the general and others, and knew what was what. Although I never complained, she'd seen me red-eyed on several occasions and understood a great deal without much being said. Only once did she share her thoughts on the matter. "Hump," she said to me when I'd finished doing Custer's hair in the parlor on that afternoon described previously, and after the general had smiled sweetly and thanked me and kissed Libbie before departing to inspect his troops, and Maggie had noticed my mouth quivering just a bit and my eyes moistening. "Hump, there ain't a lot of good men in this sad world and that bastard you got is no damned prize, I'll warrant you that." Then she put her hefty arms around me and gave me a big squeeze, leaving me momentarily breathless.

After Maggie and the other wives left that afternoon, Libbie and I were alone. I was sweeping up the general's hair and she was staring out the window. "Oh, look," she said. "Our men! My, Hump, aren't they both just *so* handsome? Come see." I did and there they were: the man I loved best in the world and the one I hated most, talking together on the parade ground. My misbegotten husband had his hand on Long Hair's shoulder and was pointing to the sun overhead. Then he moved his hand from the general's shoulder to the bottom edge of his curls and rubbed a strand of blond hair between two fingers and grinned at Custer. Son of the Morning Star smiled back and nodded. At that moment, a cold hand unexpectedly clutched my heart and squeezed. "You know, Hump," Libbie went on, "Autie does so admire and respect your husband. He's often said to me, 'I don't know what I'd do without White Man Runs Him. He's the best scout I've ever had.' And, as I say, such a good-looking man. Oh, Hump, aren't we both lucky women?"

I said nothing. I couldn't. "Yes, Hump," Libbie went on, "I'm certainly lucky. Autie and I are so happy together. And it's so comforting for us to have our family all around us—Captain Tom, brother Boston, Maggie and Jimmi, and now young Armstrong. The only thing is, well, it would be so nice if we had children of our own. That's what I miss most, Hump. We've tried, you know, but ... well, I suppose I can't reasonably expect all the blessings in the world. Lord knows, Hump, I've been among the most blessed of women over the twelve years Autie and I have been one in the eyes of our creator." Then she walked back to the kitchen humming a tune which I recognized as one that she and the wives had often sung during the parlor afternoons, "Nearer, My God, to Thee."

Alone in the parlor, I thought about what Libbie had said. Children, she longed for. I remembered the night my child and I had first met Custer. It was after the Washita battle and we were among the fifty or so captives—women and children all—who had been taken to a log hut north of the destroyed Cheyenne village, in a place the wasichus called Camp Supply. Most of the women were wailing and tearing at their hair to demonstrate their great grief over their slain men, and some had started to rip at their flesh as well. Young Grass and I joined in the wailing only, purely for the sake of appearance since, of course, we were not unhappy about Little Rock's violent demise. Soon General Custer and three other officers entered the hut and looked over the captives. Being a woman of the world, I knew immediately what they sought: belly-warmers for the cold winter nights ahead. Inasmuch as Young Grass That Shoots in the Spring was by far the best-looking of the captives, I also knew that she would be first choice. Indeed, the general spied her out immediately and approached hastily, casting but a brief sideways glance at me. "Ah," he said, "quite an enchanting and comely young squaw." My daughter and I did not know who Custer was at the time, but we were both stricken—me with the man himself and she with his obvious position of power and authority.

Poor Long Hair had no idea what he was getting into. He was used to simply charging ahead and overpowering all foes, but in Young Grass That Shoots in the Spring he'd finally encountered one even more strong-minded and capable of achieving her ends than he. My daughter had eighteen winters when we met Custer and had already been through one husband, Hairy Legging. One night, while intoxicated, Hairy'd sought her favors, she'd declined, and he'd foolishly pressed the issue. Without warning, Young Grass shot her husband in the right knee with Little Rock's pistol, thus dissolving their union. Now she'd met the great war chief of the wasichus, was favorably impressed, and—after her fashion—immediately set her goals and went after what she wanted. She and Custer made the beast in his tent that very night and every night for the next week.

At the end of that week, Young Grass took Custer's hand and led him to a sitdown with another of the captives, a wrinkled old crone named She Who Knows the Clouds, who immediately placed their hands together, mumbled some words in Cheyenne, and blew smoke from a decrepit pipe to the four main compass points. Custer didn't know it then or later, but he'd just married my daughter. She, of course, capitalized on their one-sided union for years thereafter and was highly regarded among the plains tribes for being a wife to the famed wasichu warrior—for although the Lakota and Cheyenne hated Son of the Morning Star as a foe, they greatly admired him as a fighter.

Nor was Young Grass done with him. In late spring of the following year, 1869, I noticed that she looked different: her face was a bit more fleshy, her waist thicker, and her breasts larger. "Who is the father?" I demanded.

"Long Hair," she replied. "My husband. Who else?"

I slapped her face hard, leaving a red mark across one cheek. "He is NOT your husband!" I screamed. "You tricked him, you shameless one. And now you have made a child with him! Leave my sight."

"Shameless? Who are *you* to talk?" she hissed. "You who have married that worthless Crow so soon after my father's death, and now you are working for the wasichus who killed him! All the women are talking. Leave your sight? You have your wish."

That was the last time I saw Young Grass That Shoots in the Spring. She stayed around for a short while following our confrontation and even assisted Long Hair as an interpreter and intermediary in some difficult negotiations with several Cheyenne warriors near Fort Cobb. Yet she and I never spoke again. Then by mid-summer, having finished with Custer and gotten from him what she wanted, she left Indian Territory and joined up with a band of the Northern Cheyenne near the Powder River in Wyoming Territory. It was there, in the early winter, that she gave birth to Yellow Swallow and made it clearly known that he was the progeny of her husband, Son of the Morning Star, thus enhancing her status even more.

I never saw my grandson and only heard about him and his mother from friends and relatives. By the time she departed, I was unhappily stuck with White Man Runs Him and regretting our marriage, but was happy—happier as time went on—with my beloved Long Hair, and was in a way glad that my daughter was out of the way. Young Grass had only used Custer but never loved him as I did. Nevertheless, it galled me during the early months of 1869 that he was making the beast with both of us, and after she left I gladly had him to myself—except, of course, for Libbie. Yet, though I was certainly jealous of Mrs. Custer, I never resented her. I'd liked her so very much from the first time we met, which was shortly after I learned of Young Grass's pregnancy, and her friendship soon became the best thing in my life except for making love with her husband.

So when Libbie mentioned her longing for children, I understood. My heart, at that moment, ached for my estranged child and for the grandson I'd never seen and maybe never would. It was hard sometimes even to look at the children playing at the edge of the parade ground or, when it was safe, outside the fort. But although Young Grass was gone from my sight, perhaps forever, at least I'd had a child whereas poor Libbie had not and maybe never would. At least there was that.

It was the very next day, right after breakfast, that I knew the Custers would not only never have children but that their time together would soon end forever, as would my lovely stolen moments with Son of the Morning Star. Maggie and Libbie were sipping their second cups of coffee in the kitchen of the Custer home and I was cleaning up the breakfast dishes when the general, dressed in his best deerskin jacket over a flowing white shirt, a yellow scarf tied around his neck, burst in, excited and energetic. "Ah, Hump," he exclaimed, "I'm glad to see you. I require your services immediately."

Both Maggie and I must have looked startled for Long Hair, seeing our faces, flushed momentarily. "I mean," he said, " ... that is ... well, I need a haircut."

"Autie!" Libbie cried out. "*Why?* Your hair is so lovely just now, and Hump did it so nicely just yesterday."

"Yes," he said, "I know. But, well, we're leaving in the morning to go after the Sioux, as you know, and as White Man Runs Him pointed out it's likely to be godawful hot out there and, as he said, I'll probably be a lot more comfortable with shorter hair. Very warm out there in early summer, you know, very dusty." Seeing me staring at him, he added, "Your husband gives me good counsel, Hump. He always has."

I averted my eyes from his gaze. I couldn't look at him, nor at Libbie. I considered trying to argue, to persuade him to change his mind, to get him to see that his hair was his medicine, his power, and that if he cut it now he would surely lose to the greater medicine of Sitting Bull, Crazy Horse, Gall, and the others who were out there somewhere in great numbers, I knew, probably along with my people, unwilling for now to bend to the demands of the wasichus that they report to the agencies and reservations and ready to do battle—maybe for one last and glorious, if desperate, time. But I knew just as surely that it was no use to argue; I knew that the Everywhere Spirit had, for reasons we could not know, decreed that things should come to such a pass—had determined that I would never again know the joy of my Long Hair's embrace or feel his silky yellow mustache tickle my pathetic hump as he sang "Garry Owen" to it after making love to me more beautifully than anyone else ever had or would again. All I could do was to nod, resigned, and quietly gather my combs and scissors. None of us said a word as General George Armstrong Custer sat on a wooden chair in the middle of his kitchen and I draped a sheet over his shoulders and quickly snipped off most of my darling's wavy blond tresses, my throat constricting as each clump fell harshly to the floor.

"There," he said when I'd finished, "that was easy, wasn't it? Now I'll be much more comfortable out there, and by the time we return, a great victory under our belts, it will have started to grow back again nicely. Then, Hump, you can work your magic yet again." With that he kissed his wife on the lips and his sister on the cheek and departed. "Not to worry," he said as he walked out the door. "When the hostiles see the Seventh's guidons, I wager they'll scurry back to the agencies posthaste. Then we'll return to celebrate our nation's Centennial in grand style, all of us together."

Neither Libbie nor Maggie nor I said anything for several minutes after the general left. I'd never known Maggie to be at a loss for words. Then Libbie turned to me, took my right hand in both of hers, and said, "Hump, tomorrow when the regiment leaves Maggie and I will go with them for a way. I'd like it if you'd come too. We need you to be with us."

When my husband came home that evening, stinking of whiskey, I confronted him. "*Why?*" I hissed. He merely sneered but did not reply. "WHY, you coward? I have to at least know that."

"Benteen," he finally answered, slurring the name. "He told me of you and Long Hair. His spies told him."

I stared at him for I don't know how long. I was as close to murder as I'd ever been, closer even than that last night with Little Rock. I wished that I'd retained the scissors with which I'd snipped my beloved's locks so I could plunge the twin blades into White Man's black heart. "You will not be in the battle, will you?" I finally said, practically whispering. "You and your hateful Crow friends will leave before it starts. Am I right?"

He nodded. "Long Hair has said this is not our fight. Once we lead him to the Lakotas, we are free to go. It is not our fight." Then he put his face close to mine. "We will live and I will return," he said. "I *promise.*"

I spent that night in the stable, but couldn't sleep. By dawn I was at the edge of the parade ground, watching the troops saddle their horses. It had been drizzling all night so that the ground was a field of mud. The entire fort was enveloped in a fog that muted colors so that all— men and horses—appeared spectral, strangely indistinct, as in a dream. It felt like a dream; it seemed like a dream. At first, the fog muffled the sounds of the morning: the snorting of horses, the buckling of cinchstraps, the clanking of sabers, the complaining of the doomed soldiers. But as the mist thinned the sights and sounds grew a bit clearer, the faces of the men more distinct. I saw Tom Custer making a playful obscene gesture to another officer, the blue tattooed eagle on his bare biceps fierce-looking, ready to fly. Then I spotted Benteen mounted on his big gray gelding, staring intensely in my direction. His face was friendly and he smiled warmly, inexplicably so until I realized that it was not me he was eyeing. I heard a sigh behind me and turned to see Maggie gazing longingly at her illicit lover. Libbie was behind her, dressed in a pretty light-yellow dress, looking glum. She put her small hand on my shoulder and rubbed gently.

Together, we watched for about an hour as the column formed and the troops prepared to depart. Son of the Morning Star and a group of officers gathered at the head of the line, followed by the band and then the troops, the various Indian scouts, cannons, and finally a procession of supply wagons. They began to move forward very slowly through the lingering fog. A ghostly procession. Just outside the edge of the fort, the wives of the Ree scouts—about a dozen dark-skinned women— crouched on the ground, totally silent, most staring downward. They appeared not to have the energy, or perhaps the will, to lift their heads. Some of the Ree children tried to follow their fathers and had to be re- strained by the women. A group of unrestrained wasichu children, though, mimicked the troops by forming a mock infantry column of their own. They'd tied handkerchiefs to sticks to represent flags, beat tin pans as drums, and marched back and forth in a perfect row, serious and straight-backed. Their leader was a blue-eyed, blond-haired cherub of perhaps six winters—the same age as Yellow Swallow.

Then a handsome young sergeant riding a beautiful bay and lead- ing two other horses approached us, removed his hat, and addressed Libbie. "The general's compliments, ma'am," he said. "I'm to escort you and Mrs. Calhoun to the head of the column." As depressed and apprehensive as I felt, I nonetheless found myself studying the young man with interest, my blood quickening.

I looked around to see if White Man Runs Him was among the Indian scouts. I spied that pathetic Bloody Knife and identified Goes Ahead and also saw one who I think was Half Yellow Face, though I wasn't certain, but couldn't immediately locate my despised husband. That was fine. I wished to see him no more.

Through the mist, I could hear the band tuning their instruments and feared they would play our song. If so, I wasn't sure I could retain my composure. I wondered if Son of the Morning Star would have the same reaction as I if they played it, but it proved moot speculation because they launched into a different selection, a jaunty tune that Maggie identified as "The Girl I Left Behind Me."

"Come with us, Hump." Libbie said. "You can ride near Maggie and me. I'm sure Autie won't mind. We're going to camp with the regiment tonight at the Heart River and then return in the morning."

I considered her offer for only a moment. "No," I answered. "I couldn't. Thank you, my friends. Go to your husbands. Your place is with them."

Libbie and Maggie both hugged me and then mounted the extra horses. The good-looking sergeant led them to the head of the column, which was still moving out slowly. I silently prayed that he would survive intact the coming carnage. Later, I happily learned that he did and contrived to make his acquaintance.

Standing on a barrel, I watched the departing soldiers and, in the distance, was able to make out my beloved Long Hair—now *Formerly Long Hair*—dressed in his deerskin jacket, riding his graceful sorrel mare, Vic. As the column reached the top of a promontory, he turned, stood high in the stirrups, and waved his hat toward the fort. As the soldiers disappeared into the mist, I heard the last strains of the song about the girl left behind.

A Tea Party Assistant for Lewis Carroll

I SERVED AS A TEA PARTY assistant of sorts for Lewis Carroll, the author of *Alice in Wonderland* and *Through the Looking-Glass* and the sometime photographer, whose real name was Charles Dodgson—the *Reverend Charles L. Dodgson*, if you will. I was an arguably difficult ten-year-old whom Mr. Dodgson, for some reason, liked. Of course, he liked a *lot* of little girls, not just me; I was but one of many. Little girls had always been his passion, strange man. The main young girl of his life had certainly been Miss Alice Pleasance Liddell, the skinny, dark-haired, pouty little fluffhead who'd begged Mr. Dodgson to write down the bizarre but enchanting story he'd told her and her two sisters, Lorina and Edith, during a boat trip up the River Isis to Godstow on July 4th, 1862. She'd then been ten years old herself, and now, in 1897, was a stuffy middle-aged married woman, Mrs. Reginald Hargreaves, who so bored me the one time I met her that I wondered what Mr. Dodgson had ever seen in her and why he'd taken so many wonderful photographs of her as a child, about which I was so jealous. *Queen Alice* is how I referred to her after that meeting, though not charitably so.

It was in honor of the thirty-fifth anniversary of that famous boat trip that Mr. Dodgson asked me to do something for him during a similar boat excursion on the Isis and picnic at Godstow with a half-dozen little girls. "The theme," he explained, "shall be 'All in the G-Golden Afternoon,' and it shall be my last such outing. For you see, Mimsy, I am but a s-s-sad and lonely old bachelor and shall, I am quite sure, d-d-die soon." As he told me, he considered that long-ago July day with Alice and her sisters—the "golden afternoon" of the preface poem to his first famous book—to have been the high point of his life.

Mimsy was my chosen name, not my given one. That was Margaret, which I hated only slightly less than Maggie, which was what most people, including my parents, called me. I'd chosen Mimsy when I'd been four and first heard my mother's recitation of Mr. Dodgson's wonderful nonsense poem "Jabberwocky," the first and final verse of which is:

> 'Twas brillig and the slithy toves
> Did gyre and gimble in the wabe
> All mimsy were the borogoves,
> And the mome raths outgrabe.

Oh, what a wonderful word!

My mother had initially refused to call me by my preferred name, and I'd then responded by ignoring her until she did. Finally, she'd always give in—sort of. "Oh, Maggie," she'd say, "please set the table." No response. "Uh, Maggie ... oh, well, *Mimsy* then, please do set the table."

I met Mr. Dodgson shortly before Christmas of 1896, backstage after an opening of *Alice in Wonderland* at the Prince of Wales Theater in London. My insufferable older sister, Evelyn, was playing the lead role and my younger sister, Lily, had the role of the Dormouse. Mr. Dodgson was cooing over Evelyn and telling her how *wonderful* she was and what a *perfect* little Alice she'd been and how her performance so put him in mind of the real Alice, his beloved "dream-child," and on and on. It almost made me sick. Yet, I thought, how interesting he appeared: a tall, thin man with white hair, standing quite erect, wearing a black broadcloth cleric's suit, collar turned back, and a white tie. And gentle. So gentle. I'd never seen anyone quite like him before, and was intrigued.

Evelyn had a reputation as a marvelous little actress, and I suppose she was decent enough, but she had the personality of a potato and the imagination of a turnip. *Miss Priss* is how I referred to her. Both she and Lily were mad about the Alice character, for our mother had read Mr. Dodgson's books to us ad nauseam since infancy. I too liked parts of both Alice books, particularly certain of the more violent poems, although I found the main character herself quite insipid. I even liked her cat, Dinah, better than Alice. Mother had said that the real Alice—Miss Liddell—was a daughter of the Dean of Christ Church College, Oxford University, where Mr. Dodgson had long served as a mathematics don, and that it was she who had been the inspiration for Mr. Dodgson's classics.

Whereas my sisters were pretty—they both, in fact, looked deliberately like the long-haired Alice in Sir John Tenniel's famous illustrations for Mr. Dodgson's books—I was decidedly not so: badly-complected, thin-lipped, sharp-featured, and one eye, the left, slightly higher than the other. Moreover, my right eye—the lower one—wandered, so that when I looked at someone he or she could not be sure that I was actually paying attention. My hair, which was the color of a three-day-dead mouse, stuck up every which way about my head and there was nothing to be done for it. I knew that my appearance would preclude my ever being on stage, as Evelyn and Lily were, except perhaps as one of the witches in *Macbeth*. But no matter; I harbored no such ambitions, disliking almost everything about the theatre—particularly having to watch preening egotists such as Evelyn strutting about—and preferring to spend my time alone, reading.

Still, my ugliness, if that's what it was, never bothered me much until I saw Mr. Dodgson's photographs for the first time. About a month after that opening night, he wrote a note to our mother asking if he could "borrow" Evelyn for an evening on January 27th, to have tea with him in his rooms in Tom Quad, Christ Church College, to help him celebrate his sixty-fifth birthday. She'd written back that that would be fine, but wondered if Maggie and Lily might come too? "Oh, it would be *such* a nice experience for them, Mr. Dodgson," she'd implored.

Shortly after we arrived on the appointed date, he directed us to sit on a big dark-green sofa in the largest room. "I am off to make the t-tea, young ladies, and shall be b-b-back directly," he said. "In the meanwhile, d-do sit right there—this is, after all, my sitting room—close your eyes, and think p-p-pleasant thoughts. When I return, you shall t-tell me just what you were thinking, and you shall spare *no* d-details. Are we agreed?"

"Oh, yes, Mr. Dodgson," Evelyn simpered. "That would be *ever* so agreeable."

While Evelyn and Lily closed their eyes and thought their pleasant thoughts, I explored. What first caught my attention were the photographs hung on the walls of the sitting room and adjacent hallway. They were almost all of little girls and all marvelous. There were at least five photographs of the real Alice; I knew this because of the little printed cards beneath each picture: "Alice Pleasance Liddell, 1859," "Alice Liddell as a Beggar Child," and so on. Like many of the pictures, that latter one portrayed the subject in a costume of sorts. There was another such labeled "Xie Kitchen as a Chinaman." My favorite, though, was of Beatrice Henley. It showed a smiling long-haired young girl in a dark dress leaning against the stone wall of a building, her little feet crossed, holding a pretty hat in one hand and looking into the distance off of the right frame.

Staring at that photograph for the longest time, I felt jealous of Miss Henley and of a sudden desperately wished that I, too, could be one of Mr. Dodgson's subjects. I imagined myself preparing for the sitting—washing my face, trying to get my ridiculous hair to stay in place, choosing a pretty dress to wear—and fantasized further the actual photo session: taking directions from Mr. Dodgson, standing or sitting a certain way, looking at the camera with a dramatic facial expression, being the temporary center of the great man's artistic attention. The idea of being memorialized at a particular moment in time—a moment that would never recur—fascinated me. That wonderful photograph of Miss Henley would outlive her; she would be the same healthy smiling little girl long after she herself had shriveled and died and decayed. And yet I doubted that he would ever select me; I was assuredly not pretty nor, if one gave credence to Evelyn, was I particularly agreeable.

When I returned to the sitting room, Mr. Dodgson and my sisters were cuddled together on the sofa sipping tea. Lily was sitting on his lap and Evelyn was snuggled up beside him, resting her silly head against his shoulder. "T-t-tell me, Evelyn," he said, "what were your p-pleasant thoughts?"

"Oh," she sighed, "I was just thinking about portraying dear Alice in your *wonderful* work. I was just remembering how marvelous I felt that first night, opening night, when I came out for curtain call and everyone ... oh, Mr. Dodgson, it was *such* a lovely feeling ... they applauded for me over and over!"

"I s-see," he said. "Oh, that is a pleasant thought. How p-proud you must feel! And Miss Lily, what of you? What were your, uh, thoughts?"

"Oh," she replied, "I was just thinking about the Cheshire Cat. I like it when he grins."

"You like it when he grins. Oh, my p-precious child!" Beaming at her affectionately, he pulled Lily closer to him and kissed her first on one cheek and then on the other and then directly on her mouth. A cold shiver went through me. I felt an even bigger shudder when Evelyn snuggled closer to him yet and raised her lips for a kiss as well and he complied. *Yuck!* I stared coldly first at her and then at Mr. Dodgson. He, however, didn't notice. Turning to me, he asked, "And what of you, M-Mimsy? Did you have any p-p-pleasant thoughts?"

"Oh, Mr. Dodgson," Evelyn said, "don't bother with *her*. She's as sour as any lemon and *never* has pleasant thoughts."

"Oh, but I *do*," I said, imitating Evelyn's sniveling tone. "I was just thinking about Alice—dear, *dear* little Alice. I was thinking about how *marvelous* it would be, in the scene where Alice meets the Duchess and her baby and the cook throws the plates and saucepans, for a *cookpot* to hit Alice's lovely little head and shatter it into, oh, just a thousand pieces! Oh, wouldn't that be ever so pleasant, Mr. Dodgson?" Then, on impulse, I jumped onto a low chair and loudly—perhaps a bit *too* loudly—recited the Duchess's "lullaby" to her baby:

> *Speak roughly to your little boy,*
> *And beat him when he sneezes;*
> *He only does it to annoy,*
> *Because he knows it teases.*

> *I speak severely to my boy,*
> *I beat him when he sneezes;*
> *For he can thoroughly enjoy*
> *The pepper when he pleases!*

Finally, raising my arms above my head and swaying from side to side, I shouted the chorus—*"Wow! Wow! Wow!"*—over and over until my throat ached.

Mr. Dodgson stared at me for a moment, not speaking, and then burst out laughing. "Oh m-my!" he said. "A spirited l-little wood sprite, you are."

Evelyn sat on the sofa with her arms folded across her chest, look-ing furious. "Oh, she's horrid!" she hissed. "She is absolutely *not* to be tolerated, Mr. Dodgson. I cannot *conceive* that such a vulgar being is my sister." Then she looked at him and added, "Imagine! Throwing *cookpots* at Alice!"

"Yes," he replied, looking in my direction and nodding. "Imagine!"

I DID NOT see Mr. Dodgson again for several months. I wasn't sure I ever would, given my splenetic little outburst on his birthday. So I was a bit surprised when, in mid-May, my mother received a note asking if I might accompany him on a stroll down Broad Walk to Christ Church Meadow and then back to his rooms for tea. "Why would he want to see you alone?" my mother wondered. "You've not ever been on stage, and everyone knows how much he likes child actresses." But she consented.

That caused me to wonder. "Was Alice ever an actress?" I asked. "Was she on stage?"

"Not that I know of, dear. Of course, not all his 'young ladies' have been. Many have, but not all. But why would he ... ? Well, never mind."

Since seeing Mr. Dodgson's photographs, I'd wondered about Alice Liddell. Why had he taken so many pictures of her? Why had she been the namesake for his famous character? She'd been a pretty enough child, though there was a snootiness and vapidity in her expres-sion that I disliked, but what was so special about her? Thinking about that, I re-read both the Alice books and was particularly intrigued by the poem at the end of *Through the Looking-Glass*. One verse in particular touched my fancy:

> *Still she haunts me, phantomwise,*
> *Alice moving under skies*
> *Never seen by waking eyes.*

"Phantomwise"—what an interesting word. But what did the verse mean?

When Mr. Dodgson came to pick me up for our walk, I noticed that he seemed to have aged somewhat since I'd seen him just over three months previously: he was thinner, his hair was whiter, and he seemed not to display quite the same erectness of carriage. Yet he greeted me warmly and grasped my hand and told me how glad he was that I "would condescend to walk about with a p-pitiful aging creature such as m-m-myself."

It was a grayish misty day, a bit cool. Mr. Dodgson was dressed as before in his black cleric's suit, and he wore a pair of black-and-tan gloves. He carried a small picnic basket. "Shall we take a p-pleasant walk out to the Meadow, Miss M-M-Mimsy?" he asked. "I should like to ask a favor of you a b-bit later."

I shrugged my shoulders. "'A pleasant walk, a pleasant talk,'" I replied, quoting a line from one of his poems, "'along the briny beach.'"

In truth, I was not in the best of moods, having had words with Evelyn earlier that morning. "Oh," she'd said snidely, "you're going to see Mr. Dodgson today, I'm told. Well, how very *special* for you. I'm sure you don't get many such opportunities, do you? You know, of course, that he likes to cuddle and kiss young girls, but I'm sure that in your case he will make an exception. Oh, I didn't mean to *insult* you."

"Insult me?" I'd replied. "Oh, not to worry about *that*, Miss Priss. I tend not to pay enough attention to you to be insulted at *anything* you might say. Besides, I'm sure that after kissing and cuddling you, he would never condescend to touch a mere mortal such as myself."

As Mr. Dodgson and I were walking past St. Aldates Gate toward the Broad Walk, I noticed a dowdy middle-aged woman flanked by three boys strolling in our direction. I saw them first, for Mr. Dodgson was at that moment peering into the picnic basket, probably to ensure that he'd forgotten nothing. The smallest of the boys appeared to be slightly younger than I and another slightly older. The eldest was quite tall, and looked to be about fifteen years of age. All four had serious, sour looks on their faces, and there was something—though I couldn't say what—about the woman's facial expression that seemed familiar to me. "Good day, Mr. Dodgson," she greeted him in a somewhat bored, slightly nasally voice as we neared. "I trust you're well?"

"Mrs. Hargreaves!" he exclaimed, looking up. "How n-nice to see you. Yes, thank you, v-very well indeed."

She stared at me for a moment, and then looked back to him. "You remember my sons, of course. Alan, Leopold, and Caryl."

"Indeed I d-do," he replied, shaking each of their hands in turn. "A fine-looking lot, I m-must say. You must be very p-p-proud."

"Of course. Regi and I are most pleased with our family."

"And how is M-M-Mister Hargreaves?"

"Quite well indeed. We continue to be very happy at Cuffnells. We are here to visit my parents for the week. The Dean has been a bit ill, you know."

"Has he?" Mr. Dodgson said. "I'm s-sorry to hear it. Oh, I've f-forgotten myself. This is my young friend Mimsy, sometimes known as M-M-Maggie, more rarely as M-Margaret. Mimsy, this is Alice ... uh, that is, M-Mrs. Hargreaves."

The woman looked down her nose at me, in that carefully practiced status-conscious style of the English gentility, but said only, "Yes, I see." I could feel her disapproval of my appearance; it was almost palpable. I very much wanted to stick my tongue out at her, but controlled myself. While she rudely stared, it occurred to me where I'd seen that particular slightly pouty facial expression before: on the five photographs of Alice Pleasance Liddell in Mr. Dodgson's sitting room and hallway.

"Well," she finally said, "I see you're off to an outing. Good to see you, Mr. Dodgson."

"And you, Mrs. Hargreaves. Please c-convey my very *kindest* regards to Mr. Hargreaves, and to the D-D-Dean and Mrs. Liddell as well."

We walked on through the Broad Walk, a long avenue lined by stately elm trees, crossed the bridge over the reservoir, and on toward Christ Church Meadow. We spoke little. When we got to the Meadow, Mr. Dodgson opened his picnic basket and spread the contents on a patch of grass beneath a large oak tree. "Ah," he said, "what have we here? Oh, chicken, salad, l-lovely rolls. Could one wish for anything more, Miss M-M-Mimsy?"

I looked at him. "SOUP!" I cried out. Then I stood tall directly in front of him and sang:

Beautiful soup, so rich and green,
Waiting in a hot tureen!
Who for such dainties would not stoop?
Soup of the evening, beautiful soup!
Soup of the evening, beautiful soup!
  Beau-ootiful soo—oop!
  Beau-ootiful soo—op!
Soo—oop of the e-e-evening,
Beautiful, beautiful soup!

Mr. Dodgson stared at me for a moment and then burst out laughing and reached over to tousle my unruly hair. *"Mea culpa!"* he exclaimed. "How *could* I have forgotten the soup?"

After we ate, he asked his favor. "You know, M-Mimsy, this July, on the Fourth, shall be the thirty-fifth anniversary of a very special d-day in my life. To mark it, I should like to p-p-plan a boat excursion and picnic for several of my favorite young l-ladies, including you. I would like, if you're willing, for you to do me a k-k-kindness." He explained what he wished me to do and it was then that he told me the theme of the event and said that he thought he would die soon. He had a faraway though peaceful expression on his gentle face when he said that. "I was so very happy to have you as my guest on my b–b-birthday, Mimsy," he added. "I d-doubt I'll see another."

I didn't know what to say to his request, so just nodded. "Why was that a special day, Mr. Dodgson?" I asked.

"Ah," he replied. "It was on that day those many years ago that I took a similar b-b-boat journey with three young ladies, three quite enchanting young l-ladies." He paused and looked into the distance. "One of them was a very special young lady, M-Mimsy—very special indeed." We were quiet for a bit and then, looking at me and smiling wistfully, he said, "Life, Mimsy, what is it but a d-dream?"

Those last words sounded familiar. I searched my memory, but couldn't pinpoint where I'd heard them.

After a while we walked back to Mr. Dodgson's rooms. While he made the tea, I again looked at the photographs in his sitting room and hallway and again felt jealous of his subjects—Alice, Xie, Beatrice, Florence Terry, Lorina Liddell, and the rest. I wondered when he'd ask to photograph my sisters, for surely, according to his apparent standards, they were as attractive as his other subjects. I stared particularly at the pictures of Alice, peering intently at her little face, trying to understand her appeal. I couldn't. In each photograph, she seemed more vapid than in the last. Studying the pictures, I noticed again the similarity of the young Alice's bored, somewhat stupid facial expression to that of the tiresome dowager I'd met earlier that day.

And thinking of his photographs, I recalled another reason for my dislike of my older sister. Following our evening with Mr. Dodgson on his birthday, I'd told our mother about his wonderful photographs. Evelyn had overheard me, and the next day at breakfast told a scurrilous falsehood. "Oh, did you know," she'd said, "that he's photographed some girls with no clothes on? Naked! Oh, I'm *sure* you didn't know that, did you? After all, how *would* you?"

"Do not tell lies, Evelyn," I'd replied. "It doesn't become you, not that anything you do does." Yet I wondered: Was what she said possibly true?

When Mr. Dodgson returned, swinging the teapot from side to side to hasten the steeping, I asked what was on my mind. "How did it make you feel today to see her ... you know, Alice?"

He shrugged his shoulders. "I run into Mrs. Hargreaves every f-few years. We have little to say to one another. We've taken quite different p-p-paths, you know. She looks well, I b-believe. Would you not agree?"

I nodded, but said nothing. I felt confused. All this time, I'd supposed that Mr. Dodgson had been ... well, *obsessed* with the real Alice, and yet seeing her appeared not to have affected him any more than encountering any casual acquaintance. And I wondered further why he would be so preoccupied with her, if indeed he was; she seemed as dull as most adults I knew—more so, in fact, than most. The few minutes we'd spent with Queen Alice and her insipid sons had almost put me to sleep, and had it continued longer I would, I'm sure, have been obliged to contemplate either suicide or homicide.

We were quiet then for a while. Mr. Dodgson sat at his writing desk and wrote with purple ink in his diary while I, recalling something, went to his bookshelf and found a copy of *Through the Looking-Glass* and again studied the end poem. There it was, the very last line of the final verse, the words he'd just uttered after telling me about the young lady who was "very special" to him. I read that final verse aloud:

> *Ever drifting down the stream—*
> *Lingering in the golden gleam—*
> *Life, what is it but a dream?*

He looked up from his writing, his brow furrowed, studying my face. In that moment, I felt he could read my thoughts; perhaps he could. "That July day thirty-five years ago—the d-d-day I was telling you about— that day, M-M-Mimsy, was the best and most memorable of my long life. None have been b-better, though there've been many wonderful ones since. There was a m-magic to that day on the Thames—we call that part of the river *Isis*—with Alice and her sisters. But t-times change. People change. Little girls, M-Mimsy, grow up, have lives of their own, become g-grown women. Regrettable in a sense, perhaps, but t-true. Life … yes, a dream."

I looked at Mr. Dodgson, fondly, but again didn't know what to reply, mostly because I didn't quite understand his point. I just sighed and paged back through *Looking-Glass* until I found my favorite poem in all the world, jumped up, and, with dramatic gestures, read aloud— *very* aloud—my two favorite verses:

> *The Walrus and the Carpenter*
> *Were walking close at hand:*
> *They wept like anything to see*
> *Such quantities of sand:*
> *'If this were only cleared away,'*
> *They said, 'it would be grand!'*

> *'If seven maids with seven mops*
> *Swept it for half a year,*
> *Do you suppose,' the Walrus said,*
> *'That they could get it clear?'*
> *'I doubt it,' said the Carpenter,*
> *And shed a bitter tear.*

Mr. Dodgson, staring at me, smiled just a bit. "Yes," he said. "Thank you, child. I appreciate that little k-kindness. Read the entire poem, if you p-please." I did, though in a more subdued manner, and he closed his eyes and listened, now and again nodding slightly. "Ah," he whispered when I'd concluded, "now that wasn't very n-n-nice of them, was it, M-Mimsy—to eat all the little oysters? Oh, what a *mean* t-trick!"

"*Contrariwise!*" I practically yelled, sticking my stomach out as far as possible and allowing my arms to hang straight down at my side to imitate Tweedledee and Tweedledum. "It was *quite* the right thing to do, in my opinion. Fresh oysters with pepper and vinegar and thick slices of buttered bread! Why, *who* could resist?" I paused. "Of course, I'm sure my silly sister would be oh-so horrified. 'Oh, *dear* me!'" I mimicked Evelyn's high-pitched voice, raising my right hand to my cheek and opening my eyes wide. "'How *very* ungrateful of the Walrus and the Carpenter to devour *all* the poor dear little oysters! Really, Mr. Dodgson, they *ought* to be ashamed!'"

He laughed aloud, finally. "Indeed!" he said. "They ought."

JULY FOURTH blossomed as a brilliant summer day with amazing cumulus clouds lazing along in an azure sky. It was as perfect a day as one could wish for, yet its perfection was, for me, blighted by the fact that Evelyn would be going along on our boat trip and picnic. Lily was going too, although her I minded not at all. My older sister had grown increasingly intolerable since her success on stage; the accolades she'd received for her portrayal of Alice had swollen her already-inflated sense of self-importance to the point that she was decidedly unbearable. I believe she thought she *was* Alice! Night after night, I fantasized about pushing her off the cliffs at Dover and watching her plummet to the rocks below, her long blond hair flying amok and her silly pinafore blowing about her horrified face, ultimately engulfing her nose and mouth and depriving her of the breath of life.

But worst of all was her obsequious fawning to Mr. Dodgson. The three of us met him at noon, as agreed upon, at Folly Bridge where we were to rent the boats for our journey upriver. He was there when we arrived, sitting on a low bench, and as soon as Evelyn saw him she ran over and threw her arms about his neck and kissed his cheek and again offered her disgusting little mouth to be kissed, which he disgustingly did, and then said, "Oh, thank you so *very* much, Mr. Dodgson. What a *wonderful* treat this day shall be for me, and of course what an honor—one I ... oh, one I *scarcely* deserve." Naturally, she thought this day was all about *her!* If at that moment I could have crushed her head with a rock, I might gladly have done so.

Sitting next to Mr. Dodgson was a stout, jowly, yet pleasant-looking older man with a droopy mustache. "Young l-ladies," Mr. Dodgson said, "allow me to introduce my friend and former c-c-colleague, Mr. Robinson Duckworth. Mr. Duckworth has made this journey with me b-before. Have you not, D-D-Ducky?"

"Indeed," the other man said. "Though I daresay I was leaner then about the waist by a not-inconsiderable margin."

Soon the other three girls arrived. Oddly enough, they too were sisters: Agnes, the eldest; Winnifred—*Winnie*, as she was known—next; and Olive, the youngest. They seemed to correspond roughly in ages to my sisters and me, and all three were pretty. Agnes and Olive, in fact, had long blond hair and, like my sisters—if one could believe it—quite resembled the illustrated Alice. Winnie, though, looked not like the storybook Alice but the *real* young Alice: thin; brown eyes; dark, short hair; and even a similar serious facial expression, though without Alice's pout. All three ran to Mr. Dodgson and hugged him, and he put his arms around each girl in turn and hugged her and then kissed her cheek, except that he also kissed the youngest, Olive, on her mouth as well.

Winnie was the quietest and best-mannered. After greeting Mr. Dodgson, she curtsied nicely to my sisters and me and introduced herself. She furrowed her little brow when she saw my face, and I could tell that she thought I was looking at someone else rather than at her, for when our eyes met she turned to her left to see who was behind her. No one was.

It was about three miles, Mr. Dodgson said, to Godstow. I was in the first boat with Mr. Dodgson and Agnes and Winnie, while Mr. Duckworth manned the second boat with the others. At first, we were all quiet. I'd never been on a boat before, and it was lovely: the warmth of the sun, the pretty white clouds floating overhead, the fully-leafed tree branches on both banks swaying gently in the slight breeze, the pleasant sounds of the oars creaking as the men commenced each stroke and then the oars dipping into the river and then rhythmically dripping water on each return stroke. It truly *was* a golden afternoon!

I looked at Mr. Dodgson and noticed again that he appeared older still since I'd seen him in May—his face more lined and his posture a bit more stooped. As he rowed, he had a faraway look as though his thoughts were elsewhere, and I suspected where: on that other nice summer day in 1862 with Alice Liddell and her sisters. Now and again he would peer at each of us in turn, particularly Winnie, studying our faces intently. I wondered what he was thinking then, but didn't wish to break the spell by asking.

"All right, Miss M-M-Mimsy," Mr. Dodgson whispered to me after a little while. "If you p-please."

I sighed and sat up straight and retrieved from his basket a copy of *Alice in Wonderland* and quietly read the opening poem, which began:

> *All in the golden afternoon*
> *Full leisurely we glide,*
> *For both our oars, with little skill,*
> *By little arms are plied,*
> *While little arms make vain pretence*
> *Our wanderings to guide.*

After I'd concluded, Mr. Dodgson nodded and then was quiet for a few moments. "Thank you, child," he said. "And n-next, the f-final one, if you would." I put Alice down and found his worn copy of *Looking-Glass* and, moving a bit closer to him, read the final poem:

> *A boat beneath a sunny sky*
> *Lingering onward dreamily*
> *In an evening of July—*
>
> *Children three that nestle near,*
> *Eager eye and willing ear,*
> *Pleased a simple tale to hear—*

Long has paled that sunny sky:
Echoes fade and memories die:
Autumn frosts have slain July.

Still she haunts me, phantomwise,
Alice moving under skies
Never seen by waking eyes.

I paused and looked at Mr. Dodgson's face. He was looking in Winnie's direction, though I wasn't sure if he was looking at her. His expression was blank. He said nothing, so I finished reading the poem. Agnes and Winnie looked at me curiously as I read.

After about an hour, we arrived at our destination: the meadow at Godstow. By now it was approaching mid-afternoon and quite warm. "We must find a b-bit of shade," Mr. Dodgson said, "so that we may eat our c-c-cake and drink our t-tea in comfort."

"Beside a hayrick?" Mr. Duckworth asked. "As before?"

Mr. Dodgson smiled. "Quite so, D-Ducky," he said. "Lead the way, if you will."

We followed Mr. Duckworth for a way until we came to a huge stack of hay. "Ah," Mr. Dodgson said, "this will do n-nicely." Then the two men spread a large blanket on the ground and unpacked the basket Mr. Dodgson had brought. "Oh, Mimsy," he said brightly. "No soup again today. I *do* hope you'll f-f-forgive me."

"What did he mean by that?" Evelyn whispered to me, sneering a bit.

"Not your business, Miss Priss." I gave her a look. "It's between Mr. Dodgson and me. Just the *two* of us!"

She merely glared at me, her blue eyes narrowed into hostile, threatening slits

"Come now, young ladies," Mr. Duckworth called out after a while. "Time for tea."

Eight places had been set around the blanket, each with a small plate and a teacup and a nice cloth napkin. Olive and Lily—already fast friends—sat next to one another, and began giggling. As Evelyn was about to sit, something came over me. "No *room!*" I yelled, pushing her away a bit. "No room here!"

"*What?* What do you mean 'no room'? What in the *world* is the matter with you, you lunatic?"

"No ROOM, Evelyn!" I shouted. "Not for *you.*"

At that, Lily began to giggle and then so did Olive. "That's right," Lily said. "No room. That's what the Mad Hatter and the March Hare said to Alice. Ask the riddle, Maggie. You know: 'Why is a raven like a writing-desk?' Here," she went on, standing up, "I'll sing the song":

> *Twinkle, twinkle, little bat!*
> *How I wonder what you're at!*
> *Up above the world you fly,*
> *Like a tea-tray in the sky,*
> *Twinkle, twinkle,*
> *Twinkle, twinkle ...*

"Oh, you're *hateful!*" Evelyn cried out. "Both of you! Why are you ruining my day like this?"

During this, I kept my eye on Mr. Dodgson. I thought he might be upset by our sibling scrapping, and felt bad. *Do try to exercise some self-control*, I thought to myself, *for his sake.* But he didn't seem upset. Indeed, he was looking at us—first at the younger girls and then at me—with just the warmest of expressions.

After we'd finished our cake and tea, Mr. Dodgson turned to me. "Oh, Mimsy," he said, "shall we have a little recitation? Perhaps, oh, perhaps 'Jabberwocky,' or even 'Father William'? What would you say?"

"Oh," I replied, "The former will do nicely." Standing at the edge of the hayrick, I stood erect and faced the group and began:

> *'Twas brillig, and the slithy toves*
> *Did gyre and gimble in the wabe:*
> *All mimsy were the borogoves,*
> *And the mome raths outgrabe.*

Then, on impulse, I turned to look directly at Lily and, pointing at her with my index finger and looking stern, went on:

"Beware the Jabberwock, my son!
  The jaws that bite, the claws that catch!
Beware the Jubjub bird, and shun
  The frumious Bandersnatch!"

I picked up a long, thin stick from the edge of the hayrick and waved it above my head.

He took his vorpal sword in hand:
  Long time the manxome foe he sought—
So rested he by the Tumtum tree,
  And stood a while in thought.

And, as in uffish thought he stood,

Here—again on impulse—I pointed directly at Evelyn, and raised my voice considerably:

The JABBERWOCK, with eyes of flame,
Came whiffling through the tulgey wood,
  And burbled as it came!

One, two! One, two! And through and through
  The vorpal blade went snicker-snack!

I waved the stick at Evelyn and then made a sweeping gesture with it near her neck.

He left it dead, and with its head
  He went galumphing back.

Then I dropped the stick and turned to Lily and grinned and held out my arms as though welcoming her into them.

"And hast thou slain the Jabberwock?
Come to my arms, my beamish boy!
O frabjous day! Callooh! Callay!"
He chortled in his joy.

Lily laughed out loud. "Off with her head!" she yelled.

I lowered my voice and looked directly at Mr. Dodgson, and quietly recited the final verse: "'Twas brillig ... " and so on. He, however, was looking out into the distance beyond the river, not at me.

After a moment, I noticed that Evelyn was hunched over and quietly weeping, her face buried in her hands. Agnes went over to her and put her arm around Evelyn's shoulders and stroked the back of her hair. "Are you all right, dear?" she asked. Then, turning to me, she scolded. "You ought to be *ashamed* of yourself, you know—making the poor dear cry like this." Olive came over to stroke Evelyn's hair too, looking concerned. Lily, grinning impishly, stood next to the other three girls and started to giggle. "Oh, Evelyn," she tittered. "*Really!*"

I stared at the four of them, grouped tightly—all looking like Tenniel's Alice. By now Evelyn was openly sobbing, fat wet tears falling onto her pinafored lap. I half expected a pool of tears to form and all four Alices to commence swimming around in it. Then I looked over at Mr. Dodgson. He too was looking at the girls, but said nothing. I again wished that I knew what he was thinking.

I walked slowly to Evelyn and put my hand on her shoulder. I felt bad—not much, just a bit—that I'd made my sister cry. "Oh, well, I apologize, Miss Pr ... Evelyn," I said. "You know I'd never *really* cut off your head."

On the return trip downstream, Lily and Olive and I shared Mr. Dodgson's boat. After giggling and whispering to each other for a few minutes, both girls fell asleep in the back of the boat, which Mr. Dodgson said was the "stern." The sun was just starting to lower in the sky to the west, and the light coming through the trees and illuminating the water was softer, even more pleasing, than it had been on our upstream journey. The filtered light created magical dancing dapples on the greenish river. Birds chattered in the trees on either bank, and at one point a large white one with a long narrow bill landed on the river just downstream from the boat and swam about gracefully, unruffled by our presence. There was a bit of a breeze and, although it was not yet cool, I covered Lily and Olive with the big blanket we'd used on our picnic.

"Thank you for today, M-Mimsy," Mr. Dodgson said after a while. "I shall never f-f-forget it." He smiled, and looked at the sleeping girls. "Oh," he went on, "I so wished, when you were doing 'Jabberwocky,' waving that s-stick about, that I still t-took photographs. The sight of you r-reciting, the looks on your f-f-face and Evelyn's, and then Agnes and Olive c-comforting Evelyn ... oh, I'd give anything to have those images always, other than just in my p-poor heart."

"*What?*" I exclaimed. "You no longer take photographs?"

"Oh, dear me, no. I haven't for, oh let's see, s-seventeen years—since 1880. Although there have been t-times, as I say, when ... but, oh well. Yet today, M-Miss Mimsy, I would so l-liked to have captured your spritely little f-face. Oh, very much so." He paused and looked up at the treetops. "'No r-room!'" he recalled, grinning. "'No room here!'" Then he moved his face closer to mine and, practically whispering, said, "But you know, child, that you really *ought* be n-nicer, more charitable, to Evelyn. Sisters are p-p-precious."

I was stunned at what he'd just said about his photography. Seventeen years! So that's why he hadn't asked Evelyn or Lily to pose. Yet I felt so flattered that he'd even *considered* wanting to photograph me. Thinking of Mr. Dodgson's photographs, I conjured in my mind's eye his wonderful image of Beatrice Henley, my favorite—standing by that stone wall, smiling, looking into the distance—and just then I think I truly understood: it was not at all the real Alice of today, that tedious matron, with whom he was preoccupied, but instead with his memory of the child Alice during a particular time of both their lives—that other "golden afternoon" on the river when she'd begged him to tell the story of Wonderland and to write it down for her.

Still, I didn't *completely* understand. That verse—"Still she haunts me, phantomwise ... "—had stayed in my mind. Mr. Dodgson had written that a long time ago, certainly, but what about "still"? Was that "very special young lady" of thirty-five years ago just a nice memory—the nicest of his life, to be sure—or was it somehow more than that? Did he still dream about her? Did she—ten-year-old Alice, his long-ago "dream-child"—*still* "haunt" him? And if indeed he still dreamt of her as a child, what were those dreams? Somehow, I had the idea—though I couldn't say why—that his thoughts about the young Alice were more … well, complicated, I suppose, than I could quite grasp. Yet I wasn't at all sure if that was so, or, if so, how. It was just a feeling.

I glanced at my sleeping sister and her new friend. Lily's mouth was partly open and a bit of spittle had pooled in one corner. What an interesting image the two of them made! I decided that Lily and I, and perhaps Evelyn if her personality significantly improved, which was doubtful, would make this journey on the Isis every July 4th and have tea and cake at the meadow at Godstow—to honor Mr. Dodgson, not stupid Alice. If Mr. Dodgson lasted longer than he anticipated, maybe we'd all go. Perhaps, I thought, I'd learn to take photographs and bring along my camera.

A Press Aide to President
William Howard Taft

I WAS PRIVILEGED to work as a press aide for President William Howard Taft, the overstuffed turkey who never wanted to be president but sought the office to please his ambitious wife, Nellie. I was then a new and perhaps somewhat arrogant young lawyer from Cincinnati, Taft's hometown. I'd graduated from Yale Law School in 1910—Yale was Taft's undergraduate alma mater—and was fortunate to immediately obtain a position at the White House as a legal issues intern. Well, *fortunate* is perhaps not the operative word; my appointment was more in the line of an expected political payback inasmuch as both my father and my uncle, co-founders of one of Cincinnati's biggest corporate law firms and bigshots in Ohio Republican circles, had helped ensure that Taft carried the state in 1908. My specified job duties were to pay attention to certain Supreme Court issues and to keep the president informed. However, within a short time I discovered that I had a talent for misleading members of the press and Taft, noting and appreciating that talent, enhanced my job description.

Taft was a piece of work. By the early summer of 1910, he dressed out at 388 pounds, although the official line was that he weighed 325 tops. My main job as a press flack was to convince the reporters covering the White House that he didn't weigh as much as he appeared to and, in fact, was losing weight. Now this was a hard sell since any American with half an eye could see that the president was a disgusting blimp who was expanding daily.

Of course, I was in no position to criticize Taft's bulk since I myself was no lightweight. On the day of my Yale graduation I weighed 292, mostly flab, and had one of those pale, soft, fleshy faces with three, perhaps four, chins. My sandy hair was already thinning, and, being nearsighted, I wore thick-lensed eyeglasses with black frames. I loved to eat—*lived* to eat!—and had never exercised. Not once.

Eating, as it happened, became early on one of the main bonds between the president and me. I was first introduced to Taft as he was eating luncheon alone in the Oval Office—one of his wonted, as I learned, huge midday meals. "Ah," he said as I was escorted into his presence, "the young gentleman from Yale. Louie, is it not? Welcome, my boy. Will you join me in a modest repast? Nothing special, just some nice medium rare roast beef, potatoes au gratin, buttered carrots, Caesar salad, and, of course, these wonderful Parker House rolls. Oh, I do so love them. And I've been advised by reliable sources that there'll be Dutch apple pie for dessert. Have you a hunger?"

I'd eaten an acceptable breakfast at the Washington Hotel that morning—six blueberry pancakes with warm butter and maple syrup, four Belgian waffles, buttered toast, nine thick slices of bacon, and coffee—and wasn't terribly hungry but didn't wish to be rude to the president of the United States. "Well, perhaps just a slice or two of beef," I replied, "if it wouldn't be an imposition, Mr. President."

"Nonsense, nonsense," Taft said, smiling—a wonderful warm smile that spread across his bloated face. "No imposition. None at all. A healthy appetite is nothing to be ashamed of, my boy." He chuckled aloud. "Don't *I* know that, eh?"

I dished a plate—four slices of roast beef and perhaps two dozen carrots and just a few of the Parker House rolls, no more than three—and we ate in silence for a few minutes. Between bites, the president gulped milk from a quart-sized glass with the presidential seal and the initials *WHT* beneath that. He told me that he'd arranged for a cow, Pauline by name, to graze on the White House lawn so as to supply him with fresh milk daily. He was perhaps the neatest eater I'd ever seen; rarely did a crumb escape his lips and his plate was nearly spotless after he'd finished his meal—progressively mopped, as it were, with each Parker House roll temporarily gripped in his big left hand before it disappeared almost whole down the presidential gullet. He wore an oversized white napkin—practically a towel—tucked into his shirt collar beneath his chin, but there was not a drop of gravy or other mark on it.

As we were eating our pie, the First Lady entered the Oval Office. "Ah, my dear," Taft said, standing and opening his arms to her. "Allow me to introduce you to my newest protégé, a young man from our own

Cincinnati, by George. He shares my interest in the Court, don't you know."

"Oh, *Will*," Nellie said, "won't you ever stop talking about the damned Supreme Court? The Court, the Court—sometimes I think that's all you care about. You're the president, for goodness sake! Isn't *that* more important?" I studied her while wiping the corners of my mouth with my napkin. She was a short, dark woman with thin pursed lips and wore her black hair up in a somewhat severe bun. The right side of her face twitched slightly as she talked and seemed just a bit scrunched up. I remembered that she'd had a stroke about a year ago, and hadn't been able to talk for some months. I stood and subtly bowed, one arm in front and the other in back. "A true pleasure to meet you, Mrs. Taft," I said. "I find myself graced not only by beauty but elegance."

She gave me a look. "I see," she finally said. "'Graced,' huh?" After a moment she turned back to Taft. "Listen, tonight we're having *adobong pusuit*. I'm having Oswaldo parboil it in that special way he knows. Won't that be nice? And those cunning rice patties too. So I'll see you at dinner."

After she left, Taft sat back down and sighed. "Adobong pusuit," he exclaimed. "Do you know what that is, my boy? *Cuttlefish!* Parboiled cuttlefish, for God's sake. Have you ever had the pleasure? I doubt it. It's worse than ... *turnips,* for heaven's sake, which are without question God's most pathetic creation." He paused and raised his right pinky finger to his mouth and chewed lightly on the end of it. "I love that woman to death, Louie. She's been my life. But ever since we were in the Philippines, I've had to eat this crap—strange fish, seaweed, God knows what. She's enchanted with all their silly food, plants, clothing, and on and on. Look around this room, young man. Look at those foolish tapestries and those damned bamboo or whatever-they-are floor mats—*petates*, they're called. I assure you they're not my idea." He looked at the ceiling for a moment and chuckled. "You know," he went on, "she somehow persuaded the Japanese ambassador to send thousands of cherry trees to Washington. Quite a feat! Sadly, they were infested and had to be destroyed, but damned if Nellie didn't get them to send another batch. They'll be here sometime soon, and her dream is that they be planted all around the Tidal Basin. *Cherry* trees.

Ha!" He took a huge bite of his Dutch apple pie, then another. Then he stood and opened the small hinged door to the cage of his pet canaries—Rosie and Bully, according to a little brass nameplate attached to the cage—and dropped a few morsels of seed into their tin food cup. "Oh, well," he sighed, plopping heavily into his chair. "At least tomorrow night it'll be pork chops and dressing with Gerda—a veritable feast, as it were—and none of that bankrupt Filipino fare. Gerda! Now *there's* a lady with a healthy appetite. Perhaps you'll join us, my boy, if you've no other plans. In the meantime, young man, tell me about yourself."

I finished the last bite of my second slice of apple pie and started to tell Taft about my Cincinnati upbringing and my Yale Law education and my work in the Young Republicans, but before I'd finished my fourth sentence I heard loud snoring and saw that the president was fast asleep in his big leather chair, his head slumped to the left and his mouth opened. A string of spittle was drooling from the lower corner of his mouth, part of it clinging to the end of his brown handlebar mustache. I got up to leave, but before I could exit the Oval Office I heard Taft mumbling in his sleep and turned back to look at him. His brow was furrowed and he seemed distressed. "Who's the litigant in this case, anyway?" I heard him say. "*Damn* it, boys, who's the tortfeasor here?" I walked over and put my hand on his shoulder and shook just a bit. "Mr. President," I said gently. "Mr. President, wake up."

"*What?*" he cried out, startled awake and opening his eyes. He looked up and saw me and after a moment smiled that nice smile. "Oh," he said, "I must have dozed off. Well, my boy, I'll hear your history later. Did you enjoy the pie? I must say, the crust was just right today—neither too flaky nor too moist. I have high expectations when it comes to proper pie crust, Louie. I am, after all, the leader of the world's greatest democracy, don't you know." He paused and sighed. "Well," he went on, "time to go meet with my Cabinet. Doubtless they'll be, as usual, exhaustingly exercised by the great issues and events of the day and want me to do this or that or the other and do it *now*, by God, not tomorrow, or the republic will go to hell in a hand basket. Hah!" He looked around the Oval Office. "Now where did I place that tin of chocolates? Oh, yes." He stood and ambled over to a shelf near the window and picked up a big red and white tin box. "I worked out a deal with the

Swiss ambassador, Louie. Every week I get a box of these lovely assorted Swiss chocolates. His wife delivers them personally. Gerda. Here, try one." I took a piece of dark chocolate from the tin and munched it. It had raspberry filling.

"Mr. President," I said after a moment, "allow me to opine that this chocolate is unquestionably the most wondrous in the Western Hemisphere. It is a joy such as I have never previously experienced, much less imagined. These delicacies, sir, are well worthy of your high station."

"*Hah!*" Taft chuckled. "A man after my own heart. Louie, you and I shall get on famously." He sighed. "Well, my boy, I must off to my Cabinet meeting. Say, why don't you come and sit in? We shall consider the experience, as it were, an extension of your political education. And then, thank the lord, it will be time for golf."

The Cabinet met in a big white-walled room down the corridor from the Oval Office. The members were seated around a huge oak table, and each man had in front of him a brass nameplate with his name and title in lovely script. "Good afternoon, gentlemen," Taft said as we entered. "A beautiful day, in my humble opinion. Or am I wrong?"

"Mr. President!" one of the men insisted—a thin, sour-looking individual whose nameplate identified him as Secretary of Commerce and Labor Charles R. Nagel. "We simply *must* discuss this damned tariff thing. No matter what we do, we're getting crucified. I'm telling you, Will, the press is making me crazy on this. That goddamned Oscar King from the *Times*, he's ... relentless."

Taft sat at the head of the table and set his tin of chocolates in front of him. He took one and studied it for a moment and then put it in his mouth and chewed, savoring the flavor. I noticed that his dark-blue eyes had a filmy, almost milky, appearance. Finally, he turned to Nagel and smiled. "Relax, Charlie," he said soothingly. "No need to get exercised, for gracious sake. Don't let these pygmies get to you." He took another piece of candy and stared at it admiringly for a moment before popping it into his mouth. "Tariffs," he went on. "As for me, I'm tired of the subject. Let's discuss something else."

Four or five Cabinet members began talking excitedly at the same time. The loudest was Interior Secretary Ballinger. "Mr. President," he exclaimed, "this thing with Gifford Pinchot, it's going to come back to bite us in the arse. I know you had to fire him, the damned fanatic, but you can't believe the heat I'm taking from the newspapers, Bill. They keep saying how much Roosevelt loved and trusted Gifford, and *how* could you do this to good old Teddy? ... how *very* ungrateful of you ... oh, what a betrayal of beloved old T.R.'s conservationist principles ... and on and on. They're suggesting that I resign, for God's sake! What am I going to do? What are *you* going to do?"

"And that's not all," Secretary of State Knox said. "In between snide comments to me about Nicaragua and this Panama Canal toll thing, some of these guys are starting to criticize *you*, Mr. President, for your ... well, for your size. The guy from *The Nation*, Watson, said you were 'a disgrace to the American public.'"

Taft took another piece of chocolate from his tin and eased it into his mouth and stared at the ceiling while chewing slowly. One might have thought he was oh-so-carefully considering his response to his Cabinet members' concerns, but I suspected he was just wondering whether the next piece of chocolate might have a pecan in it. I say that because the look on his face was one to which I could relate. "I see," he finally said. "Thank you for that information, Philander. Well, we shall deal with our gallant members of the Fourth Estate in due time. In *due* time, gentlemen. In the interim, let us not get unduly exercised. 'Tisn't worth the aggravation, is it? Not at all."

There was a pause while the Cabinet members waited for the president to say more. When he didn't, but instead peered into his tin to inspect the contents and finally selected a light-brown delicacy and eased it lovingly into his mouth, both Secretary of War Dickinson and Attorney General Wickersham began talking excitedly at the same time. "Goddamnit, Mr. President," Dickinson, red-faced, insisted, "if those little brown bastards in Nicaragua want to go around again, I say let's send in the Marines and this time fix them for good. Who do they think they are, demeaning us? Am I right?"

"This Sherman Antitrust Act," Wickersham practically screamed, jabbing his finger at Taft. "We've got to use it more, Will. It's the best thing we've done. Standard Oil, by God, and those arrogant sons of bitches at U.S. Steel too, and even American Tobacco, they're *not* ... "

He'd stopped because he'd noticed that Taft was asleep. That was no surprise to me. I'd been watching the president since his reply to

Knox and had observed his eyes start to glaze over and then his jowls droop and his head tilt to the left and his mouth open. No one said anything for a minute or so. Wickersham looked disgusted. He loudly cleared his throat, causing Taft to open his eyes and look around. "Well, gentlemen," the president said after a moment, "let's call it a day, shall we? I don't believe we shall settle anything of, ah, import, as it were, today. I shall, however, certainly consider all of your observations and suggestions and shall, uh, cogitate upon them at my leisure. Food for thought, gentlemen, delicious food for thought. So my most gracious thanks to all, and let us adjourn for the nonce."

Taft and I remained seated while the Cabinet members exited, some grumbling noticeably. *"Whew!"* he said when the room had emptied. "What'd I tell you, Louie? Well, my boy, no one said this would be an easy job. Here, have a piece of chocolate. I think there are a few left with that lovely caramel within. I was most fortunate to have selected both a maple nut crème and one of those delicious pecan and English walnut clusters. And now, by George, it's off to the links. Will you join me?"

"I don't play golf, Mr. President," I said. "Never took it up."

"Pity. A most relaxing endeavor, Louie. Well, not to worry. Come and tag along, as it were. I promise it shall be more enjoyable than conversing with *that* distinguished gathering—not, of course, that I don't have the highest regard for all of them. And I further promise that we shall not discourse on issues of any greater import than the weather and perhaps how to play the dogleg on that difficult seventh hole. Hah!" His brow furrowed. "That is, of course, if we can manage to avoid the damned reporters. Those miscreants can ruin a man's day quicker than a case of indigestion."

On the way to the Chevy Chase Country Club in Taft's personal automobile, a sumptuous White Steamer with room for seven people— he informed me that he'd had the White House stables converted into a garage for four motorcars, including, in addition to the Steamer, two Pierce Arrows and a small black Baker electric automobile—the president and I finished off the tin of Swiss chocolates. "By *God!*" he exclaimed. "A damned pity that candy's gone. Oh, well. Tomorrow evening, Gerda shall replenish our stock. Until then, my boy, we must, sadly, make do with lesser fare." He instructed Angus, his sallow-faced driver, to stop at a bakery for some pastry. "And be sure it's fairly fresh, Angus," Taft instructed. "I must minimally insist on that, don't you know."

I'd never been on a golf course before, and it was lovely: the acres of fresh green grass, the bright sunshine, the nattily attired golfers strolling about. But I wasn't looking forward to all the strolling about we'd be doing; the prospect of walking anywhere more than absolutely necessary was anathema to me.

As it turned out, Taft's driver was also his caddie. The president and I, munching on the assorted pastries, walked ahead while Angus, carrying a big bag of clubs plus the paper sack of sweets, lagged a few feet behind. Just before teeing off at the first hole, Taft looked around the course and then back at me and smiled warmly. "Ah," he said, "this is just fine, isn't it, Louie? This is the life, by George!" He drove the ball nicely and watched its arc. "You know," he went on, "I tried tennis before I got into golf, but it didn't quite work out."

"That's right," Angus said, nodding. "Tell him why, Bill."

"Well, for one thing," the president said, patting his protruding stomach, "this fellow precluded the possibility of any truly efficient backhand. For another ... "

"For another," Angus interrupted, "you couldn't run three steps without huffing and puffing. Had you continued that game, you'd never make it to a second term."

Taft gave him a look. "Yes," he said. "Thank you, Angus. I can always depend on you for honesty." He glanced at me and winked. "Trust the Scots to be brutally honest, my boy. Living in that godforsaken mountainous terrain as they do, eating oatmeal and thistles and those rock-like scones and God-knows-what else, what can one expect?"

"Well," Angus said, scowling, "at least we have first-rate golf courses, not like this piece of child's play. And next time you tee off, please observe your follow-through."

As we walked toward the first-hole green, the president and I split a powdered sugar doughnut. It was a bit stale, but Taft didn't complain. "A second term!" he muttered after finishing his doughnut, shaking his head. "That's the last thing I want in this life. One term, by God, is considerably more than enough."

"Why is that, Mr. President?" I asked.

"Oh, a hundred reasons, my boy. A *thousand* reasons. This is the worst job in the world, by George. Why anyone would ever wish to be president is, frankly, beyond me. It's an impossible job and, yes, a damned thankless one. No matter what you do, some pygmy's nipping at your back, criticizing your actions, second-guessing your decisions, demanding, expecting, cajoling. It's Nellie who wanted this for me ... for us. As for me, I'd so much rather be on the Court. And not ..." glancing at Angus "... the *tennis* court." He smiled and nodded. "If truth be told, my boy, I sometimes think that Nellie's better suited for this job than I. She's smarter in many ways, Louie, more industrious, more ... confrontational, as it were. Believe me, she would have dealt with Dickinson and Wickersham and those other zealots. Plus, she actually cares about the great issues of the day—not all, of course, but many. Damned shame women can't sit in the Oval Office, eh?"

The president shot one above par, as he let me know, on the first hole—*bogied*, as he indicated. "Listen, Louie," he said as we approached the second hole tee, "tomorrow I want to talk with you about some Court issues. I'm thinking of naming Charles Hughes with my next appointment. Check him out and let me know what you think." He paused and grinned at me. "You know," he went on, "I'm hopeful I may have the chance to name as many as four justices. What an opportunity, eh?"

The seventh hole was, as Taft had noted, a difficult one. I say this because playing it was the source of some of the most animated conversation between the president and his caddie—conversation that made little sense to me due to the plethora of technical, and even ornithological, terms. "All right, Bill," Angus said as we neared the green, "you've done better than I anticipated so far, particularly on that dogleg, but now you have a long putt for eagle. You can do it. Keep in mind the break ... Now concentrate, calmly, and grip ... *grip*, I said, do not choke the damned thing ... and breathe. *Breathe!* Just imagine the line, like I've told you a thousand times."

"I've got it," Taft said, breathing evenly and preparing to tap the ball. "Eagle, eagle ... quite an accomplishment that would be ... here goes ... " We watched as the ball dribbled about three feet past the hole. "*Damn!*" Taft exclaimed. "Missed the break again!"

Angus shook his head and looked disgusted. "You'll never learn! I *told* you to breathe right. Oh, well. Now you have a three-footer for birdie. A par five on this hole, for God's sake. All right, a child can make this putt. Can *you*?"

The president gave him a look, bent over, concentrated, and putted the ball into the cup. "Hah!" he exclaimed, smiling. "A child, eh? Indeed!"

By the time we got to the twelfth hole, I was exhausted and breathing heavily. Taft, noticing, put his hand on my shoulder and asked if I wished to rest for a while. I nodded and he led me to a small stone bench at the edge of the fairway. "Here," he said, "have a cinnamon bun."

After the game, we went to the clubhouse for a bite to eat before returning to the White House. I could barely stand, I was so tired. The course manager had set aside a small alcove off of the dining room for the president's use so that he wouldn't be bothered, and there the three of us sat down to a lovely selection of sandwiches and garnishes. "Excellent!" Taft opined, biting into a big chicken sandwich on dense wheat bread. "Just the right mixture of dark and white meat, sliced perfectly—neither too thick nor too thin—and precisely the proper combination of butter and mayonnaise. It's a true pleasure when a culinary craftsman does his work well, even in regard to a humble sandwich. Do you not agree, my boy?"

"Indeed, I do, Mr. President. I must say, however, that I am not an appreciator of dark chicken meat inasmuch as it has never settled well with me, although, given the opportunity, I would never simply reject it out of hand. As to the mayonnaise and butter, my preference on a sandwich is for a tad more of the former and a bit less of the latter, albeit I am by no means fanatical on that point."

Taft laughed out loud, his jowls quivering. "Indeed!" he said. "I quite understand. 'By no means fanatical ...'—an *excellent* perspective." Turning to Angus, he asked, "And how about you, my dour Scot friend? What is your opinion of the fare?"

Angus shrugged. "Food is food," he said. "One sandwich is as good as the next, in the grand scheme of things. Butter, mayonnaise, mustard, whatever—ten minutes later, what the hell's the difference?"

Taft looked at me and winked. "Well," he said, "there you have it, my boy. The masses have spoken: 'What the hell's the difference?'"

I limited myself to two sandwiches—the chicken followed by a fairly thick turkey and ham and Swiss cheese on lovely light rye bread—and several big pickles, no more than five, but the president wolfed down three sandwiches, including another chicken and then a roast beef swimming in horseradish, explaining that his dinner that evening, the adobong pusuit and rice patties with Nellie, would be "somewhat less than satisfying" and he wished "to fortify myself for the ordeal, as it were." Angus barely finished his only sandwich.

On our way back to the automobile, three reporters ambushed the president. Angus had opened the back door of the White Steamer and Taft was just about to ease his bulk into the seat when a loud, shrill voice pierced the summer calm: "*Mr. President! Mr. President!*" Taft tensed noticeably and turned around, a pained look on his face. "Ah," he said in a resigned tone, "Mr. King, is it not? Well, what can I do for you?"

"Mr. President, what about this tariff thing? What are you going to say in your speech next week in Baltimore? And for that matter, what is your intention in regard to Standard Oil? Are they not an unfair trust? Will you apply the Sherman Act? Do you ... "

"And," interrupted another reporter, a plump older man wearing a somewhat unflattering flat-topped straw hat, "forgive me for asking this, Mr. President, but I cannot avoid it inasmuch as our readers keep bringing it up. What about your weight? It appears as though you've gained a not insubstantial number of pounds since your inauguration last year."

The president's face reddened a bit and he swallowed hard. "Well," he finally said, "as to tariffs ... "

On impulse, I stepped in front of Taft and faced the three men. "Gentlemen," I said, in a somewhat harsh tone, "we *must* ask you to be patient. We shall certainly be happy to respond to your queries soon, perhaps on the morrow, but for now President Taft is quite tired and is somewhat troubled by, uh, an unfortunate case of indigestion. So thank you, and goodbye for the nonce."

"Who the hell are *you*?" King asked.

"Why," I answered, "I'm ... uh ... that is ... "

"He's my new press aide," Taft quickly said, plopping into the automobile and starting to close the door. "And as he said, thank you and goodbye."

On the drive back to the White House, the president chuckled aloud. "By God!" he exclaimed. "That was worth the price of admission. I've never seen that rapscallion King put in his place before, and that other miscreant too—Watson. Louie, I am in your debt." He sighed mightily. "Well, now it's on to less-pleasant endeavors—*considerably* less pleasant, by George. Oh, well, we shall endure. Tomorrow's another day. Speaking of which, my boy, why don't you join me for a pleasant breakfast on the morrow and we shall discuss your future as my, uh, my ... "

"Press aide?"

Taft laughed out loud. "Exactly so," he said, his belly jiggling. "Press aide. Exactly so!"

NEXT MORNING, the president and I breakfasted together in a small private dining room off of the White House kitchen. It was a splendid repast: a large T-bone steak smothered in mushrooms for each of us, lovely scrambled eggs filled with a delicate whitish cheese of some sort and sprinkled with bright green chives, a big yellow porcelain bowl filled to the brim with hefty round boiled potatoes, and both toast and Taft's wonted Parker House rolls. He informed me that he required those rolls with every meal, but added that at breakfast, when toast was an additional bread option, he tended to eat fewer of them than at luncheon or dinner. "However," he added, grinning, "I am by no means fanatical on that point." The steaks were both done medium-rare, which reflected our mutual preference.

Taft and I spoke little at first, preferring to devote our energies to the task at hand. I noticed that his habit was to carefully and methodically—I daresay *lovingly*—cut each of his food selections into five pieces of remarkably equal size before actually consuming. He cut five pieces from his steak and then ate those and then cut five pieces of potato and ate those, then took a huge bite of a roll, and then repeated the pattern. Between each five-piece set, he gulped milk from his quart-sized glass or, more rarely, sipped black coffee. Every now and again he leaned back contentedly in his chair and grasped his big milk glass in his left hand and his white coffee mug—also with the presidential seal and WHT engraved below that—in his right and drank alternately from each. As usual, there was not a drop or speck on the big napkin he'd tucked into his collar below his chin.

After we ate and were finishing our coffee, I asked Taft about his dinner with Nellie. He furrowed his brow and slowly shook his big head. "Not among my more memorable meals, my boy. I daresay, in fact, that it was one of the worst. The cuttlefish put me in mind of papier-mâché and, believe it or not, that fanatical Oswaldo had doused it with garlic and vinegar—'to bring out the tang,' as he said. And the *rice* patties? Well, let's just say that they were something less than 'cunning.' And to top it off, there was a salty dessert called bagoong, which I still don't know what the hell it was. Nellie indicated that we ate it many times in Malcanan but for the life of me, Louie, I don't recall having had the pleasure." He shuddered visibly, his jowls shaking, at the memory of his unpleasant repast and then stuck the end of his right pinky finger into his mouth and chewed on it for a moment.

"Nellie!" he went on. "The woman's ability to remember details from, oh, from years ago constantly amazes me. She can recall not just what she was wearing but what I was wearing at some silly dinner event twenty years ago, and what everyone had to eat at that dinner, and what they talked about over dessert. I, on the other hand, can't remember what the hell I ate as recently as last night. She remembers everyone's names, even if she met them just once, a decade ago." He paused and stared at the ceiling for a minute before continuing. "The woman makes me crazy, Louie, with her incessant nattering. It's impossible, by God, to enjoy a meal in her presence. 'Oh, Will,'" he imitated in a higher-pitched voice, "'you have a *crumb* in your mustache ... Will, *please* take a bite of your bagoong, I *know* you'll adore it ... Now, *don't* overeat, Will, you must try to control your weight ... '" He sighed and twisted the end of his mustache between his right thumb and forefinger. "But I'll tell you, my boy, even though she crazes me, I must admit that I truly admire that woman—her mind, her determination, her ... fortitude."

He paused again. "Oh, well. Enough of that. Let's discuss your upcoming encounter, if you will, with our gallant members of the Fourth Estate. Now I have a few ideas, and perhaps you do as well."

A bit later, I returned to my hotel for a brief nap followed by a light lunch of salmon croquettes and a side order of the Washington Hotel's famous hash browned potatoes with white onion slices and a quite acceptable bowl of peach ice cream with raspberry sauce.

At two o'clock that afternoon I met with the press in a dingy low-ceilinged room in the White House basement. I started out with a bland announcement to break the ice. "Gentlemen," I said, "President Taft is pleased to let you know of a new international policy directive today. He is, of course, very concerned about appropriate downward revisions in tariffs and intends to initiate conversations with key House members, including Speaker Cannon, to institute a reduction in the tariff on birdseed for canaries. We don't know yet whether he'll be able to speak of this in Baltimore next week, but we're hopeful that ... "

"Excuse me," one of the reporters, Oscar King from *The New York Times*, a skeletally-thin individual and one of the three who'd ambushed Taft the day before, interrupted. "Are you kidding me? *Birdseed* for canaries? What is this, a joke?"

"Not at all, Mr. King. You may consider birdseed a minor matter, but I assure you that for tens of thousands of bird-loving Americans whose wallets have been lightened by the escalating cost of this important product, it is an issue of cataclysmic dimensions."

"Look," said another, "the hell with that. *Canaries*, for Chrissake! Let me get to the point here: President Taft is significantly overweight—disgustingly so, I might add. Now many of *The Nation*'s readers have noted that and are wondering whether ... wondering if he ... I mean, what is he *up* to now anyway?"

I stared at him for a moment—perhaps a bit coldly—before answering. "Well, Mr. Watson, we certainly appreciate your readers' concerns for the president's health. The fact is that President Taft was down to 323 this morning, meaning that he's lost half a pound since yesterday. He's very hopeful that his new turnip diet will enable him to lose weight at a steady pace, since his goal is to be below three hundred pounds by Christmas. He'd love to show the American people that ... "

"Oh, *please!*" Watson said snidely. "What do you mean, 'turnip diet'? And if he's 323, Teddy Roosevelt's my mother. What's this ridiculous turnip stuff?"

"Gentlemen," I said, "I can certainly understand your skepticism. But the fact is that President Taft has started a wonderful new diet consisting primarily of turnips and turnip greens, and has actually grown rather fond of it. This diet, which has been quite popular in Europe, particularly Belgium, since the turn of the century, also consists of a breakfast of plain oatmeal, *sans* milk, and a small daily portion of cream of thistle soup. Thistles, as you may or may not know, have been used quite effectively as a weight reduction aid in Scotland for many years. In fact, ... "

"Thistles, my ass!" another man exclaimed loudly. "He's probably up there right now inhaling his third Boston crème pie of the day—that is, if he's not out on the *golf* course. Thistle soup, indeed! What about Nicaragua? Are we sending the Marines there or what? And how about this Panama Canal toll thing?"

"Forget Nicaragua for a minute, will ya George?" another yelled out. "Nicaragua's not important. And the hell with the Panama Canal, for Chrissake! I'm sick of hearing about that already. Now are you telling me that the president is actually on a *diet*? Can you look me in the eye and tell me that he's gonna be under three hundred pounds by the end of this year? I mean, that seems *unbelievable!*"

"Well," I answered, "that is indeed the president's goal. And you know as well as I that he is a very determined, very goal-oriented individual. Of course, we can give no guarantees. After all, this turnip diet *is* somewhat revolutionary. And as to golf, we are aware that some have protested that the president spends an inordinate amount of time at Chevy Chase, but you must understand that diet alone is not the answer to effective weight reduction. Exercise is, of course, the other side of the coin. President Taft has several times indicated that he would *much* rather be meeting with his Cabinet members than playing golf in the afternoons, but, as determined as he is to lose weight, has insisted on repairing to the links. *Walking*, gentlemen, that is the key."

Well, it went on like that for perhaps another five minutes, and then I had to end the press conference before I disgusted even myself. After I promised to meet with them again early the next week and as they filed out of the room, the reporters looked at me askance. But I just smiled back and told them what a *pleasure* it had been to meet with them and how *humble* I felt to serve in this important capacity.

Later that afternoon, I reported the results of my encounter to the president as he was taking his afternoon bubble bath in the family living area on the second floor of the White House, soaking in frothy water up to his collarbone in the special seven-feet-long by nearly four-feet-wide bathtub he'd ordered constructed after an embarrassing episode the previous year in which, as he related, he'd been stuck in a normal-sized tub and it had taken six men, including Angus, to pull him out. "I vowed not to let *that* happen again, my boy," he explained, puffing on a big dark Cuban cigar. "That damned Scotsman has never stopped ribbing me about it."

Taft chuckled when I told him about my meeting with the reporters. "*Excellent!*" he said. "I can just see the faces on those miscreants— particularly that emaciated jackanapes King. Birdseed for canaries. *Hah!*" He paused and stared at the ceiling for a moment. "Actually," he went on, "there might be some merit to reducing that tariff, if there is one. I'll have to look into it."

Holding his cigar to his mouth with his left hand, he reached over the side of the tub with his right and scooped a handful of Macadamia nuts from a bright blue bowl. "Have some, Louie," he said. "They're quite acceptable." As we munched, I noticed that the crest of the president's hairy stomach protruded through the bubbly water, looking for all the world like one of those lovely big sand dunes in northern Indiana on the shore of Lake Michigan. Taft noticed me staring and laughed. "Not exactly a thing of beauty, eh? Well, my boy, as you indicated, by Christmas we hope to be but a shadow of our present self. *Hah!*"

He offered me a cigar, which I accepted although I'd never previously indulged. The president had to show me how to cut off the end and light it properly and even how to puff and draw to keep it lit, and I must say that cigar smoking was not something I initially enjoyed, but after a bit it felt somehow empowering to hold that long brown thing between my thumb and forefinger and to lift it to my lips every few moments to puff on it and to see the bluish smoke spew forth and linger in the air above Taft's oversized bathtub, mingling with the smoke from the president's cigar.

"Well," Taft said after a few minutes, "let's talk about the Supreme Court." He sat up straight in his tub and, looking serious, drew on his cigar and, after a moment, exhaled. "Now, what are your thoughts about Hughes?"

"Good man," I said. "Young ... popular New York governor ... possible presidential candidate down the road ... even-tempered, and generally conservative. He'd be a good appointment, in my opinion."

Taft nodded enthusiastically. I noticed that his eyes were bright and clear. "My thoughts exactly, my boy," he said. "Precisely. And let me tell you my other idea. Justice Ed White. I don't particularly *like* the arrogant egotistical son of a bitch, but, damn it, he *looks* like a Supreme Court justice should: tall, powerful, that shock of gray hair, that chiseled face, those steely blue eyes. I'm thinking of naming him chief justice. He's a staunch conservative and he's ... well, malleable, Louie. I think I can get him to champion my 'rule of reason' idea. I'm anticipating that this year or next we'll have to break up Standard Oil, maybe American Tobacco too, and of course they'll sue and eventually the Court will have to rule. Now I've given this considerable thought, my boy, and I want the Court to apply a reasonableness standard to the Sherman Act. Unreasonable restraints of trade are, of course, prohibited, but, by George, not all corporate actions are that. The 'rule of reason,' my boy, must ever be our *obiter dictum*; business, after all, is the backbone of our country." He paused and tapped his cigar ashes into a tall shiny metal ashtray to the left of his tub. "That damned fanatic Roosevelt!" he went on. "He fancied himself the great trustbuster, but it was all ego—*all* ego, young man. We must adopt a more balanced approach to preserve, as it were, the fundamental structure of our government as our fathers gave it to us."

I didn't know what to say. In our brief acquaintance I'd never seen the president quite so exercised.

"My other vision, dream if you will, is for a new home for the Court," Taft said, continuing to draw on his cigar. "They've been housed in that pissant old Senate Chamber since before Lincoln was president, for God's sake, and that overheated conference room stinks to high heaven. A *pig* could gag in there! Now here's my idea ... " He proceeded enthusiastically to describe his plan for a totally separate Supreme Court building, a marvelous palace with sixteen scrolled columns in front, like a Corinthian temple. "Classical architecture, Louie. Four stories high it'll be, with marble stairs ascending to the main entrance, and big—*massive*, by God!—bronze doors. There'll be a huge corridor called the Great Hall, with busts of all the chief justices, also with lovely marble columns. And the Court chamber—*magnificent*, my boy, with twenty-four pillars, constructed of the best marble from around the world … Italy, Spain, Africa … ."

Well, he went on for perhaps ten minutes, describing the dimensions of his envisioned Court chamber and his plan for the justices' conference room and on and on, and on the one hand it was all quite fascinating; on the other, it was tiring. My eyelids started to feel heavy and before I knew it I'd fallen asleep in my chair, snoring lightly. I only awoke when I heard the president laughing aloud. Opening my eyes, I saw him standing beside the tub, drying himself with an oversized red, white and blue towel, his cigar clamped in one corner of his mouth, and smiling that wonderful smile. It was, frankly, a rather startling sight to which to awaken: the president of the United States naked, pale, disgustingly obese, the loose flesh around his torso jiggling, hanging loose, his round gut protruding, his meaty hairy buttocks prominently displayed. It was a vision for which I hadn't been mentally prepared, and I quickly looked away.

"Well, my boy," Taft chuckled, "perhaps my idea isn't all that exciting. Did you enjoy your brief nap? Quite refreshing, eh?" He looked up at the ceiling and took a huge puff on his cigar and then scooped a handful of Macadamia nuts and devoured them, three or four at a time. "Oh," he went on, "hopefully it will come to pass before I ascend, as it were, to that highest of all courts. It's a lovely dream, and I shall work toward its fruition as best I can. Of course, I've never told Nellie; she'd think it was, well, silly. She gets irritated by anything regarding the Court."

He dressed and brushed his hair. Staring into a dressing mirror, he carefully combed his mustache and applied a bit of wax to the ends and then delicately twisted each end so that it pointed north at a rakish angle. "Excellent!" he said. "Now to dinner with Gerda. The pleasure of your company, my boy, shall sweeten our repast even more."

Then we were off to the same private dining room off of the White House kitchen where we'd breakfasted, where the president received his weekly supply of assorted chocolates from the wife of the Swiss ambassador. This woman was practically a carbon copy of Taft, dressing out easily at three hundred pounds and maybe more. She was the biggest woman I'd ever seen and the most enthusiastic. As soon as we walked into the room, she jumped up from her chair and laid a crushing bear hug on Taft. "Ah, Villy," she boomed, pulling his massive bulk against hers. "Iss good to see you vonce again. Here iss your treat and now ve eat, *ja?*"

"Gerda!" Taft intoned, accepting a twin of the big red and white tin box from which he and I had snacked during the Cabinet meeting and on the way to Chevy Chase. He opened it and immediately popped a dark chocolate into his mouth and then extended the tin toward me. I selected one, a lovely vanilla crème. "Thanks ever so much," the president went on, chewing his candy slowly. "And have you a hunger today?"

"Oh, *ja*, surely I do. Great hunger, sure. Vat ve gott tonight?"

"Pork chops ... delicious dressing, I'm quite certain ... gravy. And I've been advised by reliable sources that there'll be a marvelous cake for dessert. But before we indulge, allow me to introduce my young friend, Louie. He is, in addition to being my esteemed press aide and a wonderful judge of jurisprudential talent, a fellow connoisseur and appreciator, as it were, of culinary accomplishment."

I offered my right hand. "A true pleasure to meet you, ma'am," I said. "I find myself graced to be in the company of ... " But before I could go on Gerda smartly brushed away my hand and laughed aloud—a raucous, healthy laugh that echoed off the walls of the room—and threw her arms around me and pulled me tightly against her. "*Ja!*" she intoned. "Iss good to meet you, young man. You eat *mit* Villy and me, I insists!" I felt momentarily breathless both from the sheer power of her embrace and the fact that my mouth and nose were crushed deep into her humongous pillowy breasts, and started to push away. "*Oh!*" Gerda exclaimed, giggling. "Dat's a riot."

The president chuckled. "You'll find, Gerda," he said, "that my protégé has a fine healthy appetite, don't you know. Let us, then, commence without further ceremony."

We sat down and both Taft and Gerda tucked their oversized napkins—towels, practically—under their jowly chins and both grinned like children on Christmas morning as three young men in starched white uniforms carried in trays of steaming food and served us. The meal was splendid: huge pork chops, lightly browned; mounds of fluffy dressing; piles of mashed potatoes; small peas mixed with delicate little round onions; and the most delicious brown gravy I'd ever experienced, much less imagined. Naturally, there was a basket of Taft's Parker House rolls, and also individual silver bowls filled to the brim with applesauce. We went at it without speaking much. The president carefully cut each of the six pork chops he ate into his usual sets of five symmetrical pieces. I noticed that as neat an eater as Taft was, Gerda was the opposite; employing a fork in her right hand and a tablespoon in her left, she shoveled huge mouthfuls down her gullet, invariably dribbling peas or gravy back onto her plate or, as often, her sleeve. She seemed not to care; I doubt she even noticed. Perhaps her most charming quality was that she hummed steadily as she ate, a Germanic-sounding tune with just a hint of a yodel—*lil-lol-LA-HEE-hoo*—here and there. She even hummed while chewing, though she certainly didn't devote much time or energy to that task. Instead, as soon as her mouth was full she'd casually move her jaws up and down two or at most three times in an almost token effort before swallowing mightily and noisily, all the while using her fork and tablespoon to carefully position the next pile of food at the dark entrance to her gaping mouth.

Taft, as was his wont, downed impressive quantities of milk from his quart-sized glass. Occasionally he sipped from a glass of wine—Pinot Noire, I believe—but not enthusiastically. Gerda, however, was a beer drinker. She apparently kept a personal stein at the White House for use during her weekly visits—a big, colorful thing with scenes of fat peasants cavorting in a Tyrolean village at the base of the Alps. It was one of those devices with a pewter cover that opens with a thumb latch. One of the servers stood directly behind her with a large glass pitcher from which he'd refill her stein with foaming dark beer the moment she emptied it. Now that was fairly often, for Gerda was a healthy drinker. Toward the end of the meal, she raised her stein—refilled five or six times by now—and toasted her host. "To you, Villy," she said. "Dat vas goot repast, ja? I don't tink I can eat not anyting more."

"Surely, Gerda," Taft said, frowning, "you've saved room for some cake, have you not? I've ordered some excellent cake for us, lemon with German chocolate frosting, which I know you'll enjoy. Can you not, Gerda, find it in your heart to eat just a slice or two for dessert?"

"Not in my heart, Villy. Not in mine heart, but *here, ja?*" she replied, laughing robustly and patting her disgusting stomach.

I thought it was mildly droll at best, but the president had apparently never heard anything quite so hilarious. His face turned bright pink and he commenced to slapping his left knee and guffawing furiously, his mustache twitching and jowls quivering. Soon his eyes began to water and he wiped them with his oversized napkin. "Oh, Gerda!" he squealed. "I must say that you are a breath of fresh air. A breath of fresh air, indeed! And now let us have the cake. Some cake," he said, turning to me, "is just what we need at this moment in our nation's glorious history. Would you not agree, my boy?"

"Indeed, Mr. President," I replied. "I daresay the very future of democracy depends upon it."

Taft and Gerda each wolfed down two huge slices of the lemon cake, but I only had room for one and then a small portion of another. I, too, had eaten six pork chops, in addition to five rolls and several huge helpings of the dressing and mashed potatoes and the peas, all swimming in that lovely gravy, and was stuffed—more so than ever before in my young life. I felt I had to move around. "Mr. President," I said, standing, "I hope you will excuse me, but I must take my leave for the nonce so as to properly digest." I turned to Gerda and bowed formally, one arm in front and the other behind. "A sincere pleasure to meet you, ma'am. I look forward to the honor of once again ... "

"Oh, *sure!*" she boomed, standing and again enfolding me in her wonted bear hug, again causing me to become breathless for a moment. "Iss goot to share repast mit a young man vitt good appetite. You come again next veek, I insists."

"Well, my boy," Taft said, grinning, "I shall see you upon the morrow for a pleasant breakfast, at which time we shall discuss plans for your briefing of our esteemed members of the Fourth Estate, if you will, in anticipation of my Baltimore speech. We shall also, no doubt, seriously consider other issues of great, uh, import. As it were. *Hah!*"

While exiting the small dining room, I heard hearty laughter and turned around to see President William Howard Taft and his hefty guest sitting across from each other at the dining room table, grinning and holding their drinks at arm's length in front of them—Taft his oversized

milk glass and Gerda her Tyrolean beer stein. Gerda commenced singing in a rather loud but only slightly off-key voice:

> *Du, du, liegst mir im Herzen,*
> *Du, du, liegst mir im Sinn.*
> *Du, du, machst mir viel Schmerzen,*
> *Weisst nicht, wie gut ich dir bin.*

Then, as if at a signal, the two of them raised their drinks higher yet and
swung them from side to side while wagging their heads in rhythm with
their arm movements and loudly concluded the verse:

> *Ja, ja, ja, ja,*
> *Weisst nicht, wie gut ich dir bin.*

I walked south on Seventeenth Street, past Constitution Avenue,
until I came to a sizeable body of water. A small sign identified it as the
Tidal Basin. Aside from yesterday's golf outing, I couldn't remember
the last time I'd walked anywhere except to get from one place to another as soon as reasonably possible and with as little annoyance as
necessary. I sat on a green wooden bench and stared across the water
and recalled Taft telling me of his wife's vision to have Japanese cherry
trees planted all around the Basin. I'd never seen cherry trees, but could
only imagine how beautiful they'd be in this nice place. What a legacy!
I remembered all that Taft had said about Nellie, even that he'd opined
that she'd probably be a better president than he. "She's been my life,"
he'd said. I wondered what she'd been doing while her husband and
Gerda and I had been gluttoning out on the marvelous pork chops and
dressing and lemon cake.

I thought too about the president's idea for a separate Supreme
Court building—all those marble columns and busts of chief justices—
and imagined how nice it would be to work in such a grand place. I'd
like that. Hopefully, there'd also be a spacious and well-provided restaurant or cafeteria there for the justices and lawyers and law clerks and
interns. I was surprised Taft hadn't mentioned that. And thinking thus-
ly, I wondered what the bill of fare would be for our breakfast next
morning. As for me, another T-bone steak, medium rare, and more of

those magnificent scrambled eggs with that delicate whitish cheese, or perhaps a large stack of nice pancakes with warm butter and plenty of maple syrup, maybe even a dozen or so lovely fried sausages, and of course the Parker House rolls, would be quite acceptable.

A Maid for Gertrude Stein
and Alice B. Toklas

I WAS PRIVILEGED, in retrospect, to serve very briefly as a maid for Gertrude Stein and Alice B. Toklas at their apartment at 27 Rue de Fleurus near the Luxembourg Gardens in Paris in the mid-1920s. I was then a comely young woman with creamy skin, green eyes, and wavy red hair that cascaded nicely past my tiny waist.

On the day after my eighteenth birthday, a rainy Saturday afternoon, my mother and I were visiting Shakespeare and Company, Mademoiselle Sylvia Beach's wonderful bookshop on the Rue de l'Odéon. We were conversing alternately in French and English, our custom on our habitual Saturday outings, about books in the shop and about the interesting photographs of writers hung on the walls. I was especially interested in the portrait of Monsieur Poe, author of my favorite story, "The Tell-Tale Heart."

Soon two women entered the shop and engaged in a spirited conversation with the proprietress and her lover, Adrienne. Within a short time, the two began staring at my mother and me—somewhat rudely, I thought—and my mother stared right back. What an interesting pair they seemed. Gertrude Stein, although I didn't know who she was at the time, was short and stout with a broad peasant face and wore a short brown jacket and a loose-fitting brown corduroy skirt. On her head was precariously perched a small straw cap and she carried a silver-tipped cane. Alice B. Toklas was smaller and darker, almost pretty, with a sharp-featured little face, a hooked nose, and intense dark eyes. She wore a shiny black coat, black gloves, and a funny little black hat that sprouted colorful artificial flowers.

They continued to study my mother and me for the longest time and then began whispering to each other. "What would you think of her, pussy?" I overheard the larger woman say.

"Oh," answered the smaller one, "I suppose she'll do as well as the next. You ask her, lovey."

At that, the larger one—Gertrude, as I soon learned—approached. "Pardon, mademoiselle, but my friend and I are desperately in need of assistance this very evening inasmuch as Marie, our maid, has resigned in an inexplicable snit. I wonder if we might offer you a position?"

That's how I started my short-lived employment with Gertrude Stein and Alice B. Toklas. My mother advised me against it, thinking the pair too strange. "Antoinette," she cautioned, *prends soin de toi. Have a care. Would it not be better to remain safe and quiet at home with me?" But I, who had led the most sheltered of French Catholic schoolgirl lives, was ripe for any adventure.

I reported late that afternoon to their apartment, where Alice gave me a lovely black uniform and advised me as to my duties. "On Saturday evenings," she said, "we receive various artists who have come to Paris—now mostly writers, many our expatriate countrymen. Several will come with their wives, most of whom are quite small-minded. Gertrude will hold court, as it were, in the salon while I converse with the wives in the kitchen. That is the way it is and you must not question it. Gertrude Stein is a genius, you see, and cannot be bothered with or distracted by the silliness of the wives. I am not a genius, and accept that. Your job shall be to serve the hors d'oeuvres and the aperitifs which I shall have prepared and later the meal, all of which are quite wonderful. You are NOT, however,"—and here she glared directly at me, her little dark brown eyes cold and menacing—"to act the coquette with Gertrude Stein in any way. You'll be *sorry* if you do, I promise you that."

Now this caught me by surprise, but I maintained what I thought to be a proper demeanor and composure appropriate to my new position. "Certainement, mademoiselle," I replied, curtsying perfectly. "As you please." Now that I saw her without her odd little hat, I noticed that her hair was cut like that of the deluded Sainte Jeanne d'Arc.

I helped Alice in the kitchen until shortly before the guests arrived. We spoke little. She seemed upset about something, but I couldn't tell what. Now and again she muttered to herself under her breath. "Oh that overinflated egomaniac," I heard her say. "How he fawns to her always. He is *not* to be trusted!"

At one point Gertrude came into the kitchen and immediately pronounced that thenceforth she planned to call me *Teresa* after her favorite saint, Teresa of Avila. Then she examined the dishes Alice was preparing. "Oh, pussy," she exclaimed, "your fabulous duck pâté. It is perhaps your signature dish, is it not? And the lovely red crayfish. *Magnifique!*"

Alice smiled for the briefest of moments, gazing at Gertrude with a look of pure devotion and affection—the first evidence I noted of any warmth in her—before resuming her scowl. "Well," she said, "duck is a duck is a duck, *n'est-ce pas*? I'm sure your brawny Oak Park protégé will enjoy it. Will he not, lovey?"

"Oh, pussy," Gertrude implored. "Don't be silly. Please, please don't be silly. Can't we just have a good time without being silly? We can have a good time, but let's not be silly. *Please*, pussy." When Alice didn't answer, Gertrude's big face hardened and she turned to me. "My, Teresa," she exclaimed loudly, "how *lovely* you look in your new uniform. And *how* it flatters your slim hips." And with that she stormed out of the kitchen, her nose saluting the ceiling.

Alice's face turned darker than usual for a moment, but then she recovered. "Well," she murmured, "I suppose even a genius is not above pettiness. Do you not agree, Miss Slim Hips?"

Soon, the guests came. The first to arrive were Ernest Hemingway and his wife, Hadley. Hemingway was a big, handsome, dark-haired man with a fine mustache. Beneath his long green overcoat he wore a patched jacket of a nondescript color and on his feet a pair of scuffed, battered brown work shoes with no socks. My first impression of his wife, on the other hand, was that she was somewhat plain—short, a bit thick in body, large-bosomed, a round freckled face, and short auburn hair. She was not someone you'd pick out on the boulevard. Then I noticed her eyes. *Qu'ils étaient beaux!* They were light-gray, friendly and warm, inviting. When I asked to take her wrap, she said nothing but simply handed me her coat and smiled and looked with those eyes directly into my girlish soul. I was not the same after that.

Other guests arrived shortly after. Among these were the Fitzgeralds, Scott and Zelda. I barely recall their entry, for my heart was aflutter. I do recall that Monsieur Fitzgerald was quite handsome, kind and polite, whereas his wife was a pain from the start. I believe that she hated me the moment she saw me, for she stared at me with intense hawk's eyes with a look I can only describe as pure malice—*le mauvais oeil*. She spoke not a word to me until much later in the evening, not even "*merci*" for the wonderful food and drink I served her dutifully, the ungrateful little piglet. And when, finally, she did address me, it only confirmed my suspicion, formed more firmly as the evening deepened, that Zelda Fitzgerald was quite mad.

My consolation was that I was not the only target of her malevolence. During the first ten minutes after her arrival, I observed Madame Fitzgerald's interactions with the others. Gertrude allowed the wives to remain in the salon for a brief time before being dismissed to the kitchen and tried to discharge her hostessly obligation by engaging in small talk with them. "And how are you finding Paris these days?" Gertrude politely asked Zelda at one point.

Zelda peered at Gertrude through slitted eyes that seemed somehow not to focus quite properly. Finally she answered in a shrill, high-pitched voice with a bit of a Southern American accent. "How do Ah fine Paris? Ah just stick mah precious ass out the window each mawning and theah it is, usually drizzling and cold and miserable. *That*'s how Ah fine Paris." Then she glared at her husband, who was staring at his shoes and smiling weakly. "It's enough to block anyone," she went on, "if you know what Ah mean."

"Indeed, my dear," Gertrude answered agreeably. "The weather this time of year can be quite demoralizing. Do you not find it so, Ernest?"

"Certainly, Gertrude," Hemingway replied, puffing out his big chest and extending to his full height. "You're right, as always. And yet it is satisfying on these rainy mornings to sit outside a pleasant café— the Café de la Paix, say, or even the Rotonde— wrapped in a fine slicker against the weather, drinking a café au lait and listening to the rain falling softly on the awning. It is good to talk with Emíle, the morning waiter, and to hear who is expected to run well at Auteuil. Or to walk quietly along the Lycée Henri Quatre past the old church of St.-Etienne-du-Mont and the Place du Panthéon and finally end up at the good café I know on the Place St.-Michel, a clean well-lighted place where, on a cold rainy day, you can order a rum St. James and feel the good Martinique warm your body and spirit. There the writing goes well and truly and you can watch the pigeons searching for morsels, bobbing their heads. One thing about a pigeon, he's always ready to screw."

While Hemingway went on and on, both Alice and Zelda glared at him, their faces hard and cold. It was my impression that neither cared much for him. I, however, initially found him somewhat charming and quite masculine, although of course I also felt jealous of him for being with Hadley. She, all the while her husband was talking, gazed adoringly at him, her lovely unblinking eyes soft and light, her round face radiant, beatific. She said nothing. She could have been a saint. To me she almost was—a saint more real and pure than all those whose dull deeds and virtues had, in an unending litany, been force-fed by the nuns of my timid youth. In a moment of epiphany, I at last understood that they, those nuns who seemed so certain, knew nothing of true passion.

Gertrude Stein was impassive during Hemingway's monologue. She merely stood unmoving by the fireplace, short and stout and solid, dressed in a shapeless brown corduroy gown, wearing a pretty lapis lazuli necklace that hung to her ample waist. "Yes," she said when he'd finished. "Interesting observations. Noteworthy remarks, Ernest … Well, Miss Toklas, will you escort the ladies? The shadows are lengthening. Lengthening are the shadows. They are lengthening. Lengthening."

"As you wish, Miss Stein," Alice replied deferentially yet, I thought, sarcastically. "I shall in all endeavor to please."

My first assignment was to serve the salon contingent. I have not yet described this room, the largest in the apartment, but it was quite fascinating. There was a great fireplace on one wall, although the salon was heated by a big iron stove. In front of the fireplace was a large, low wooden coffee table and surrounding this on three sides were heavy chairs that looked as though they would be uncomfortable to sit on. The room was quite cluttered with furniture—big tables, little tables, chests of drawers. Some of the tables were covered with piles of papers which, I learned, were Gertrude's manuscripts, of which she was quite proud. The walls were covered with paintings by such as Cézanne, Matisse, Picasso, that madman Gauguin, and others more obscure. I knew the works of some of these for my mother was a great admirer of the arts and had taken me to the Musée du Luxembourg, the Musée d'Orsay, and other wonderful galleries and museums on our pleasant Saturday excursions.

Those nice outings also served my mother's purpose of getting me away for a while from my brutish father, a mean-spirited and detestable opportunist who, thankfully, spent most of each weekend unconscious in a drunken stupor in his bedroom.

Gertrude held court, as Alice had said, while sitting in a high-backed Italian Renaissance chair with scrolled extensions on either side, which resembled horns growing out of her head. Like a queen on her throne, she observed everything going on and all the supplicants in her minor queendom deferred to her. Hemingway was the worst. Leaning forward in his chair, his hands pressed together as in prayer, he gazed at Gertrude as though she was the Madonna and hung on her every word. "Hemingway," she said at one point, "allow me to advise you of one thing: remarks are not literature. You must remember that. And you would be well-advised to remove that disgusting erotica from your Michigan story. It has no place and is quite false. Even the suggestion of ... well, I find it false and small-minded. Your story must not be, shall I say, *inaccrochable*."

He looked momentarily shattered at her pronouncement but brightened up a bit when I served him a drink in a small glass, a marvelous distilled aperitif made from purple plums. Gertrude had by then turned to Fitzgerald and the others, so Hemingway stood and shifted his attention to the paintings on the wall to the left of the fireplace. He seemed particularly fascinated by two: a Matisse entitled *Blue Nude*, of a lush naked woman with large breasts and ample thighs and buttocks, relaxing invitingly in a pastoral setting; and another by someone named Felix Vallotton, *Reclining Nude*, of a healthy-looking young woman, also naked, lying on a white-sheeted couch, her right arm hanging listlessly, her left knee bent carelessly upward, her gaze focused seductively on the viewer.

Hemingway studied these paintings for perhaps five minutes, fondling his chin with the thumb and forefinger of his right hand, his head cocked to one side. Finally, he turned from the wall and stared at me for the longest time, in a way that made me feel quite uncomfortable, as I was serving the other guests. Then he walked over to me, looked into my face, and placed his meaty paw on my left shoulder. "Daughter," he said, "we've not met before tonight, but I hope that I will see you again. Hadley and I come here often, you know. We are quite fond of Gertrude and Alice, as they are of us ... I, uh, as I say I hope to see more of you ... that is, when we come here. You understand." On the one hand, I enjoyed his attention and the feel of his manly touch on my thin shoulder. On the other hand, I wanted to plunge an icepick into his eye. How dare he mention my beloved Hadley while leering at me and having, as I supposed, impure thoughts?

"Pardon, monsieur," I answered demurely in my best little girl's voice, my eyes averted from his gaze. "I understand little English ... I must go now to the kitchen ... Please to excuse me." I then lowered my shoulder so that his hand dropped away and slithered out of the room as quickly as I could.

In the kitchen, Alice B. Toklas was entertaining the wives, of whom there were two in addition to Zelda and my Hadley. I did not know who they were and was in any case indifferent to their existence. Alice sat on a tall stool with three cushions, which raised her considerably above the level of the others. As she talked, she continuously manicured her nails, cutting snippets with a tiny scissors, smoothing the edges with a little file, and even at one point using her teeth to gnaw on a particularly irksome area of the nail on the thumb of her left hand. Every few minutes she would form one or the other of her hands into a rigid claw, fingers spread far apart, and examine each nail. With her head cocked back and her sharp little chin raised, she carefully inspected the end of each finger in turn as though they were relics from some long-departed saint. If anything she saw displeased her, her dark face would pucker into a frown and she would work furiously to correct the deficiency, employing her scissors or file or her pointy little teeth. She worked on her silly nails the entire time, except for now and again when she would tiptoe to the door of the kitchen and peer down the hallway toward the salon to spy on Gertrude and whatever was going on in there.

Until it was time to serve the meal, Alice conversed with Zelda and Hadley and the other two about gardening, French cooking—there was considerable mention of the intricacies of preparing *poulet en cocotte*, places to go in Paris, Gertrude Stein, and people of note. Perhaps *conversed* is not the most appropriate word; from her three-cushioned height advantage, Alice chose every subject and monologized on each as she obsessively perfected her nails. The others listened politely and chimed in now and again—mostly the two whose names I didn't know. Hadley said little but merely listened, marvelous and serene, to Alice's rambling.

That horrible Zelda, however, stared maliciously at me from the moment I entered the room carrying my tray of hors d'oeuvres. When I silently offered her some tiny crevettes, she scooped up a dozen and glared at me, saying nothing, her tawny face tight and threatening, as though I had that very morning gleefully garroted her parents and all of her siblings. The woman frightened me. Part of me wanted to prostrate myself before her and beg her forgiveness for whatever sin or slight I had committed to so earn her enmity, yet another part wanted to grab hold of her short blond hair and snap her head back and stuff crevettes down her nasty throat until she turned blue and expired on the spot. But, of course, I did neither.

Lovely Hadley, though, was the soul of grace. My hands were trembling slightly as I proffered my tray to her. She noticed and reached out to cup one of my small hands in both of hers for a moment, just the briefest and most precious of moments, before delicately accepting two of my offered crevettes. Her hands were warm and soft, her grasp confident and wonderfully comforting to one such as I. Again our eyes locked. "Thank you, Teresa," she murmured in a soft voice that put me in mind of the Mediterranean evening breeze blowing gently across the beach at St. Tropez, where my mother had taken me on holiday —just we two—at a time when that seemed necessary. "Is it truly Teresa? Your name?"

My face felt warm. "Pardon, madam," I think I replied. "It is Antoinette ... my name ... If you wish to call me Antoinette ... *par ce que c'est mon nom* ... I would be happy."

"Yes," Hadley said just to me, smiling tenderly. "Antoinette. It's a lovely name. I didn't think you were Teresa."

"*Teresa!*" Alice's sharp voice shattered my short-lived reverie. "Teresa," she said, "come here at once. It's time to serve the dinner."

Reluctantly—that is the word—I parted from my sweet Hadley to attend my employer. "*Oui, mademoiselle?*" I asked.

"Listen," Alice B. Toklas said, "let me ask you something. When you were in that other room, the salon, did you remember what I told you about your demeanor with Gertrude? I hope, for your sake, that you did. And when you were in there, was Hemingway? ... Did Gertrude? ... I mean, did you notice if? ... Oh, hell, never mind. You wouldn't understand. Just help me serve the damn food. I give up on everything." She then rang a little bell and within a short time all the guests were gathered in another room to the side of the kitchen, around a big oak table covered with a delicate white lace tablecloth. On the walls of this room were a few more paintings, including one that particularly disturbed me: a long and narrow oil portrait of a tall, bearded monk in a dark brown cassock holding up his right arm and staring, horrified and bewildered, at his torn and bleeding hand. I almost cried out when I saw it, and for a moment wished to flee the apartment and return at once to the safety of my mother. But, of course, I had my duty and so simply averted my eyes, took a deep breath, and went on.

Gertrude Stein sat at the head of the table. The others were seated in no particular order. Hemingway and Fitzgerald sat next to one another and Fitzgerald, whispering to the other man, looked mildly agitated. Alice and I served the meal which, as she had immodestly but accurately claimed, was "quite wonderful." In addition to the delightful duck pâté and the red crayfish, the meal included such delicacies as partridge, big tomatoes—the largest I'd seen, small new potatoes in parsley and butter, and wild strawberries. There was a pretty salad with pungent chives and several bottles of the best white wine of the Loire. There was also a nice sampling of bleu de Bresse cheese, although not everyone partook of this.

As I served the men, I overheard Fitzgerald. "Honest to God, Ernie," he whispered, "she says I'm too small to satisfy her. Just last night she said, and I quote, 'You are, I believe, somewhat less than average.' Now how the sweet Christ does she know *that*? Jesus, Hem, what the hell do I do? I couldn't write a goddamned paragraph this morning." I couldn't hear Hemingway's reply, but he puffed himself up again and his answer went on and on as though he were an archbishop expounding upon the lessons of the Sermon on the Mount to an assemblage of fresh-faced neophytes. At one point I noticed him glancing toward Zelda with a look that was mostly disdain but, I thought, partly fear. I wish I *could* have heard what he was saying because I wondered what it was all about, but that was not possible because a gramophone in the corner was playing a scratchy rendition of a song that Gertrude proclaimed was her favorite and to which she sang along, looking directly at Alice, waving her butter knife as a conductor's baton:

> *In the Blue Ridge Mountains of Virginia,*
> *On the Trail of the Lonesome Pine,*
> *In the pale moonshine, our hearts entwine,*
> *Where she carved her name and I carved mine.*

At that point Alice, at the other end of the table, joined in too and the group quieted as the hostesses, both waving their knives, performed a duet:

> *Oh, June ...*
> *Just like the mountains I'm blue,*
> *Like the pines,*
> *I am lone-some for yo-o-o-u.*

And then everyone joined in for the chorus finale:

> *As I sit repining in Virginia,*
> *On ... the ... Trail ... of ... the ... Lone-some ... Pine!*

Only Hadley declined to accept the dessert I soon offered, a luscious chocolate cake with raspberry sauce. "No, merci, Antoinette," she said, so softly that I could barely hear her above the din of the self-important conversation of Gertrude Stein and Alice B. Toklas and their guests. "Thank you anyway, child." I wanted to answer her, wanted so to touch the silky back of her neck and tell her that I understood, but her husband's gruff voice interfered. "Oh, take the damn cake," he said to Hadley. "Hey, I'll eat it for you. I'm always glad to do a lady a favor." Hadley said nothing but merely looked into my eyes, blessed me yet again with her smile, and nodded once. I then placed a second piece of cake in front of Hemingway and he devoured it in three huge forkfuls, the pig, raspberry sauce dribbling down his chin.

After dinner, Gertrude and the men returned to the salon while Alice and the ladies remained seated around the big oak table.

After clearing the dishes and then serving coffee and liqueurs to all, I was granted a brief respite by Alice and allowed to sit by myself in the kitchen to eat what I wished of the remains of the dinner. I was glad to be alone for a bit, away from the dining room and the picture of the bewildered monk. For the moment, anyway, I wanted only to not be assaulted further by images of punctured and bleeding hands, to be free of such wounds, and to be for a time alone or with just my beloved in a gentle and peaceful place, perhaps a quiet pine glade in the Blue Ridge Mountains of Virginia, with a soft breeze caressing my face like that I recall so fondly from my time in St. Tropez, the evenings there, with my mother.

While I was sitting in the kitchen alone, picking at some buttered potatoes and bleu de Bresse cheese, Zelda stalked into the room and leaned over me from behind, her hands tightly grasping the edge of the table. With her face close to mine, she hissed the following: "Listen, you li'l tramp, you stay the *hell* away from mah husband. Ah *know* what you're up to and will tolerate it no *longah!*" Then, just as abruptly, she turned and marched back to the dining room, her rump held indignantly and self-righteously high, her hands balled into vicious little fists.

Up to the time the guests departed, the remainder of the evening was somewhat of a blur. I flitted back and forth between the salon and the dining room—refilling drinks, clearing dirty dishes and glasses, emptying ashtrays. I primarily looked at the floor and avoided eye contact as much as I could. My face felt flushed. I tried to make myself as small as possible and sought to stay as far as I could from F. Scott Fitzgerald. I noticed that the more he drank, the less appealing was Fitzgerald's demeanor and behavior. He became louder, obnoxious even, and looked progressively disheveled—his eyes bloodshot, his fine light-brown hair messy, his shirt untucked. At one point he turned to Gertrude and said, a bit louder than perhaps necessary and with a slight slur, "Frankly, I don't know what the hell you're talking about. Ezra is a terrific writer, a great poet. And Joyce? Don't talk to me about Joyce. The man is wunnerful. Whattya mean you don't wanna hear his name again? *Joyce, Joyce, JOYCE!* So there."

Gertrude, ensconced upon her Italian Renaissance throne, appeared angered. Her big face had the same threatening look as earlier in the evening when she'd complimented my uniform and said it flattered my slim hips and then huffed out of the room. She glared at Fitzgerald. "That was a most interesting observation," she said darkly. "I have always admired your discretion, Fitzgerald, but now I must wonder. There is nothing I detest more than one who cannot hold his liquor and, as a result, displays poor discretion. It is quite unnerving and, I daresay, disheartening."

Poor Fitzgerald, well-rebuked, offered no reply but looked as though he might start crying at any moment; his eyes were moist and he blinked rapidly. I felt bad for him and wished to comfort him, but, of course, was afraid to approach or even look at him. Hemingway, however, put his hand on Fitzgerald's pale forearm, squeezed slightly, and said, "You know, Scott, I think Gertrude's right about Pound. Don't you agree he's overrated?"

Fitzgerald ripped his arm away. "Don't TOUCH me, for God's sake!" he screamed. "You *know* I'm not like that."

Hemingway looked surprised but did not reply. I noticed that he glanced at Gertrude for just a moment, for approval perhaps or sympathy. But she, stone-faced and imperious, still seething at Fitzgerald's impertinence, offered nothing more.

That event was the death knell for the evening's festivities and the party broke up soon after. When I handed Hemingway his coat—an ugly vomit-green piece of trash with frayed sleeve ends, smelling faintly of spilled gin —he looked as though he wanted to say something to me. For a moment I feared he was going to call me "daughter" again, in which circumstance I would have terminated my employment on the spot and fled screaming into the Rue de Fleurus.

When I gave sweet Hadley her wrap, my heart pounding within my chest, she took my hands in hers. "Antoinette," she whispered in my ear, our cheeks touching ever so lightly, "it is for you to be strong. I know you can. *Je suis sûre que tu peux le faire.* Within you is the strength you need." For the final time I gazed into the lovely gray eyes, calm and serene, the remembered beauty of which I would depend upon, I knew, in my years to come. Hadley quietly spoke her final words to me: "Forgive them, child. They can't know." Then she was gone from my sight but not my heart.

Fitzgerald and his wife prepared to leave shortly thereafter. He was still apparently affected by Gertrude Stein's rebuke and seemed a shattered man. I helped him on with his beautiful camel's hair coat and he mumbled a gracious thanks. Zelda glared horribly at me yet again while I assisted her husband, and all at once I had a proverbial bellyful of her. When I'd finished with Monsieur Fitzgerald and he had exited the apartment, I snatched up her coat, strode boldly over to her, and shoved it into her chest. With our faces close, she curled her ugly little upper lip and showed her yellowing teeth. "What did Ah *tell* you, you li'l bitch?" she sneered viciously. "You keep your whore's ass away from mah husband or Ah'll ... " But she never finished telling what terrible thing she'd do because, with what strength I had, I crowded her closely into a corner and looked directly into her eyes. "Heed me, madam," I said, quietly but firmly so that only she could hear. "I have had quite enough of you. Please to keep your vile mouth closed and leave now without speaking further. *Comprenez-vous?*"

She was so startled she said nothing. Her mouth opened as though she was about to speak, but no words emerged. She looked at me once, unsure of herself, and then abruptly turned and left to catch up to her husband.

Neither Gertrude nor Alice saw. The hostesses were occupied with saying goodbye to one of the other couples—a pretentious pair of aesthetes, both rail-thin, with obnoxious laughs. However, in the mood I was in, I would not have cared had they witnessed it all. I was ripe for a confrontation; I felt ready to stand up for myself at last. Had my employers chastised me, I believe I would have made the very welkin ring.

With the guests departed, Gertrude and Alice collapsed into large stuffed chairs in a corner of the salon and had their nightcaps. I busied myself emptying ashtrays. "Oh, pussy," Gertrude said. "What an evening! Quite distressing in some ways, to be sure, but satisfactory in others. Your meal was *superbe*. I must say that the crayfish was the best you've made, and you know how fond I am of it. And the partridge! It was certainly the equal of your marvelous *château-briand* of last week, if not superior."

"Yes," Alice replied, looking pleased. "Thank you, lovey. I must admit that I am quite satisfied with my efforts. And may one ask how your literary explorations proceeded?"

"Well, as for that let us have an understanding. If Mr. Fitzgerald calls again to ask if he may be received, I intend to inform him that he is unwelcome—indirectly of course. 'Oh, dear, Fitzgerald,' I'll say, 'I am so sorry, but the fact is Miss Toklas has a bad tooth and we are not entertaining this evening ... nor the next, nor the next, nor the next.' Hah! We shall see how fond he is of Mister James Joyce then."

"And does that go for Mister Hemingway as well?" Alice asked, indifferently examining her nails. "Will *he* be welcomed by you?"

Gertrude gave her a look. "Oh, pussy," she said, "I thought we agreed to not be silly. Hemingway is harmless—as harmless as his insipid little wife, for all his masculine posturing. We both know that."

"As for the insipid wife, there I agree with you, lovey. As for the aspiring writer, I am not so sure." She paused. "Oh, Teresa," she said, turning to me, "would you like a little nightcap?"

"Yes, Teresa," Gertrude added. "Have a nice cognac."

"It is NOT Teresa!" I snarled, dropping a full ashtray and turning to face the pair. "That is not my name and you are to stop calling me that right now! I am not some silly saint, and never could be. *Je m'appelle Antoinette.* Do you hear? ANTOINETTE!"

They looked surprised. "Well," Gertrude said after a moment. "Of course. Antoinette. If that is what you prefer ... if that is what you wish ... "

"How *dare* you raise your voice like that!" Alice scolded. "Just as I was about to suggest to Miss Stein that we keep you on, perhaps in a permanent capacity. But now ... well, really, such impertinence simply cannot be brooked. You *must* apologize."

"Now, pussy," Gertrude said soothingly. "She's just upset about something. However, Ter ... Antoinette, Miss Toklas is right. Such an outburst is not acceptable. After all, you are ... "

"*Ha!*" I interrupted, rudely to be sure. "It is to laugh! Stay on here? *Surely* you are not serious. Surely you cannot think that I ... " I was about to go on and unburden myself, to tell all that was within my heart, but then my anger faded as I looked at those two interesting women sitting in the salon grasping their little glasses. I looked at Gertrude's broad peasant-like face with her open and direct American gaze and at Alice's almost-pretty face as well—smaller and more well-defined, her dark-brown eyes intense. I remembered my first sight of Alice at Mademoiselle Beach's bookshop, with her strange little black hat with the artificial flowers. I recalled the image of the two at opposite ends of the dinner table waving their butter knives and singing their silly song together, to each other. At that moment I felt affection for both women, despite anything. Part of me wished to hug them both and to be hugged, but the greater part of me wished suddenly just to go home to my mother and to lie on our soft blue sofa while she rubbed my aching feet and to tell her of my evening.

"Mademoiselle Stein," I said politely. "Mademoiselle Toklas. I do not apologize for my 'impertinence,' as you say, but that is no matter. Thank you for employing me tonight and for considering to employ me further. *Ce n'est pas possible.* I hope, however, that I will see you both from time to time, perhaps in Montparnasse, and that we might share a cup of tea or a glass of Chardonnay. That would please me, for I have much to learn."

They both just stared at me for a bit and then Gertrude got up from her chair, put her stout arms around me, and drew me to her substantial bosom and held me for a few nice moments. "Certainement, Antoinette," she said gently. "That would be nice. And we would be pleased if you would call on us now and again. Yes, pussy?"

Alice, still seated, perusing the nails on her left hand, nodded. "Of course, lovey," she said. "Most welcome."

Walking home in the rain, it occurred to me that tomorrow would be Sunday and my mother would expect me to accompany her to early Mass. I decided that I would decline, at least this week, and would instead take a long walk alone through the Left Bank. Perhaps, I thought, I would seek that clean well-lighted café on the Place St.-Michel and watch the pigeons.

A Fortuneteller for Marilyn Monroe

I SERVED AS A FORTUNETELLER, and I suppose too a sort of sur-
rogate mother, for Miss Norma Jeane Baker, the fragile drug addict and
film actress popularly known as Marilyn Monroe. By late May of 1953,
when Norma Jeane asked me about her future, I was a burnt-out, chain-
smoking, bleached blonde living in a little brownstone just off Parsons
Boulevard in Queens with my husband, Eugene, a groundskeeper at
Yankee Stadium. He also worked part-time in a cut-rate paint store,
mostly stocking shelves. I supplemented our meager living reading
palms, which was mostly a scam though not entirely. Mostly, I just told
people what I thought they wanted to hear—silly generalities they could
take to the bank—but sometimes I truly knew what was ahead for a person. I had my own way of knowing that. But if what was ahead wasn't
good, I usually wouldn't tell them; I'd lie, I'd fudge, I'd shrug my thin
shoulders.

That's what I did with poor Norma Jeane. She wanted to know if
she'd marry Joe DiMaggio and have children and live with him happily
ever after, or at least for a while. She wanted to know if she'd become
and be regarded as a serious actress, not just some silly breathy-voiced
blonde with big boobs and a great ass wriggling around in tight outfits.
She even wanted to know if she'd someday be Mrs. Arthur Miller, wife
to the tall, serious, morally admirable pipe-smoking playwright whom
she so respected. "Oh, Aunt Jean," she said, "wouldn't that be *marvelous?* He'd write wonderful plays and I'd be in them." And she wondered and wanted to know if she'd someday go crazy and have to be
locked away, like her mother.

On a more mundane level, she wanted Eugene to give her some
ideas for talking about baseball with DiMaggio, the recently-retired
Yankee great and her current beau—a man whom I detested but my
husband idolized. "That's about all he likes to talk about, Uncle
Eugene," she said. "We hardly ever talk about anything except baseball—that is, when we talk at all. Please help me."

133

Eugene and I'd first met Norma Jeane when we briefly served as her foster parents in the early summer of 1934 in Hawthorne, a Los Angeles suburb, when she was seven years old. I'd known her mother, Gladys, a little from when she'd come twice for palm readings, and knew even then that Gladys was ... well, sick. Unstable. A marginal mother, at best. She was in and out of mental hospitals, and her little girl spent time in one goddamned foster home after another—in some of which she was treated like an indentured servant, in others of which she was slapped around and even felt up by perverted scumbags, and in almost all of which she was yelled at and demeaned and made to feel like trash.

Not in ours. Eugene and I and our three sons, George and Lou and young Waite—named, respectively, for New York Yankees George Herman "Babe" Ruth, Lou Gehrig, and Waite Hoyt—led a simple life, a quiet life, though we were poor. I loved those boys and was okay with Eugene. He'd never been the brightest light in the chandelier but he was kind and simple and had no apparent interest in other women or gambling, and in fact few interests in anything except baseball—particularly the Yankees. Many were the nights that I fell asleep to the sound of his nasally but soothing voice detailing that day's triumphs: how this one had stolen second in the bottom of the fifth inning; how that one had made an amazing over-the-shoulder catch in the outfield with two out in the top of the seventh; how another had patiently worked such-and-such a pitcher to a three-two count, fouling twice down the first base side, before blasting a game-winning homer deep into left-center. He wasn't exactly exciting—no Clark Gable, about whom I'd fantasized for years, usually at night in bed with Eugene asleep and snoring beside me—but was just the right kind of man for me: dull and steady if you please, predictable, no emotional extremes. And he was nice to that girl, talking to her and reading her stories, and I knew he'd never dream of getting weird with her.

Anyway, we happily had the kid for five months before that bitch Grace McKee, Norma Jeane's legal guardian, took the child from us to live with her. Well, that didn't work out because Grace's gaping asshole husband, Erwin—*Doc*, as he was known—took to sticking his tongue in her mouth and having her sit on his lap and rub against him, the wretched son of a bitch, and eventually she wound up in the Los Angeles Orphans Home on North El Centro Avenue. She wasn't really an orphan, but might as well have been for all the use her wacko mother was to her.

I would have taken that lovely little girl back and raised her as our own if I could have, except that in 1935 we moved back to New York City, where Eugene and I'd been raised, to help my sister take care of our dying mother. It took the old lady almost a year to finally tip over and during that time Eugene landed his job with the Yankees and loved it to the extreme, being close to his heroes and feeling that he was in heaven, and we decided to stay. I hated the winters, but other than that never missed California much.

I often thought back to the time we'd had Norma Jeane. Having a daughter had always been my precious dream, and that was as close as I came. I remembered holding her on my lap, brushing her silky light-brown hair and sometimes braiding it or arranging it into twin pony-tails; reading *Alice in Wonderland* to her while she munched graham crackers and sipped chocolate milk; talking to her about what outfit she could dress in next day and sometimes letting her play dress-up with my skirts and blouses and ivory-colored lace shawl and my high-heeled shoes; teaching her how to put on lipstick and mascara; sometimes washing her little back or shampooing her hair when she bathed. I thought about the times I'd taken her shopping, though we had little money, and bought her inexpensive bright-colored dresses—blue was her favorite—and once a nice pair of black patent leather Mary Jane shoes that she said she adored. I remembered teaching her to set the dinner table and how she liked to fold the napkins just so and place the fork perfectly in the center of each one. I even remembered that some-times I'd had to remind her to flush the toilet when she went tinkle. And always I recalled her looking up at me, her pretty blue-gray eyes clear and big, sometimes calling me "Mommy." Once I took her to see a Shirley Temple movie and remembered how, when we got home, she did a perfect Shirley impression, cocking her head and forming her mouth into a cute pouty little O and opening her eyes innocently wide and singing the song from the movie:

> *What makes life the sweet-est?*
> *Best-est and complete-est?*

Not a big dull house,
Or a Mickey Mouse,
But the right some-body to love!

Ice cream, cake and can-dy
May be fine and dan-dy,
But if you ask me, they're not one-two-three
To the right some-body to love!

We shared a birthday, June First, and I'd made her a little party with a lovely angel food cake and her very favorite, chocolate pudding. After that, she and I made pudding together every few days, cooking it on the stove and pouring the thickened contents into dessert cups and covering it with waxed paper while it cooled so that there'd be just a thin dark skin on top, which Norma Jeane loved to skim off and eat before she spooned the warm pudding itself.

After Grace took the child from us, I often wondered what had become of her. And as life soured for me, I thought of that girl—the daughter we could have had—more and more.

By the late 1940s I was a bitter woman. George had been killed in World War II on Guadalcanal, a godforsaken piece of shit jungly island in the Pacific, and Lou was a bona fide paranoid schizophrenic, spending most of his hopeless time in a mental hospital in Jersey City getting messages through the radio from God and Satan and Harry S. Truman. Waite lived at home with us for a time, but couldn't hold a job for more than a month or two and drank more Schlitz each night than I approved of and smoked like a goddamned chimney, and after a while he packed his Nash and left for Hollywood, hoping to get work as an extra in westerns and war movies, after which we rarely heard from him.

After George's death, I too had taken up smoking—two packs a day, minimum—and cussing as well, mostly at my husband. It was, "Goddamnit, Eugene, I thought I told you to take out the fucking *garbage!*" or "I wonder when that cocksucker's gonna bring the sonofabitching mail?" or "Pass the motherfuckin' salt." I somehow couldn't control my potty mouth. Poor Eugene didn't like it, but didn't give me a hard time. He knew my pain.

On top of all that, I was going through the change. One minute I'd be okay, floating along, and the next I'd be feeling lower than a worm's ass and weeping. One minute I'd be freezing and the next sweating and burning up. Nights were the worst. Sometimes I'd hog all the blankets and couldn't get warm and had to snuggle against my husband and shortly thereafter I'd kick off all the covers and be flushed and drenched with sweat, and then I'd go through the whole goddamn cycle again and then again. Eugene nicely talked me to sleep, but then, when I'd finally fall asleep, as often as not I'd be jarred awake by his snoring and/or further nocturnal ramblings about—what else?—the damned New York Yankees. I'd usually have to jam him in the ribs to shut him up, at least temporarily.

I mostly felt that I was just going through the motions of living—taking care of my husband and our modest little house, doing palm-readings most afternoons, and visiting Lou a few times a week. I smoked my Chesterfields a lot and cried a lot and sometimes went to movies, either alone or with my sister or now and again with Eugene during the baseball off-season. We saw a few movies with Marilyn Monroe—*Niagara, Monkey Business, The Asphalt Jungle,* and my favorite, *All About Eve*—and liked her, but I had mixed feelings: it was great to see my little girl making a success of herself, but I hated to see her caught up in the cutthroat Hollywood sex symbol bullshit.

The good thing that happened was that on Mother's Day of 1948 I actually heard from Norma Jeane. She'd somehow tracked me down and phoned from Los Angeles and we both blubbered like fools. She told me she'd been married for a while to a Jim Dougherty, but that was over and now she was trying to get good movie roles with Twentieth Century Fox. I knew all that, of course.

After that, she called me every Mother's Day—always my toughest day of the year—and on our mutual birthday, and we also exchanged cards at Christmas. Those times were the highlights of my otherwise gray existence.

Then I had an even more pleasant surprise. In 1953, she called as usual to wish me a happy Mother's Day and to ask if she could come to see me on our birthday. She was, she said, going to be in New York for a screening of her latest movie, *Gentlemen Prefer Blondes,* and asked if she could stay with us for a day or so. Oh, the anticipation of seeing that girl almost made me feel alive again.

And exactly three weeks later, on the last day of May, when I saw Norma Jeane in person for the first time in almost twenty years, I could have peed my pants—I was that glad to see her. She was beautiful! She'd been pretty in the magazines and movies, of course, but in the flesh was prettier yet; her perfect pale skin practically glowed and her blue-gray eyes sparkled. It was a bit strange to see my little girl with hips and breasts—big ones—and wearing lipstick and makeup and, of course, that trademark well-coifed blond hair. "Oh, Aunt Jean," she squealed, "it is so good to *see* you! Oh, my *God!*" She pulled me to her and hugged me and we held each other close and then I felt her shudder and she grasped me tighter and began sniffling and sobbing just a bit, and then more, and soon she was shaking in my arms and crying.

I pulled her closer and stroked the stiff hair on the back of her head. "What's the matter, honey?" I asked gently. "What is it?"

She shook her head and said nothing, but continued to clutch onto me. I didn't press it and after a bit led her to the couch, sat her down, dried her face with my handkerchief and straightened her hair. I put my arm around her shoulder and just held her to me and stroked her cheek a bit, and we were quiet then for a time. Oh, it felt good to hold my girl again!

After a while she looked up and maybe really saw my face for the first time, and I could tell she was a bit shocked. I couldn't blame her; I was a different woman from the pretty foster mother she'd known nearly twenty years ago. Then, my boys were young and healthy. Life was ahead for all of us. Since then, life—at least part of it—had turned to shit, I'd aged, my face was lined and had started to sag, my teeth were yellow from smoking, and, of course, my dry and thinning hair was bleached a horrid whitish-blond.

Soon she began sniffling again and blew her nose twice into my handkerchief and then sneezed four times in a row—and not delicate little kertie-choo ladylike sneezes either, as one might have expected from Marilyn Monroe, but loud and fat splotchy ones that sprayed green mucousy crap everywhere. "Oh, God!" she moaned. "I have a rotten cold. I feel like shit, Aunt Jean. Plus, my damned throat is so sore I can hardly swallow. And ... well, never mind."

"What?" I asked. "Tell me."

She looked sheepish. "Oh, I have my period. It hurts like hell. It *always* hurts like hell. I bleed like a stuck pig and have just the most *horrible* cramps." She paused and rolled her eyes and then put her face in her hands. "Oh, God, Aunt Jean, I am a goddamned *mess!*"

"Stop swearing, Norma Jeane," I said. "C'mon, let's get you to bed."

I led her by the hand to a small bedroom in the far corner of the house, George's old room. I helped her out of her clothes, fluffed the pillows, got her under the covers and pulled them snug around her. "Warm enough?" I asked. She nodded. Then I went to the bathroom for a wet cloth and gently washed her face. With the makeup off, she looked more like the little girl I'd known than the sexpot movie star she was.

I went to the kitchen and put on the kettle for tea and took two slices of Wonder Bread from the breadbox to toast. While the water heated I sat and smoked a cigarette, taking deep drags and exhaling through my nose in two even streams and staring at the streams as they dissolved. I had a big glass ashtray that I'd stolen from a hotel, and one of my pleasures was to tap the ashes into it—two rhythmic taps at the burning end of the cigarette, using my index finger. The whole goddamned smoking ritual calmed me: taking a cigarette from the pack, tamping the end of it three times on a flat surface, sticking the cigarette between my lips, lighting the match and seeing the orange flame appear and smelling the sulfur odor, lighting the fucking thing, flicking my wrist to extinguish the match, holding the cigarette between my index and middle fingers, inhaling, exhaling, watching the exhaled smoke, tapping the ashes off, grinding out the stub.

When I brought Norma Jeane her tea and buttered toast, as well as a hot water bottle for her cramps, she was dozing. I cleared my throat and she opened her eyes and looked around. "Oh, Aunt Jean," she murmured after a moment, "I almost forgot where I was. I was dreaming about Joe. I dreamt we were getting married, a big wedding in a church, and hundreds of people, Hollywood people, were there. Mr. Zanuck was there, smoking one of his big smelly cigars. Jane *Russell*, of all people, was my maid of honor. Oh, he was so handsome. *My* Joe!" She paused. "Gee, what a beautiful bride and groom we made."

As she ate her toast and sipped her tea, I sat on the edge of the bed and rubbed her toes through the blanket. I realized this was one of the few times I'd been in George's room and not crying since that horrible day in 1943 when we'd received the news about his death. "Umm," she said, "this is good. *God*, I feel like I could sleep for a week."

"You can, honey. You can stay here for as long as you like. I at least want you to stay until you feel better. I'll take care of you. Eugene, too. You *know* we love you, kid. Right?"

She looked at me, her eyes moist, and nodded. "I wish I could, Aunt Jean. But we have the screening tomorrow night, and then it's back to California." Then she grimaced and clenched her teeth and put her hand over her lower abdomen. "*Goddamn!*" she moaned. "Jesus H. Christ! Can you get my purse, Mom?" I did and watched as she shook three pills from a brown container and washed them down with her tea. She took a few deep breaths. "Aunt Jean," she said after a moment, "I want to ask you something. I want you to tell me about me and Joe." She extended her right hand, palm up, toward me. "Are we really going to get married, me and Joe? Will we have some little DiMaggios? Is he my ... you know ... my Prince *Charming*?"

I reached under the covers with my left hand and rubbed one of Norma Jeane's feet. That was my method. There were calluses on the bottom, near the ball of her foot. As I massaged, images of my girl's future with DiMaggio flashed through my head like previews of a coming attraction. I saw them out in public together, flashbulbs popping, both dressed so nicely. He was tall and muscular and handsome in a gray pinstriped suit, and she, blond and red-lipsticked and smiling, was wearing a tight-fitting low-cut blue dress and was balancing precariously on a pair of silver high heels. Yes, I saw them getting married, but not in a church, instead in some kind of official-looking building, and Norma Jeane looking so happy, smiling again. I envisioned them in some Asian country on their honeymoon, surrounded by slant-eyed black-haired admirers—maybe the goddamned Japs who'd killed my son—and then Norma Jeane by herself on an outdoor stage somewhere, dressed skimpily and freezing her ass, with thousands of wild-eyed American soldiers cheering for her and my girl thrilled at their adulation. And I saw the two of them in their apartment or maybe a house somewhere, stonefaced DiMaggio silently watching baseball on television and ignoring her and Norma Jeane lonely, wanting to talk, and then another image of them arguing, him screaming, enraged and jealous—about what I didn't know—and then slapping her face hard, a back-handed wallop that sent her reeling, and her crying and red-faced. And finally I saw them separated, living apart, both angry and hurt, him contrite and wanting to reconcile but her not, unwilling to be further ignored, abused, humiliated. No little DiMaggios.

I took Norma Jeane's offered hand in mine and smiled and then studied her palm. "Um-hmm," I murmured, "I see your life line. Now let's see, where's that heart line? Well, there's your line of marriage. Oh, yes. Ah, look at that Mount of the Moon, that fleshy little pad. And your line of fortune. Um-hmm." And other such crap. I knitted my brow and nodded my head, pretending to be trying to get a handle on her future. "Well, kiddo," I finally said, "I just don't know. I do see marriage, but somehow the rest isn't all that clear to me. Maybe it'll be clearer later. Maybe later, huh?" I took a Chesterfield from my pack and lit it. Norma Jeane asked for one.

"Absolutely *not*, young lady," I answered. "I do not want you to start smoking. It's a filthy habit and it'll ruin your health."

She looked at me strangely and sneered a bit. "*Start?*" she said, "Why, I've been smoking since ... "

"Norma Jeane, I do not want to hear of it. You may not smoke while you're under this roof. And you with a sore throat, too. *Honestly!*" I paused. "And to be blunt, young lady, I don't know what you see in that DiMaggio anyway."

"Oh, Aunt Jean, he's so *handsome*, and he always dresses so well, you know, and ... oh, I don't know, he's just got this quietness and dignity, or something." She sniffled and blew her nose into my handkerchief, which I'd placed near her, though one little glob of greenish snot managed to avoid the handkerchief and plopped instead onto the left side of the white pillowcase. "And I don't know if I should tell you this, but he's just the best lover I've ever had. He's ... well, *big*. Gee, Aunt Jean, sometimes it hurts when we ... you know ... "

"Norma *Jeane!*"

"The only thing is, it's hard to talk to him. Except for baseball, he's so ...quiet, reserved. In a way, I love him for that 'cause he's not always bragging on himself like other men. He doesn't feel he has to.

141

He's just so, I don't know, *dignified*. But, oh, I wish we'd talk more about things."

I didn't say anything. *Dignified*, my ass! I knew about DiMaggio. I'd watched him play, had seen Eugene and others kidding around with him, had stared at his muscular butt while he stood bent forward in the batter's box, and had even met him once at a Yankees organization Christmas party. Part of me wanted to tell Norma Jeane that the reason DiMaggio didn't talk more was that he was basically a dumbfuck; he didn't say much because he had nothing much to say. He was a big, good-looking, gifted athlete who was otherwise little more than an ignorant garden-variety dago who, yes, could be charming but whose jealousy and insecurity and need to control would always break through, if not sooner then later. He was one of these guys who, because they look so good and are so accomplished at one thing, you can't conceive that beyond that they're really just a self-centered chucklehead. I knew the type. So he'd been able to hit a goddamn baseball safely in fifty-six consecutive games in 1941. So he'd made hundreds of wonderful, seemingly effortless catches in center field. So everyone idolized him. So he had a big dick! He was *still* entirely unworthy of my daughter. But I knew I couldn't tell her that; she'd have to find out for herself. You can't protect your kids all the time. Life had taught me that.

Eugene, of course, was among DiMaggio's legion of admirers. As much as I was comforted listening to my husband go on and on in bed before sleep about the stupid Yankees, I had to tune out when he mentioned "the ole Clipper," as he called him. I chose not to take issue with him; what would be the point?

I felt depressed, seeing that part of my girl's future. Norma Jeane noticed me looking sad and took one of my hands in both of hers, looked into my eyes, and began singing softly in that breathless Marilyn voice, her eyes big in feigned innocence, like her long-ago Shirley Temple impression:

> *A kiss on the hand may be quite con-tin-en-tal,*
> *But diamonds are a girl's best friend.*
> *A kiss may be grand, but it won't pay the rental*
> *On your humble flat or help you at the automat.*

Men grow cold as girls grow old,
And we all lose our charms in the end.
But square-cut or pear-shaped
These rocks don't lose their shape ...
Diamonds are a girl's best friend.

"That's from *Gentlemen*," she said, grinning. "I'm the lovely Miss Lorelei Lee"

I had to smile, she was so damned cute. It occurred to me how funny she could be. "Thanks, kid," I said. "Listen, you get some rest now and later I'll bring you some nice soup. We've gotta get you feeling better if you're gonna conquer the world. Do you still like chicken noodle?"

Her eyes brightened and she nodded. "Can we make pudding later, Mom? Oh, please!"

"Sure, I said. "Tomorrow. I bought us some. Jell-O brand."

"When will Uncle Eugene be home?"

"Around dinnertime. Now you rest. I'll bring you some orange juice. Okay?"

She snuggled back under the covers. "Okay, Mom. Thanks." I got up to leave. "Hey," she said softly, "I love you."

I looked at Norma Jeane in George's bed, cozy under the covers, and remembered the nice times I'd put her to bed at night, kissed her, told her, "Goodnight, sleep tight, don't let the bedbugs bite," and remembered how once I'd had to give her a little whack on her little behind when, in a moment of childish anger, she'd kicked Rusty, our cocker spaniel. And now that behind, not so little anymore, encased in tight shiny dresses, was glimmeringly displayed on the big silver screen as she slithered from room to room for millions of men to stare at and drool over, and the rest of her womanly curves too, and that soft and sensuous red-painted mouth that was supposed to make men think of her twat and to fantasize about screwing Marilyn Monroe. I padded over to her and kissed her cheek and again stroked her hair and held her to me for a moment, and she put an arm around me too. "I love you too, kid," I whispered. "You *know* I do. Now you rest."

After bringing her juice, I went back to the kitchen and mixed a gin and tonic and lit a Chesterfield and sat at the table. Poor baby! I

143

smoked my cigarette down to a stub and lit another from the dying remnants of the first and downed my drink and made another and damn near finished that off in three gulps. I would gladly have gotten drunk except that I wanted to take care of that child, to make her soup, and my husband would be coming home soon, too.

When he did, I was glad to see him. My heart was sad, but I was happy to see steady, smiling Eugene. "They won, babes," he said. "Four in a row now, 7-1 against Philly. Old Johnny Sain goes the distance, gives up six hits. Hey, where is she?"

I told him that she was sick and resting in George's old room. "Let her rest, for Chrissake," I said. "You can see her later." But he'd have none of that and went in to see Norma Jeane right away.

I heard her squeal when he came in to her room and then heard her murmur, "Uncle Eugene! Oh, Uncle *Eugene!*" over and over. I looked in and saw them hugging, her golden arms entwined around his scrawny pockmarked neck. Within three minutes she was asking him about baseball, things she could talk about with DiMaggio. I left for a while to smoke and to open a can of Campbell's Chicken Noodle Soup to heat up for Norma Jeane and to start dinner. When I returned a little later, Eugene was sitting on the bottom corner of the bed, smiling, going on and on. "Now if you *really* want to impress him," he said, "the first thing you wanna do is talk about his playing center. See, everyone thinks he makes it seem so easy out there, just getting under every fly ball, runnin' 'em down like it's nothin'. But, see, they don't give him credit for studyin' guys on the other teams, *knowin'* where they're likely to hit. The ole Clipper, he knew his opponents' tendencies, so he always knew where to stand out there and which way to run when they hit the ball. Ya see what I mean? Plus, he knew all the ballparks—the wind patterns, the way the balls would go. Now you could mention that to him, Norma Jeane, and he'll appreciate it." He paused and looked up at me, as if for approval, and then went on. "And the other thing is, you should let him know that you know his, uh, his *accomplishments.* Everyone knows about the fifty-six-game hitting streak, but there's more. Did you know he was American League MVP three times—in '39, '41 and '47? Lifetime batting average of .325. Hit 361 home runs, and—get *this*—1,537 RBI's. That's runs-batted-in, kid. And of course ... " Well, my husband went on about Casey Stengel's philosophy of platooning players and then somehow got onto the mechanics of the double play, and soon I noticed Norma Jeane's eyes starting to glaze over.

"Okay, you two," I said. "Let's go in to dinner. Norma Jeane, do you like lamb chops? I'm making some nice lamb chops. C'mon. You two can talk later, huh? Enough with the baseball for now."

"Oh, *yuck*, Aunt Jean. I *hate* lamb chops." She paused. "You know what I'd kinda like though?" She beckoned me over and whispered in my ear. I nodded and went back to the kitchen.

When Eugene and Norma Jeane came to sit down at the kitchen table, I put her soup and her requested sandwich in front of her. "Oh, *gee!*" she squealed, sniffling and wiping her nose with a napkin. "Peanut butter and jelly. God, I haven't had this since ... well, I can't remember. And oyster crackers for my soup!" She swallowed two spoonfuls of the chicken noodle soup and looked up at me warmly. "Thanks, Aunt Jean," she whispered. "Umm, this feels good on my throat." Then she grimaced and clenched her teeth and, clutching her abdomen, doubled over a bit.

"What's the matter?" Eugene asked.

I gave him a look. "Nothing. Don't worry about it."

"But she ... "

"Hey!" I hissed. "Don't fuckin' *worry* about it."

We ate quietly and then the three of us went into the living room to watch TV for a while. I set up Norma Jeane on the couch and covered her with a light blanket and sat on the end of the couch and held her feet. Eugene fell asleep in his easy chair within ten minutes and began snoring lightly. Norma Jeane sneezed twice, sniffled and shivered a bit, and pulled her legs up to her chest and pulled the blanket snugly around her shoulders. "Gee," she whispered, "I am *so* exhausted, Mom."

I got another light blanket and covered her and again sat and rubbed her feet, one at a time. As I did, the visions in my head disturbed me but I didn't let on. I just smiled and asked if she wanted another hot water bottle for her menstrual pain.

"No," she said softly so as not to disturb Eugene, "but I want to ask you another thing. I know you'll think I'm weird since I asked you about marrying Joe, but I have to know something. You know Arthur Miller, the guy that wrote *Death of a Salesman*? Well, I met him in

Hollywood a couple years ago, and ... well, I think he likes me and, oh, I like him so much, and I admire him a lot and all ... and sometimes I sorta fantasize about being with him." She paused and sat up and looked right into my face. "Oh, Aunt Jean, I know I'm horrible, but I want you to tell me: Will I be with him someday? With Arthur? Will we be a couple?" She went on to tell me her dream of being a serious stage actress, of playing Natasha in Chekhov's *Three Sisters*, maybe Shakespeare—possibly Lady Macbeth or Ophelia—and how she envisioned Miller writing marvelous plays for her, just for her, and she being in them. Serious theatre roles, not the movie fluff she'd been doing. "Will it happen, Aunt Jean?"

I shrugged. "Let's talk about it tomorrow, kid. It's late. You need to get some sleep. C'mon."

Back in George's room, Norma Jeane fumbled in her purse and found a brown bottle of pills, bigger than her last bottle, and popped two into her mouth. "What's that?" I asked.

"Nembutal," she answered, swallowing. "I need them to sleep."

"I thought you were so goddamned tired. Why do you need those pills?"

"Oh, Mom, *please!*" she said, looking irritated. "C'mon, don't give me a hard time. I'm not a little girl anymore, for God's sake. I need them to sleep. I always do."

I nodded, but said nothing. I just looked at her, that pretty pale face. "Well," I said after a bit, "I wish you wouldn't, but what can I say?"

After another gin and tonic and four cigarettes in the kitchen, one after the other, each lit from the expiring stub of its predecessor, I went to bed. I snuggled against my husband and he groggily filled me in on the day's details: Johnny Sain had had a shutout going against the Athletics until the seventh inning; ole Mickey Mantle had tripled in the third to score Bill Renna from second; Phil Rizzuto, Billy Martin and Joe Collins had executed just a great double play—"*textbook*, for cryin' out loud!," he exclaimed.

I couldn't pay much attention. *Son of a bitch!* I thought. Son of a fucking *bitch!* Can't life turn out okay for just one of my kids? I knew what was ahead, knew it when I'd just rubbed Norma Jeane's callused foot: how the Hollywood studio assholes would use her up; how she'd get more and more hooked on booze, pain pills, uppers and downers; how she'd spread her creamy legs for dozens of men—movie types, powerful fat-assed politicians, others—giving them her body because she figured that's what she had to offer: a gift, a search for warmth, nurturing; looking always for protectors, saviors, caring daddys, over and over, but inevitably setting herself up to feel let down, disappointed, betrayed, and then rejecting them, sometimes cruelly, or being rejected by them; yes, marrying Miller, but after a time treating him horribly, impatient with him, and finally driving him away; studying hard to be a serious actress, obsessing about that, but how she'd actually be in only a couple of quality movie roles, if that, as something more than just tits and ass, but never being much appreciated for her acting, even her obvious—to me anyway—comedic talent, and never getting on stage. No Natasha or Ophelia. I'd even had a brief vision of Norma Jeane in a serious movie, black-and-white, with Gable, my late-night fantasy man, and felt jealous of her for that. No children, though she desperately craved them, but instead abortions and miscarriages, disappointment, pain. Suicide attempts. Overdoses. A few brief hospitalizations, but at least not for long times, lost and useless, like her mother.

And finally, worst of all, I'd seen my daughter dead young, blond and perfectly-coifed and beautifully made-up in an expensive coffin, thousands crying at her premature demise, and that dumb cocksucker DiMaggio at her funeral, red-eyed but stern-faced and running the whole fucking show, saying who could be there and who couldn't.

Son of a goddamn BITCH anyway!

NEXT MORNING, my husband left early for the paint store and I woke up alone. I was sweating and felt hot, flushed. I'd kicked off all the sheets and the blanket. My nightgown was damp. It'd been a rough night. Though I hadn't dreamt, I'd been agitated by my vision and had been awakened twice by my husband's blathering. "C'mon, Mick," he'd pleaded at 3:07 a.m., "you can do it. Get ready for the slider now. *Slider*, Mick, I'm tellin' ya." I'd had to elbow him in the ribs. "*Goddamnit*, Eugene," I'd said, "shut the fuck up and let me sleep." And then again at 4:58: "Double play, baby ... yes! ... Pick it up, Phil, relay to two ... Jump, Billy ... throw ... Good stretch, big guy! ... *Got* him!" I'd also heard Norma Jeane sniffling and sneezing and blowing her nose a few times.

Shortly after Eugene left, I padded in to George's room to check on Norma Jeane and saw her sleeping, curled into a semi-fetal position, her right thumb ensconced in her mouth. I pulled her blanket to her chin, watched her sleep for a few minutes, and then went back to the kitchen.

I made my coffee and sat at the table and smoked a few Chesterfields between sips—my silly morning routine. I watched the steam from my mug merge with the exhaled cigarette smoke before both disappeared. I was fifty-four years old today. Norma Jeane was twenty-seven. How many more birthdays would there be? Then I gathered my flour and butter and sugar and eggs and milk and started the mix for my daughter's angel food birthday cake.

I waited until a bit after ten o'clock and still she hadn't emerged. I waited another half hour and then began to feel anxious; we only had this day together, or part of it. Finally, I went in to George's room to wake her up and bring her some juice. "Norma Jeane," I whispered, gently shaking her shoulder. "Norma Jeane, c'mon, wake up. It's your birthday. Happy *birthday*, kiddo! Wake up now. C'mon."

After a while, her eyelids fluttered and she opened her eyes a bit, though doing so seemed a struggle. Her eyes looked glazed and her mouth hung open. I wasn't sure she even recognized me. I opened the window shade to let in the sunlight, and noticed how pale my girl's face looked in the bright light.

"Happy birthday, honey," I repeated. "Look, I have something for you."

"What?" she murmured groggily, squinting. "Where am I? … Oh, Aunt Jean. I almost forgot." She sat up and rubbed her face hard with both hands and scratched the back of her head, and then took a Kleenex from the box and blew her nose and tossed the tissue on the floor. I looked down and saw maybe three dozen wadded, used Kleenexes and also a bloody menstrual pad wrapped in two tissues. Oh, a few tissues had found their way to the wastebasket beside the bed, but not most.

"Aunt Jean," Norma Jeane practically whispered, "where's my purse?"

I handed it to her and she took yet another pill bottle and shook out two and washed them down with the orange juice. "Now what's *that?*" I demanded.

"Oh," she answered, "Dexedrine. They help me wake up."

"*Hey!*" I said sharply. "C'mon! Enough is enough already. You need goddamn pills to go to sleep and other damn pills to wake up and still more pills for cramps? Norma Jeane! You've gotta get off this. It's no good. It's gonna kill you."

"You're starting again? Please, Mom, don't give me a hard time."

"*What?* A hard *time?* Listen, young lady, I don't like to see you popping pills all the fucking time. Do you *hear* me?" I paused and took a deep breath. "C'mon, Norma Jeane," I said gently. "This isn't a good way to be, kiddo."

She sighed and nodded. "Yeah, I know. I know you're right. But it's just that I'm under so much *stress* right now, Aunt Jean, what with the studio and the publicity and me and Joe and all. It's just a lot. I'll kick the pills when I can. I promise, Mom. Please don't worry about me."

"That's just it, kid," I whispered. "I *do* worry about you. There's just … I mean … well, look, this is for you, sweetheart. Happy birthday."

"Oh, my," she said, opening my package. "A robe. *Terry*cloth! Oh, thanks so much, Mom. Oh, I love the color." She touched the back of my hand. "I'll be okay. Really. I just gotta get through what's going on now. But, gee, I'm so glad to see you, Aunt Jean. And, hey, happy birthday to you too. Look, I got *you* a present." She reached into her purse and pulled out a small package beautifully wrapped in delicate light blue paper and tied with a pink ribbon. "Go ahead, open it."

It was a beautiful pearl necklace with the most lovely bluish-white pearls and a delicate silver clasp. "Oh, Norma Jeane!" I squealed. "You shouldn't have spent money on this. Oh, lord! *Thank* you."

"Well, how many moms does a girl *have?* Gosh. *C'mon*, you deserve it."

I kissed her cheek and told her to take a bath while I started breakfast. I heard the water running and then after a few minutes heard her call out. "Oh, Aunt Je-e-a-n, can you come in here? I need you to wash my b-a-a-c-k."

149

Her skin was the smoothest, most flawless I'd seen. Even wet and maybe a bit bloated from her period, Norma Jeane was incredibly beautiful. As I gently ran the washcloth over her white dimpled back, she turned her head and smiled and sang to me again:

> *There may come a time when a lass needs a lawyer,*
> *But diamonds are a girl's best friend.*
> *There may come a time when a hardboiled employer*
> *Thinks you're awful nice, but get that ice ...*
> *or else no dice.*

"Thanks, kiddo," I said, rubbing the top of her head. "You're cute. Cute as hell. Now get dressed and come to the kitchen."

"Wait a minute, Mom. Before you go, I need you to tell me something. You never told me about me and Arthur. And, also, I have to know something else." She looked down at the scummy bathwater and looked serious. "You know that my mother ... my real mother ... she was, you know, not well. She was ... they had to ... oh, she wasn't well. I want you to tell me, Aunt Jean, am I going to be, umm, like her too? Am I going to be put away ... like she was?" She extended her right hand, palm up, to me. I took it and held it in both my hands and stared at it but said nothing.

"You're going to marry Miller, Norma Jeane," I whispered after a while. "Sometime down the road. I see that for you. But you should try to be kind to each other. You should ... I mean, you have to be *patient*. Can you do that?" She nodded and looked into my eyes. "Listen," I went on, "I can't tell you anything about your mother." I sighed and squeezed her soft hand and held it tighter in mine. "I'm sorry, baby. Life is tough, you know. You've gotta hang in there, kid. You've gotta ... "

"What? Gotta what?"

I stood up and sighed. "Look, I just don't know, Norma Jeane. *Okay?* Hey, I'm not God, for Chrissake. I can't see everything. I have enough trouble running my own fucking life here. I mean, ... "

She looked hurt, and sneezed twice. "Well, okay, Mom. I know you're not God. Gee, I know that. I never said you were. But you can see things from hands, and I just want to know stuff. What's the *matter* with you, anyway?"

I shook my head and looked down at her, at the tops of her firm breasts in the scummy water, her white shoulders, her pale face. "I'm sorry, honey," I said. "Get dressed and come to breakfast. I started to make a cake. We can finish it together. Okay?"

"Hey, fuck the cake. Let's make chocolate pudding. Okay? That's what I *really* want"

"Do not swear, Norma Jeane. I *told* you that, young lady."

"Yeah, yeah. No swears. Sure. I'll see you in a minute."

In the kitchen, I made another pot of coffee and mixed four eggs and a bit of milk in a plastic bowl and poured it into a buttered pan to cook, low heat, and dropped two slices of Wonder Bread in the toaster and poured two tall glasses of orange juice and then scrambled the eggs with my spatula, slowly and carefully, until they were just right. You have to cook the eggs slowly and you have to be right there all the time, paying attention. Otherwise, they can get too hard too quickly and then there's not a goddamn thing to be done.

In a bit, Norma Jeane, wrapped in her new aqua bathrobe, came in and set the table. She placed the folded napkins to the left of the plates and set the forks perfectly in the center of each. Then she buttered the toast and set a slice on each of our plates. When the eggs were done, I dished them the way we liked: Norma Jeane's on top of her slice of toast and mine plop in the middle of my plate, flanked by toast slices. I noticed that Norma Jeane'd remembered how I liked my toast—sliced diagonally, crusts removed. Eugene had always laughed at me for that, in return for which I usually deliberately burned his toast—not much, just a bit.

"Mom," Norma Jeane said after we'd finished, "I feel a little better today. My throat feels better." She paused and sipped her coffee and winced. "Of course, I still have my goddamn cramps. Jesus H. *Christ,* Aunt Jean, why does this happen to me every fucking month?"

I shrugged. "I don't know, kiddo. I don't know why anything happens to anybody. You're asking the wrong goddamned woman. And stop swearing! I don't want to have to tell you again."

"Oh, listen to yourself. You cuss like a sailor. Gee, you didn't do that when … when … I was with you. I mean, what's *that* all about?"

I didn't say anything. I couldn't. I was doing all I could to stay in control.

Norma Jeane stood up and kissed my cheek and stroked the back of my head. "I'm sorry, Aunt Jean," she murmured. "I didn't mean to upset you. C'mon, let's make that pudding."

I nodded. "Here," I said, handing her the Jell-O Pudding box. "Open it and pour it in this pan. I've put the milk in. There we go. Do you want to stir?"

"Sure, Mom. Slowly, right? And scrape the bottom so the pudding doesn't burn. I remember."

I peered into the pan to see if the pudding was starting to thicken. Then the sweet chocolate smell transported me back to my little kitchen in Hawthorne in 1934, to the time before that goddamn Grace McKee took Norma Jeane from Eugene and me. I took a Chesterfield from my pack and tamped it on the counter and lit it and took a deep drag and then another, but it didn't help, and I sat down and snubbed out my cigarette and tried to hold myself together, but it was no good, and I started to shake and my jaw quivered and then, sweet *Jesus!*, I was bawling like a goddamn baby, tears pouring out, and pounding my fist on the table. Norma Jeane, startled, put the pan on a back burner and put her arm around my shoulder. "Mom," she said gently, "what *is* it? What's the matter?" I shook my head. "Hey," she went on, "what'd I say?"

I put my hand over hers and shook my head. "Nothing, sweetheart," I murmured between sobs. "Nothing. You didn't say anything. It's just that ... just ... oh, Norma Jeane, please stay here for a while—a day, a few days. A week. Don't go. *Please don't.*" I paused. "George is gone. He's gone, Norma Jeane. Shot in the back of his poor *head*, for Chrissake. And Lou?" I looked at her face and slammed the table again with my fist, hard, and then again. "Crazier than a fuckin' *loon*, Norma Jeane! Cocksucking NUTS! Thinks I'm reading his goddamn thoughts. *Why*, Norma Jeane? Can you tell me that? Can anyone fuckin' tell me WHY?" I picked up the glass ashtray and considered throwing it at the wall but instead just slammed it down on the table, causing ashes to fly everywhere, including on Norma Jeane. "And *Waite!*" I screamed. "Who the fuck knows? Son of a fucking *BITCH* anyway! And then YOU, goddamn it! You're gonna ... it'll be ... " I was crying again and quivering now, and couldn't stop, but didn't say more. I put my face in my hands and rocked back and forth, sobbing into my hands, gulping air, until finally I quieted and was calmer. "Norma Jeane," I pleaded, quieter now and more in control, "I'm sorry, honey. I didn't mean to scare you. I just want you to stay here for a few days, with me. Me and Eugene. Just until you feel better. Just let me take care of you. *Please*, honey. Oh, *please!* Just let me do this for you. I'm asking you this."

"I *can't*," she whispered. "I'd like to, but I can't, Aunt Jean. I have to meet Joe in a couple hours."

"Oh, you *can!*" I pleaded. "Yes, Norma Jeane, you can stay, I'm telling you. All this other stuff, screenings, it's bullshit! It's all just *bullshit*. They're gonna eat you *alive* out there, kid. Sooner or later, kiddo, they're gonna fuckin' eat your heart out. *Please!* And this DiMaggio … oh, Norma Jeane, he's … he's … "

I sighed and knew then it was no use to go on, knew that just then too clearly, knew there was nothing I could do that would make a difference. All I could do was to be here for her for as long as she lasted. *Screw* everything else! "Listen," I went on, trying to smile a little, "I don't know what the hell I'm saying. Don't pay any attention to me. I'm just a crazy old cigarette-smoking broad living in Queens. C'mon, kid, let's have that pudding and then get you ready to see your Prince Charming and go to your silly screening. Put that pudding back on the goddamn front burner."

Norma Jeane looked at me strangely and nodded her head but said nothing and went back to cooking the pudding. When it had sufficiently thickened, she poured it into the four dessert cups I'd set out and then covered each with a piece of waxed paper and secured the paper to each cup with a thin brown rubber band and then put them in the fridge. Then she sat down at the table, across from me, and looked directly into my eyes. "Hey," she said, "what aren't you telling me?"

I shrugged my shoulders and shook my head. "Nothing. Not a goddamn thing." She continued to stare, not smiling. "*Really*, Norma Jeane! And stop looking at me like that. It's *very* rude."

"'Rude,' huh? Right. Okay, I gotta pee and then let's eat." I listened for the sound of her tinkling and then for the flush. No flush. "Norma *Jeane*," I called, "don't forget to flush the *toi-let*." When she returned, she took the puddings from the refrigerator and removed the wax paper from one of the bowls and gently tapped the contents with her finger to see if the skin had sufficiently hardened. "Oh, *goodie!*" she squealed, and quickly ate the thin dark skin with a spoon, licked her lips, and then devoured the rest of the creamy warm pudding. "Oh, God, Mom," she whispered, "isn't this *heavenly*? C'mon, you have some too. Gee, this is just the best."

I nodded and ate one of the puddings and then we each gulped down a second one. "Lord almighty," she said, "that was wonderful." I smiled and lit a cigarette and Norma Jeane reached over to take one from my pack too and lit it and we both smoked in silence. I didn't care anymore. Screw it! Fate's ugly hand had written what it would and there wasn't a goddamned thing to do. I even mixed myself a gin and tonic and took a long sip and, when Norma Jeane looked longingly at my glass, asked if she wanted a drink. She nodded and I made her one, though lighter on the gin than mine, and we smoked and drank in silence. She tried to imitate my exhaling in twin streams through the nose, but couldn't and had a minute-long coughing jag instead. She stuck out her tongue when I laughed at her. "Hey," she said after a bit, "I have to go get ready. You okay, Aunt Jean?"

"Absolutely," I said. "Couldn't be better." And for a while anyway, a little damned while anyway, I was. While my daughter put on her face, I sat quietly in my kitchen smoking and sipping my drink and looked at my new pearl necklace and rubbed the pearls against my cheek. I'd let it all go. I felt okay. I heard Norma Jeane sneeze loudly, disgustingly, three times and heard her sigh, "Oh, *God!*" and went into the bathroom to bring her some aspirin.

She was standing naked in front of the mirror, bent forward, her springy round bottom sticking out and boobs jiggling. I watched as she shaded her pretty face with pancake and then carefully did her eyes, white over the lids and shadow in the creases, then created her arched eyebrows with a golden-brown eyebrow pencil, using short strokes, and then curled her eyelashes and delicately put on her false lashes, and finished by protruding her lips and painting on her usual cherry-red lipstick. She gently blotted her lips with a tissue and looked at herself in the mirror from every angle and made faces—first a warm smile, showing her teeth; then a subtler and more tender smile without teeth; then a hearty laugh look with head thrown back and eyes half-closed and lips parted nicely and mouth opened wide; then a little downturned-mouth pout with forehead crinkled and head cocked to the right; and, lastly, a direct open-eyed expressionless stare. "Well, Joe," she whispered breathlessly, eyebrows arched, now gazing seductively into the mirror, "are you ready to make an honest *woman* of me? Hmm?" Then she turned sideways, arched her back and stuck out her chest, and turned her head to again stare at herself. "Jesus H. Christ!" she said. "My goddamn ass is *way* too big, Aunt Jean."

I laughed out loud and gave her a loving pat on the bottom. "Get dressed, kid," I said. "The world awaits."

Norma Jeane nodded and grinned. She put her hands on her hips and turned toward me. "Let's hear it, ladies and gentlemen," she murmured, spreading her arms to her sides, palms up, "for the lovely Miss Lorelei Lee singing one of her *greatest* hits!"

> *He's your guy when stocks are high,*
> *But beware when they start to descend ...*
> *It's then that those lou-ses*
> *Go back to their spou-ses,*
> *And diamonds are a girl's best friend.*
>
> *Oh, diamonds are a girl's best friend.*
>
> *Yeah, diamond's are a girl's ... best ... friend.*

I helped her into her new terrycloth robe and tied it in front and pulled her to me and embraced her tightly. "The hell you say, kid," I whispered. "They're not. Hey, come see me on our birthday when you can. Whaddya say?"

Norma Jeane nodded and rested her head on my shoulder. She sniffled and began shaking in my arms just a bit, like when she'd first arrived. I didn't like the perfume she wore; it was too sickly sweet. "I will," she said. "Promise." She looked up at my face. "Mom," she whispered "how about I get you good tickets when I play Natasha. Will you come—you and Uncle Eugene? Will you come see me? *Please?*"

"Sure, kid," I said after a moment. "We'll be there."

A Spy for Vince Lombardi

I SERVED AS A SPY of sorts for that temperamental grouch Vincent T. Lombardi in 1962, during the fourth year of his tenure as coach and general manager of the Green Bay Packers. My formal job was assistant to George "Dad" Braisher, the Pack's equipment manager. My specialty was cleaning and adjusting shoulder pads—perhaps not a noble or sexy profession, but, damn it, an important one. My informal job, though, was to report back to Lombardi about the social exploits of his two main wayward "sons," left halfback Paul Hornung—the "Golden Boy"—and split end Max McGee.

It was well-known that Lombardi loved Hornung and was quite fond of McGee and tolerated their antics—breaking curfew, drinking, and womanizing— *to a degree* because he had affection for them and because they were such good and dependable players on Sundays and because they, particularly McGee, kept things loose in the locker room. Some speculated that he even somewhat envied their charm and life-style, and that there was a part of him that wanted to be more like them but he didn't have the personality for that—being somewhat stiff and formal outside of his regimented world of men and football. He felt he had to maintain a conservative and straitlaced image. Plus, he was an observant Catholic who went to Mass every morning of his life, at St. Willebrord's on the corner of Adams and Doty. All that was accurate enough as far as it went, but the truth, as I learned, was more subtle. The truth was that Lombardi didn't just *somewhat* envy Hornung and McGee their lifestyles; he was actually, I believed, *insanely* envious of them—perhaps pathologically so—and had a compulsive need to know all the lurid details of their good times and sexual conquests. That's where I came in.

Dad Braisher had hired me to be his assistant in the summer of '62. I'd grown up in the Green Bay area, in DePere, and had been one of the equipment managers for the DePere High football team. Dad had coached football there for more than three decades before joining the

156

Packers staff in the mid-fifties, and my fat-assed father had played for him—a lineman on both offense and defense. That connection helped me get a spot as one of the equipment guys for the Redbirds, and later with the Pack. My old man worked for Fort Howard Paper Company and my mother was a part-time clerk in the children's apparel section of H.C. Prange's, the biggest department store in town. She was a shy woman, mousy even, always walking around with her eyes down, and all my life I wished to hell that she would have stood up to my gaping asshole father now and again when he yelled at her, berated her, which he did incessantly and for the slightest of reasons. Of course, he yelled at me and my older brother, Rocky, too. I always hated and dreaded that man's loud foul mouth and desperately wished that I too could have stood up to him. But Rocky didn't seem to mind the old man. He'd been a football star at DePere, a quarterback, and reportedly got a lot of pussy—not just the usual cheerleaders and pom-pon girls but also Miss Ganos, the statuesque algebra teacher.

I, on the other hand, had a total of two dates in high school, neither of which were memorable, and graduated a disappointed virgin—perhaps not surprising inasmuch as I was short, arguably ugly, and an unathletic nearsighted nerd whose biggest high school glory was a semester as vice-president of the Chess Club. Plus, guys named Percy probably don't get much poontang. By the time my Packers career started, three years after high school, I'd still not lost my cherry, so to speak.

I was thrilled to get my job because I'd been a Packers fan all my life, and idolized a lot of the players—not just McGee and Hornung but guys like Bart Starr, Forrest Gregg, Bob Skoronski, Willie Davis, Fuzzy Thurston, Willie Wood, Ray Nitschke, certainly, and others. That said, my favorite pro player was nasty defensive tackle Alex Karras of the Detroit Lions. He was ferocious, with a non-stop motor; had a mean mouth that he used to intimidate and demean opposing players; and wore black horn-rimmed glasses like me. He loved to punish offensive linemen. He'd said in interviews that he was proud of his Greek heritage.

The Packers had won the championship of professional football the year before I started working for them, beating the New York Giants

37-0 in the title game, and everyone in Wisconsin hoped they'd do it again.

Like many Packers followers, I'd been skeptical when the board of directors hired Lombardi to be head coach in 1959. He'd been an obscure offensive coach for the Giants, with no previous pro head coaching experience. *Who the hell is this short, stout, bespectacled wop?* many perhaps wondered. But he'd quickly turned the team around from their losing ways under the previous coach, the inept Scooter McLean, with the force of his dominating personality and his constant demand for excellent performance and intolerance for anything less, and his absolute obsession with winning. His volatile temper and incessant screaming at his players were, after a short while, legendary.

The first time I saw Lombardi in person was on the night after Thanksgiving in 1961—a gray, cold, wet early winter evening. I was out with my family for the famous Friday night fish fry at Proski's on Washington Street—somewhat of a dive, to be sure, but good food and plenty of it. Deep-fried perch with french fries and a generous side of tasty coleslaw was the house specialty. The place was, as always on a Friday evening, quite crowded. We were seated at a corner table and had just ordered when Lombardi and his wife came in along with another couple. The coach was dressed in a camel's hair overcoat and a brown fedora and wore transparent plastic galoshes over his shoes. I don't recall being all that impressed with him.

But I was with his wife. Oh, my goodness! Marie Lombardi was dressed in a luxuriant dark-brown fur coat and black high-heeled shoes. When she took the coat off after a few minutes, I saw that she wore a lovely russet-colored dress and a big pearl necklace. She was taller than her husband and by no means beautiful—quite the contrary—but there was something about her sharp-featured face and upswept blondish hair and, especially, her straight-backed regal bearing that awed me. The woman was a patrician. The woman was a queen. She should have been walking the magnificent marble halls of Buckingham Palace, not the sloppy snowy streets of Green Bay, Wisconsin. She should have been dining at The Ritz in Paris, not Wally Proski's Food and Cocktail Lounge in boring blue-collar Green Bay, with the bone-chilling November wind blowing in off of the water. I must have stared at her for the longest time, probably with my mouth hanging open like some rube who'd just gotten off of the late shift at the paper mill and now was stopping for a quick shot and a beer and maybe some pickled pig's feet before slinking home, when into the bar boldly strides the magnificent Jacqueline Kennedy. Mrs. Lombardi must have noticed, because she stared back at me for just a moment, taking a long ladylike drag on her cigarette, and then turned away to chat with the woman from the other couple.

After that night, I thought often about Marie Lombardi. The image of her sharp-featured angular face and her erect carriage stayed in my mind. I imagined what it would be like to be the child of such a noble being. I had the feeling she didn't suffer fools gladly. I hoped I'd see her again.

My first exposure to Lombardi's famous temper was the first day of practice at training camp in late July. The players had just returned to the City Stadium locker room from the morning practice session and many were exhausted, sweating like anything and just gasping for air. Dave "Hawg" Hanner, the huge defensive tackle from Arkansas—his jersey soaked, his face beet-red—fell to the floor and looked as though he was about to expire any second. And no wonder. Dad and I had watched part of the practice, and it was brutal. It started with everyone running three laps around the goalposts, followed by calisthenics—including the so-called "grass drill" in which the players had to run in place, lifting their knees to their chests, while Lombardi, striding tense-ly among them, would yell "DOWN!" and everyone would drop to the ground and go prone and then he'd yell "UP!" and everyone would jump up and commence running in place again. Over and over, like that. It went on for what seemed the longest time, and after a while some of the guys could barely get off the ground when the coach screamed "UP!" One kid, a rookie from Missouri named Blaine, had at one point turned an ugly shade of green and puked right on the grass.

Not all of the guys in the locker room were in as bad a shape as Hanner, though. McGee, for one, was fine. He was sitting relaxed on the bench by his locker grasping a bottle of Coke in his left hand and holding a lit cigarette in his right and singing a tune that I later learned was the Tulane fight song:

Green Wave, Green Wave, hats off to thee,
  Fight, fight, fight, for our vic-to-ry,
Shout to the skies, the Green Wave's war cry,
  The bravest we'll defy,
Hold that line, for the Olive and Blue,
  We'll cheer for you,
So fight, fight old Green Wave,
  Fight on to Vic ... to ... ry!

He noticed me looking at him and his brow furrowed a bit. "Hey, Horn," he said, "look at this guy. Danged if he don't look just like old Fuzz. Same ugly crewcut, kinda squished-in face, big nose, and bugged-out eyes. Even the same horned-rim specs. What's your name, son?"

"Percy, sir," I answered. I paused. "I can't say it's a name I'm fond of."

"Well, kid," Hornung said, taking a drag on a Marlboro and exhaling through both nostrils, "Maxie's right. You're the spittin' image of number sixty-three. Hey, Fuzzy, check this out. This kid could be your son."

I was in awe. Paul *Hornung* had spoken to me! The Golden Boy had been my hero for years, since he'd won the Heisman at Notre Dame in 1956 and had then been drafted by the Packers—first pick in the draft—in '57. As a football player, he was a dream—a great running back, incredibly effective from inside the twenty-yard line, but not just that: he could also catch the ball nicely out of the backfield and was a threat to throw the option pass as well, having played quarterback, among other positions, at college. Plus, he was a decent field goal kicker as well as a punter. He'd been named the league's Most Valuable Player in 1961, despite missing four games while serving Uncle Sam. As a man, he was as advertised: charming, utterly self-assured, and ruggedly handsome with wavy blond hair, high forehead, crinkly blue eyes, and a warm smile.

"Listen, kid," he said to me, grinning, "you ever gotten laid yet?"

Thurston approached, studied my face from about a foot away, and guffawed out loud. McGee was right: we *did* look alike. I was about to answer Hornung and lie and tell him yeah, sure, of course I'd gotten laid, when Lombardi strode into the locker room. He was dressed in dark slacks and a gray sweatshirt with GREEN BAY PACKERS in green lettering on the front, a whistle on a lanyard hanging around his neck. "Gentlemen," he said, smiling nicely, "that was a good morning, huh? You did fine. Just fine. Just the first of many productive mornings to come, gentlemen. Well, let's rest for a while and get something to eat and then we'll go at it again this afternoon. Pretty warm day, huh, fellas?" He paused and smiled, showing the gap between his two front teeth. A few players nodded. "Say," he went on, in a soothing, seemingly concerned tone of voice, "is anyone feeling tired?" There was a stirring in the room, and several players meekly raised their hands. Lombardi's face quickly darkened and his facial muscles tensed. "What the hell you mean you're TIRED?" he yelled, his deep voice booming across the locker room. "I don't wanna hear *that* horseshit! You're Green Bay Packers! You're the goddamned champions of professional football! *Tired?* Don't tell ME you're tired! Don't ever tell me you're tired! Let me tell you something, men, fatigue makes cowards of football players. I will NOT tolerate cowards! You wanna be *tired*, you wanna be a *coward*, go play somewhere else, not HERE, not in Green Bay, Wisconsin! Not for ME!" Then he stormed out of the room, slamming the door behind him.

I looked at the players. *"Damn!"* exclaimed Earl Gros, a rookie fullback from LSU. His eyes were huge and he looked scared. "What the hell was *that* about?"

McGee chuckled and took another drag of his cigarette. "Don't worry about it, son," he said gently. "That's just the Old Man trying to intimidate y'all. Don't pay him no never-mind. But by the same token, don't ever admit to him you're tired."

"Or that you're in pain," Hornung added. "He doesn't want to hear that crap either."

The afternoon practice was just as brutal as the morning's. Maybe worse. The assistant coaches, Bill Austin and Red Cochran and Norb Hecker and others, ran some drills, and of course they did some yelling, but none of them could hold a candle to Lombardi. He stalked the field and just mercilessly berated the players. "C'mon, Skoronski," he'd scream, "show some effort, for Chrissake! You wanna be a team captain? *Captain*, my ass! Let me tell you something, mister, you'll be lucky to *make* the team this year!" Or, "Let's go, Nitschke. If you don't *practice* with abandon, you won't *play* with abandon. Now let me see some *fire*, mister!" And so on.

Dad had warned me about Lombardi's carryings-on, but nothing could have prepared me for that penetrating baritone voice. I found myself wondering if he ever yelled at people besides players—the assistant coaches, the trainers, the equipment guys like Dad and me, the office people, and so on. I hoped not. I didn't want to be the object of that man's wrath. I wondered, for that matter, if he yelled at Mrs. Lombardi.

Later that week, after the Thursday afternoon practice, Hornung approached me in the locker room. He was carrying his shoulder pads and had stripped off his jersey and I noticed, surprisingly, that he had somewhat sloping shoulders. "Hey, kid," he said, "my pads are kinda fucked-up on the left side. Jordan laid a nasty hit on me. Can ya get 'em right for me? Thanks." He paused and winked at me and then called out to Jordan, who was on the other side of the locker room. "Hey, *Henry*," he yelled with mock outrage. "What the hell! I thought we were buddies. Who you tryin' to impress?"

Jordan, a big defensive tackle from Virginia, standing naked beside his locker, toweling off his balding head, laughed. "Ain't nothing personal, Paul," he yelled back. "Ah was just fixin' to rub some of mah ugly off on you so's to maybe save the virtue of some of them stewardesses and barmaids and Prange's clerks and whatnot that y'all meet up with."

Hornung chuckled and turned back to me. "Listen, kid," he said. "Now and again me and Max and sometimes a couple other guys, Thurston and others, go downtown to have a few cocktails and maybe meet a generous young lady or two. Maybe we'll bring you along sometime so you can, uh, expand your horizons. Know what I mean?" He winked again.

I nodded. "Thanks, Mr. Hornung. I'd like that."

"Call me Paul, kid. Don't worry, we'll take good care of ya."

But training camp progressed and the team played their usual six pre-season games and the guys never asked me to accompany them. It was no secret that Hornung and McGee often broke eleven o'clock curfew and snuck out of Sensenbrenner Hall at St. Norbert College in De-Pere to visit their favorite watering holes—The Spot or King's X or Piccadilly or Candlestick or the Buzz Inn or even that firetrap The

Chatterbox. Now and again, I overheard one or the other of them talking about their successes. "Man oh man!" Hornung once said to Jim Taylor, the muscular cigar-smoking fullback from Louisiana. "I tell ya, Jimmy, that little broad kept me up till dawn. '*More*, Paulie,' she kept squealing. 'I want MORE!' Man, I'm beat! I'm gonna have to start sewing my pants shut when that little twitch's around, I'm tellin' ya."

Lombardi somehow knew about some or maybe all of their transgressions because he fined them and, of course, yelled at them in the locker room and during team meetings. "You guys think you're special!" he'd bellow. "You think you can get away with breaking my rules just because you think you're hotshots. Horseshit! You're *not* special. You're average football players, at best. Heisman winner, my ass, Hornung. *MVP*, my ass! You're slow and you're weak. And you, McGee, you're the laziest sonofabitch on this team. When the hell are you two gonna take this game seriously?" I noticed that Hornung, during these tirades, looked directly at the coach and sat up straight and nodded, as though seriously taking in the rebuke and agreeing wholeheartedly with Lombardi's criticisms. McGee, however, usually got red in the face and stared at the floor and looked pained.

Yet, at other times, Lombardi kidded around and laughed with both Paul and Max. Once, after a Friday afternoon practice, I saw the coach on the sideline with his arm around Hornung's shoulder and laughing uproariously, his mouth wide and teeth gleaming. Hornung was grinning too. Then McGee sauntered over and said something, I couldn't hear what, and both Lombardi and the Golden Boy guffawed.

By the time the regular season started on September 16th, I'd almost forgotten about Hornung's offer. So I was surprised when he approached me in the locker room after the game. "Hey, kid," he said, "wanna come along with me and Maxie and Fuzzy tonight? We're going to The Spot for a few cocktails." He was in a good mood. The Packers had beaten the Minnesota Vikings 34-7 at City Stadium and Paul had rushed for three touchdowns and kicked all the extra points and had also, for good measure, kicked a forty-five yard field goal in the second quarter.

Later that night, I met the three players at The Spot on Main Street. There was a decent crowd, including a good assortment of nicely dressed young ladies, a fair number of whom wore decidedly tight sweaters and skirts. By the time I got there, Hornung and McGee were sitting at a round table in the middle of the main room, smiling and laughing, with a quartet of adoring young women flanking them and a fifth, a thin-lipped whey-faced brunette with outsized boobs, sitting on Hornung's lap, her arm draped around his sloping shoulders. Now and again she ran a hand through his wavy hair. There were two bottles of scotch on the table. Almost everyone was puffing away and there were three big green glass ashtrays, each filled to overflowing with cigarette stubs. Thurston was standing behind McGee's chair, a tall glass gripped tightly in his right hand, talking with a middle-aged man wearing a gray business suit, who had a ridiculously bad toupee, and at one point laughing hugely at something. Now and again Fuzzy'd take a healthy gulp from his glass, throwing his head back and practically pouring the liquor down his throat. It occurred to me that number sixty-three was an accomplished drinker.

"Hey, kid," Hornung said, noticing me, "have a seat. Let me order you a drink." I took a chair between two sort-of-beauties, a blonde with short frizzy hair and a horsey-faced redhead with way too much garish blue eyeshadow and a nasty two-inch scar to the outside of her left eye, partly hidden by her hair. Taking a long drag on a thin brown cigarette, she looked askance at me. "*You* sure as hell can't be a player," she said. "Are you?"

"He's our reserve punter," McGee quickly said. "Punters don't have to be pretty, you know. But by the same token, don't let his looks fool ya. He's strong as a damned bull. *Great* leg. And let me tell ya something else about him ... " He leaned over and whispered into the redhead's ear, whereupon her eyes opened wide and her plucked eyebrows arched and she pursed her full lips and stared at me for a moment and then nodded. "I see," she said. "Well, that *is* impressive."

THE NEXT MORNING, Monday, my phone rang at seven o'clock. It was Dad Braisher. "Listen," he said, "the Old Man wants you to come see him at his house at nine. He'll be back from church by then." He paused. "Any idea why?"

My head hurt so bad from the previous evening's festivities that I could barely answer. "No," I answered. "No idea."

I was petrified. I expected the worst. What had I done? How had I screwed up? I was sure of a severe ass-chewing at the least, and getting canned at worst. I just hoped it would be quick, and he wouldn't yell at me too much. I hoped I wouldn't cry or otherwise embarrass myself.

At eight forty-five I was ringing the doorbell at Lombardi's nice-looking red-brick ranch house on Sunset Circle in suburban Allouez. I'd overheard some of the players saying that, according to the Old Man, if a meeting was scheduled at a certain time you were late if you didn't get your butt there at least fifteen minutes *before* that time and could then expect to experience Lombardi's wrath. I braced myself for the coach to answer the door and to immediately commence reaming me out in that booming baritone voice. So I was surprised to be greeted instead by his wife—tall and regal-looking with that upswept hair, holding a drink in one hand—a gin and tonic, by the smell—and a lit cigarette, a Salem, in the other. Even though it was early, she was dressed impeccably in a well-tailored light-blue dress and high heels and a pearl necklace—perhaps the same one I'd seen her wearing at Proski's the evening after last Thanksgiving, the night I was first blessed to look at her. "Who the hell are you?" she asked in a somewhat loud, gravelly voice with, I believed, a New Jersey accent. I couldn't answer right away. I was again awestruck. I'd never seen anyone like her. She was stunning. She was amazing. In her majestic presence, I again felt like the lowliest Midwest hayseed hick in all of Brown County. It must have taken me a minute—maybe longer—to answer, to tell her who I was. She took a deep drag on her cigarette as she listened. "Ah," she said, "lovely. Assistant equipment manager. Well, come with me. The great man's in his den, no doubt contemplating the subtleties of the power sweep."

Lombardi was sunk deep into a brown leather recliner in his wood-paneled den watching a Tom and Jerry cartoon on a big console TV and drinking coffee from a blue mug with NEW YORK GIANTS and their logo in white. To my great relief, he was laughing at the antics of the cat and mouse antagonists, slapping his left knee hard at some parts. He was particularly amused when Tom and Jerry cooperated to capture a runaway baby after the brat, in some kind of infant hissy fit, mercilessly beat Tom on the head with a brick and then fled. The Old Man pointed to a smaller chair and motioned for me to sit. He said nothing for maybe three or four minutes, until the cartoon was over. I tried to calm myself with deep breathing. *Here it comes*, I thought when the show ended. But he merely turned the TV off and smiled nicely, that gap-toothed grin, and asked politely how I was, how I liked my job, if I enjoyed working with Dad Braisher, and so on. He listened to my answers, and nodded at each. "Well," he said, "we're very glad to have you with us." He paused and took another sip of his coffee. "Say, I understand you were out last night with Paul and Max, and Thurston too. Did you, uh, have a good time?"

"Well," I answered, "if I broke any rules, Mr. Lombardi, I'm very sorry, sir. I promise I won't do it again. I'll certainly try to be more ... "

He waved his right hand dismissively and smiled again. "No, no," he said, "not a problem. A young man should have fun now and again. You just have to be careful, not drink too much and watch who you associate with—certain types of women, and so on. You represent the Green Bay Packers, after all. A *great* organization." He paused and yelled to his wife. "Hey, *Rie*. Can we get some goddamn snacks here? This young man's starving. Bring some more coffee too." He turned back to me and asked, almost casually, "So, uh, Percy, tell me what happened last night."

"How do you mean, sir?"

His face tensed and he seemed a bit impatient. "I mean, what *happened?* C'mon! With Hornung and McGee. What did they do? Who'd they meet? Who'd they leave with?"

"Sir, I'm not sure I should ... "

"Listen, mister," Lombardi said gruffly, standing up. "These guys ... I absolutely need to know ... I *have* to know ... " He stopped and took a deep breath, and sat back down in his recliner. He glanced up at a framed black-and-white photo on the wall that showed a younger him standing next to an older, taller man wearing a light-colored shirt with WEST POINT in block lettering on the front. Both men cradled footballs in their hands and were grinning into the camera. "Look, young man," he went on, "I'm sure you'd like a future with our club, wouldn't you? Not everyone gets a chance to work with an NFL team. It's a rare goddamned opportunity. Am I right?"

I understood the implied threat. "Well, sir," I said, "there were definitely a number of attractive young ladies there, at, uh, ... "

"The Spot. Yeah, yeah. I know. Go on."

"Yes. The Spot. Well, uh, Mr. McGee was really quite entertaining. He told some funny anecdotes, quite delightful really." I chuckled. "There was one story I remember, something about an outside linebacker with a foot problem, bunions I think, and several of the young ladies found it rather amusing. One in particular, a redhead, said it was the ... "

Lombardi, leaning forward in his chair, held up his right hand, palm toward me. "Son," he said quietly, "let's understand each other. I'm not interested in stories about linebackers with foot problems. I'm not interested in *bunions*. I've *told* you what the hell I'm interested in."

Just then Mrs. Lombardi entered the den carrying a tray of snacks, lemon bars and peanut brittle, and two tall glasses of lemonade. "Here you go, boys," she said. "Enjoy." I had to catch myself from just staring at her. I wanted her to talk more so that I could listen to her deep queenly voice. A queen is quite what she seemed to me, the first I'd known and the only one I ever wanted to know.

"Goddamn it, Marie," Lombardi growled. "I told you to bring *coffee*. What the hell's so damned hard to understand about that?"

She looked down her nose at him and frowned. "You've had enough coffee today, Vin. Three cups, and it's still early. You're going to ruin your stomach. And don't snap. I'm not one of your candy-assed players, and I'm not intimidated." Then she turned and abruptly left the room. I could hear her high heels clacking on the wooden floor in the hallway.

Lombardi was silent for a moment. Then he sighed loudly and looked at the floor and scratched his head vigorously with his right hand. "*Christ* almighty! Okay, mister, what do you have to tell me?"

I couldn't stall anymore. I told the coach what I knew. Hornung had left The Spot with the whey-faced broad who'd sat on his lap for the better part of an hour, giggling foolishly at his every remark, sometime after one o'clock. They'd driven off in his cream-colored Cadillac convertible, she so close to him that she was practically in his lap, again. She was nuzzling the Golden Boy's right earlobe with her thin lips as they exited the parking lot, and may have had her left hand on his crotch as well. He was smiling nicely, white teeth gleaming, wavy hair mostly unruffled by the open air. As for McGee, he'd left shortly thereafter with the blonde with the short frizzy hair, in her green Dodge

Dart. Thurston had left alone and, in fact, had barely spoken to any of the women in the joint—instead spending most of the evening drinking and talking football and telling stories with fawning male admirers, including the guy with the horrible rug. One impressive thing about number sixty-three, though: he'd downed more drinks than either Paul or Max over the course of the evening, or maybe both combined, yet was seemingly unaffected and appeared quite capable of walking and talking just as competently at the end of the festivities as at their start. I didn't mention that observation to Lombardi, however.

Nor did I tell Lombardi of my own successes, such as they were. I'd had a fine time just watching the masters, McGee and Hornung, at their work over the course of the evening; they seemed equally as accomplished at womanizing as at football. That pair were clearly consummate professionals in all regards and what impressed me the most, I believe, was the *effortlessness* of it all on both of their parts. They had those women eating from their hands all night and could have had any of them, and without having to beg either. Impressive! Hornung's success wasn't at all surprising, but McGee's was, at least a little, because, though charming, I didn't think he was particularly good-looking. He was, in fact, a bit homely and had a big, ungainly nose and a bit of a receding hairline. Still, I found myself looking forward to more of their life lessons.

What worked out best for me, though, was that toward the end of the evening the redhead—Sheila, by name—had suggested that I accompany her to her apartment, not far from The Spot. *Here's my chance to lose my cherry*, I remember thinking. Well, that didn't happen, as it turned out, though I did get to second base, and I didn't quite understand what she meant when, at her command, I'd lowered my pants. "Fucking McGee," she'd muttered. "Goddamn *liar*."

Lombardi listened patiently, and now and again asked pointed questions. What exactly did Hornung say to the woman he left with? In particular, what did he say that made her laugh? Did she really sit on his lap for such a long time? Did he seem to like that? How often did she run her hand through his hair? Did they kiss? If so, were they deep kisses or just pecks? Did he touch her? Where? Did he ask her specifically to leave with him, or did it just happen? Were they touching as they walked out of The Spot? How did the other women react to him? Did they laugh too? At what? How much did he and McGee drink? What did they drink? What about McGee? What did he say to the women? How'd they react? How did he get the blonde to leave with him? He didn't ask about Thurston at all. I answered his questions as best I could, giving the least amount of information I felt I could get away with. I noticed that he appeared increasingly upset, angry even, the more I talked, his face darker and jaw muscles working.

I was surprised at his need for such details, and wondered why he wanted to know so much. I figured he thought his star players were breaking rules of some kind and needed information to nail them, and I felt bad that my snitching was maybe going to get them in trouble.

But that still didn't explain his apparent escalating anger. Why would my information on those two guys, whom he reportedly liked a lot, so upset him? It didn't make sense.

After a bit, Lombardi stopped asking questions and grew silent. He took off his glasses and rubbed his right earlobe with his thumb and index finger. I noticed that his hands seemed unusually large for a man his size. He seemed lost in thought. Finally, he stood up, looked me in the eyes, and said, "Well, thanks for coming."

As we walked toward the front door, Marie came out of the kitchen. "Well, Mr. Assistant Equipment Manager," she said, "*do* come again." I could see she'd refreshed her gin and tonic; the glass was almost full and fresh ice cubes clinked around in it. I noticed that her eyes were just a bit glazed. "Did you boys have an enlightening conversation? Are we quite ready to reprise the glories of 1961?"

"Shut up, Marie!" Lombardi growled. "That was a *stupid* thing to say."

MONDAY WAS the players' day off. When they returned on Tuesday, the first part of the morning was devoted to reviewing film of the Vikings game. Dad and I got to sit in on part of the offense's meeting since the guys wouldn't be on the practice field much, and not at all until the afternoon for a light no-pads workout. Lombardi ran a film projector and commented on plays. Sometimes he'd run a particular play about which he was critical two or even three times. I was surprised that he was so negative, considering that they'd won the game convincingly. I was particularly surprised that he went after Hornung.

At one point he showed a power sweep in the first quarter in which Paul had taken the handoff from Starr and run to the right behind blocks from the pulling guards, Jerry Kramer and Thurston. The left outside linebacker, Cliff Livingston, had fought off a block from our tight end, Ron Kramer, and tackled Hornung for a gain of only three yards. "God*damn* it, Hornung," the coach growled, "that was terrible. That was *horrible!* All you had to do was cut outside and you would have gotten at least five more yards. You have to watch the 'backer and read the tight end's block, for Chrissakes. When the hell are you gonna get the lead outta your ass?" On another occasion, he ripped his left half-back for what he called "a totally half-assed effort" to pick up a blitzing linebacker, Clancy Osborne, on an unsuccessful pass attempt by Starr to Boyd Dowler. I didn't get it. Hadn't Hornung practically single-handedly won the game? But, as usual, the Golden Boy seemed unaffected by Lombardi's withering criticism—merely sitting up straight and nodding, chain-smoking Marlboros, his brow furrowed with concentration, his face devoid of emotion.

The Old Man singled out McGee too. He'd caught two passes for thirty-four yards. One of his catches was magnificent: he'd put a great juke move on the cornerback and reached high to snag Starr's pass with one hand, pulling the ball to his body to secure it with both hands just before being pushed out of bounds. But Lombardi didn't note that play at all. Instead, he showed a play in the third quarter in which Jim Taylor ran off-tackle and McGee was supposed to block downfield but had whiffed on his block on the Vikings' rookie safety, Chuck Lamson, who'd then tackled Taylor. He showed the play once, saying nothing, then rewound the film and showed it again, and then again. After the third time he glared at Max and said, rather loudly, "Mister, that was horseshit. Just *horseshit!* You oughta be *ashamed* of yourself for that kind of effort. You better start playing with some abandon, mister, or your ass is gonna get splinters 'cause you're gonna spend a lot of god-damn time on the bench." McGee, clearly embarrassed, turned red and took a long drag on his cigarette and just stared at the floor.

At another point, the coach showed a play in which Thurston had been pushed aside a bit by the onrushing right defensive tackle and had momentarily lost his balance. But before Lombardi could say anything, Fuzzy leaped up and slapped his forehead hard with the palm of his right hand and pointed animatedly toward the screen. "Oh, my God!" he bellowed, his eyes bulging. "Oh, *sweet* Jesus! Did you guys see that? DID you? That was absolutely the *worst* block I've ever seen! That was just pathetic! *Horrible!* I'm telling ya, fellas, that was just horseshit!" A few of the players snickered or even laughed out loud, and I noticed that even Lombardi was stifling a little smile.

Still, I felt bad that the coach had yelled at Paul and Max as he had. I felt particularly bad for McGee, who seemed to be more affected than Hornung by the Old Man's splenetic ravings. There was a part of me that wanted to tell Lombardi to back off, to leave those guys alone. "Listen," I wanted to say, "these guys have been good to me. They tried to help me get some pussy. They're nice guys. They're fun. They're *great* players. So just shut the fuck up! Please! OKAY?" And recalling how he'd talked to his wife the previous morning, I felt even more angry. "Shut up, Marie," he'd said. "That was a stupid thing to say." At that moment, I wished I were as big as Skoronski or Forrest Gregg, as tough as Nitschke or Karras, as intimidating as Willie Wood, who could wither a person with his stare. At that moment, I wanted to pick up Lombardi by the collar of his camel's hair coat and fling his ass into the Fox River. "There!" I'd say. "Now you leave that lovely queen the fuck *alone!* You stop talking nasty to that amazing regal woman, you grouchy bigmouthed bully. You need to *appreciate* her. And, goddamn it to hell, I MEAN it!"

But, as during the preseason, Lombardi was nicer to Hornung and McGee as the week progressed—kidding around with them, slapping them on the shoulder, grinning at them with that gap-toothed smile. "Maxie," he said at one point. "You played a hell of a game on Sunday, Maxie. Hell of a game! That was a great sideline catch! You're gonna have a fantastic season, I *know* it. I want you to know I'm depending on you. We all are, Max. I'm glad you're on my team." McGee beamed. "Thanks, coach," he murmured. At another point the coach singled out Hornung during the Thursday morning practice after the Golden Boy had burst through the line for an eighteen-yard touchdown, eluding what I thought were half-assed tackle attempts by Hanner and Nitschke and even normally-sure-tackling cornerback Herb Adderley. "Now *that's* what I wanna see!" Lombardi bellowed, so that everyone within a mile of the Oneida Street practice field could hear. "Way to run, Paul.

You keep that up, and we'll win another championship, I guarantee it. Good effort!" Then, glaring at Hanner, he added, "C'mon, Hawg, you gotta do better if you wanna keep your job. Any of the goddamned Little Sisters of *Mercy* could tackle better than that, for Chrissake."

After the practice, as the players headed toward the locker room with their helmets under their arms, I saw Lombardi watching Hornung walking away, playfully jabbing Elijah Pitts's upper arm. He turned to Phil Bengtson, the defensive coordinator, and shook his head. "Boy, I just love that guy," he said. "Him and Maxie, they're like sons to me, Phil."

But Lombardi ignored me. Now and again, he'd pass me in the locker room and say nothing. Once, Dad and I were working in the equipment room when the coach walked in. "Hey, Dad," he said, patting him on the shoulder. "How's it going? Anything you need?" But it was as though I was invisible. He said nothing to me and didn't even acknowledge my presence. I wondered of I'd offended him somehow. Had I disappointed him in some way during our little discussion at his house? I wasn't sure where I stood with the great man.

However, I certainly heard from him after the third game, a 49-0 merciless drubbing of the Chicago Bears at City Stadium. Hornung hadn't done much—two rushes for fourteen yards and no touchdowns or field goals, though he'd kicked seven extra points. Taylor and Pitts had done most of the running, and Taylor'd scored three times. The weakside fullback slant had worked to perfection all day. Even Earl Gros had a somewhat decent day, running five times for thirteen yards. McGee's day was as unspectacular as Hornung's, with just one pedestrian catch. Naturally, the post-game locker room was joyful. McGee downed three Cokes and sang his Tulane fight song and Taylor, strutting naked through the room, his chiseled body gleaming with sweat, puffed away on a big dark Antonio and Cleopatra Grenadier cigar and looked pleased. As Dad and I were picking up the shoulder pads and helmets and smelly uniforms, Hornung motioned me over. "Listen, kid," he said softly, "you wanna come out with me and Max tonight? Maybe we can find you someone a little more, uh, generous than that last one, that scary-lookin' redhead. What the Christ was her name?"

"Sheila."

"Yeah, yeah. So, whaddya think?"

Later that evening, I met them at King's X on North Broadway. It was pretty much a repeat of the night after the Vikings game, with a bevy of anxious-to-please women in tight outfits and stiff hair and carefully applied makeup, usually including a fair amount of eyeshadow, all vying for the opportunity to copulate with the gridiron heroes. Hornung and McGee were their usual charming selves, drinking and smoking and telling jokes and stories and laughing healthily, and Thurston was in even rarer form than usual. Number sixty-three downed his wonted prodigious quantity of alcoholic beverages, mostly martinis, and around midnight entertained the gathering by standing on the piano bench and crooning a poor man's version of "He's Got the Whole World in His Hands" and then rolling up his sleeves and doing pushups—at least fifty, by my informal count—on top of the piano. Jim Ringo, the center, was there too, but was fairly quiet.

At one point, Hornung had me sit next to a petite dark-haired woman wearing a light green cashmere, I believe it was, sweater. She had on pinkish lipstick. I liked her perfume. "Hi," she said huskily, offering her small hand and looking directly into my face with her pretty, smoky eyes. "I'm Lorraine. Are *you* a player too?"

THIS TIME IT was the coach himself who called at seven o'clock on Monday morning to request—*demand*, more accurately—my presence at his Sunset Circle house after he'd returned from church. I wasn't surprised at the call. But this time I wasn't as scared. I arrived the usual fifteen minutes early and, happily, was again greeted at the door by the splendid Marie. "Well," she said nicely, taking my hand, "if it isn't the assistant equipment manager in the flesh. How are you today, young man?" I was practically speechless. "Fine, ma'am," I think I said. "Okay, I guess." She waited politely for me to say more. When I didn't, she smiled warmly and nodded her magnificent head and led me into the den. Lombardi was standing in the middle of the room putting golf balls into a blue plastic tumbler on the floor. "Sonofabitch!" he muttered as he missed a one-footer as I entered. I noticed immediately that he didn't look well. His face looked drawn and even pale, less swarthy than usual. Finally, he turned and gestured toward the smaller chair, motioning for me to sit. This time there were no pleasantries. "Well, young man," he simply said, "tell me about last night at King's X."

I didn't bother to soft-soap it. I knew the game. Hornung had left late with Lorraine's friend Penny, a skaggy bleached blonde with severely plucked eyebrows. He'd entertained her and the rest of the usual female contingent all evening long, and at one point I'd overheard Penny murmur, barely audibly, "Hey, Paul, guess what? I'm not wearing any panties." Perhaps foolishly, I mentioned that quote to the coach. McGee was equally seductive in his way—telling good-natured stories and jokes, including something to the effect of how you can tell about the size of a man's penis by how big his nose is. "But I'll tell ya," he'd added, "you can't always take *that* to the bank." I didn't tell Lombardi, however, that McGee had gotten huge laughs with his dead-on imitation of the Old Man standing on the sidelines yelling, "Hey, what the HELL'S going on out there?" McGee'd left shortly before Hornung with two sisters, Bev and Pauline. Bev had her hand on his butt as they exited the premises.

As for me, I'd happily gotten to third base with Lorraine. But, of course, I didn't mention that.

Lombardi listened patiently, interrupting now and again to ask for details—similar queries as before. Again, he seemed increasingly angry and upset the more I revealed. But he also appeared increasingly wan, and was clearly less animated than during our first meeting. There was a big bottle of Rolaids on the coffee table near his leather chair, and on three occasions he shook two tablets from the bottle and popped them into his mouth and chewed and followed with a gulp of coffee from his Giants mug. I was a bit worried. "Are you okay, Mr. Lombardi?" I asked at one point, after telling him how Pauline had said to McGee that she very much admired football players with large noses and he and Hornung had laughed so hard at her remark that they'd practically fallen off their chairs.

"Yeah, yeah," Lombardi said, "Fine. Just fine."

But he wasn't. I could see that. So could Mrs. Lombardi. I saw her studying him for a moment as she entered the room, gin and tonic in one hand and carrying in the other a tray of chips and crackers and a lovely crabmeat dip that, she explained, was left over from the postgame party in their basement rec room the night before. "It's my specialty," she said, in that gravelly voice. "Crabmeat, cream cheese, mayo, mustard, and ... "—she looked at me and smiled—"just a special touch of sherry." Turning to her husband, she said, "Vin, I want you to stay home this morning and rest. They can get along without you for one day. *Please.*"

He glared at her for a moment, his brow furrowed. "Goddamn it, Rie, you *know* I can't do that. We have to look at film of the Bears game and then start getting ready for the Lions. I should be there right now, for that matter. Phil and Norb and those guys are there already. The players come in tomorrow morning, and we have film review. You know that, goddamn it to hell. Christ! You *know* my goddamn schedule. What the hell's the *matter* with you?"

"Well, you're not going to do yourself or anyone else any good if you're sick. You're human, you know. You're not invincible, despite what you think."

I was embarrassed to be in the middle of their quarrel. Part of me wanted to leave as soon as I could. But another part wanted nothing more than to stay in that den, in that house, being in that woman's presence, just listening to that woman's royal voice, just looking at her face, for as long as possible. More than any concern I may have felt for her husband, I was yet again totally enchanted by Marie Lombardi.

I had to use the bathroom before leaving, and thought I'd say goodbye to Lombardi before I left. But when I got to the entrance to his den he was standing in the middle of the room with his back to me, his face buried in both of his big hands, a bit bent over. "Goddamn it to hell, anyway!" I heard him murmur to himself. "Why is it so *easy* for these guys? *Why?*" I said nothing.

But when Mrs. Lombardi took my right hand in both of hers as I left a few minutes later and said that it was nice to see me again, I could have fainted from joy. I could smell the gin on her breath. She looked worried. "He's a stubborn man, isn't he, Mr. Assistant Equipment Manager? Oh, well. That's partly why he's done so well for all these years. But it hasn't been easy, young man, I'll tell you that much. It isn't easy, Percy."

THE NEXT morning was a repeat of the Tuesday following the Vikings game. Lombardi, looking better than the day before, ran the film projector and mercilessly criticized selected players, again particularly singling out McGee and Hornung. I felt embarrassed for poor Max when the coach ripped into him for failing to catch a pass from Starr that looked, on film, somewhat overthrown. "Goddamn it to hell, McGee," he growled. "You have to make *adjustments* on your routes once in a goddamn while. Haven't we gone over that? Over and over, for Chrissakes! And you have to *sell* the fake, for God's sake. I've told you twenty thousand goddamn times that on this play you gotta fake the cornerback on a post and then cut back to the corner. What's so damned hard to understand about that? Now when the hell are you gonna get your big nose out of Playboy and into your playbook?" As usual, McGee looked pained. As for Hornung, he hadn't done much in the game except kick extra points. But that didn't stop the Old Man. "Jesus, mister," he said, "look at that. Taylor's out there running his ass off with abandon on every play, and what the hell are you doing? You're supposed to be blocking downfield and Petitbon's tossing you around like a goddamn rag doll. That's not okay! Lemme tell you something, mister, the women in this town aren't going to be quite so damned *enchanted* with you when I park your lazy ass on the bench for a few games." The Golden Boy, I noted, absorbed this tiresome tirade with his wonted equanimity.

Listening to the coach's ranting, it occurred to me that it wasn't just the volume and timbre of his big voice that was so overwhelming, but also the simple fact that he talked so fast. He was, of course, an Easterner—born and bred in Brooklyn. A fair percentage of the players, however, were Southerners: McGee and Gregg were from Texas, Taylor from Louisiana, Starr from Alabama, and Hornung from Kentucky, to name a few. If Lombardi's staccato delivery was intimidating to a Midwesterner like me, it must have been doubly so for these slow-talking Southern boys. I felt glad that my asshole father—no slouch himself when it came to ranting and raving—at least didn't talk as rapidly as the Old Man.

Standing in the back of the room with Dad, I felt terrible. I felt responsible for the ass-chewings that my friends were getting. On the one hand, I liked the coach—well enough, anyway—and felt concerned for his health. On the other hand, I hated him for what he was doing and there was a part of me that still wanted to punish him. Part of me wanted to stand up to him—fantasy though that seemed—and tell him in no uncertain terms that I would absolutely no longer meet with him to snitch on my friends and he could curse me out from here to eternity and fire my pathetic ass, I could simply care less. But another part of me—maybe a bigger part—didn't want to do anything that would jeopardize my seeing the wonderful Marie Lombardi again.

THE NEXT Sunday, October 7th, we played the Detroit Lions in City Stadium. I'd been looking forward to that day so that I could see my favorite player, Alex Karras. I was also looking forward to that night, hopefully going out with Paul and Max, and, hopefully, finally hitting a home run.

It was a tough game. It'd rained a lot during the week and the day was gray and wet and the field sloppy. The Lions' only score was a touchdown by some guy named Lewis, on a six-yard run in the second quarter, but the Packers had only managed to kick two field goals by the time the game wound down to the two-minute mark in the fourth quarter. Still, Taylor'd rushed twenty times for close to a hundred yards and McGee'd had a decent game too, with five catches for sixty-nine yards. Yale Lary, the Detroit punter and right safety, had intercepted a pass meant for McGee after cornerback Dick "Night Train" Lane had bumped him off his route. Hornung, in addition to his two field goals, had run ten times for thirty-seven yards. On his first run of the second quarter, a power sweep to the right, Karras had caught him from behind and dragged him to the ground, and I thought I saw the big tackle knee my friend in the ribs while he was on the ground. I thought I heard Paul let out a little yelp, but maybe I was wrong.

I wasn't wrong, though, about a play shortly after halftime. It was a second-and-four, just after Taylor had run for six yards behind nice blocks by Jerry Kramer and Forrest Gregg, and the mammoth right defensive tackle, Roger Brown, had just *flattened* Thurston. After the play, while Fuzzy was lying on the ground trying to get back up, Karras ambled over to him and, bending over a bit at the waist, wagged a fat finger and loudly yelled, "Hey, assface, whaddya doin' down there? Takin' a little *nappie-pooh*, are we?" I didn't appreciate his smart-assed remark. After that play, I had to help adjust Fuzzy's pads a bit.

With less than two minutes remaining, the Lions had the ball at their own forty-nine yard line. It was third down, eight yards to go for a first down. All of us on the Packers sideline were glum; we knew that all the Lions had to do was run the ball once more and then, if they did-n't get a first down, punt. We knew that Lary was a great punter. There wouldn't be much time left when we got the ball back and there'd be a long way to go, and the Lions defense had been ferocious all day long. But, inexplicably, quarterback Milt Plum tried a pass. The receiver slipped and Herb Adderley intercepted and zipped down our sideline. All of a sudden every one of us—players, coaches, trainers, Dad and I—were animated and jumping up and down. "Bingo! Bingo! Bingo!" Nitschke and others yelled, meaning that the Packers defensive players should block every Lions player they could. Adderley got to the Lions twenty-two yard line before being tackled. Starr handed off a few times to advance the ball a little and run time off the clock and then, with just over thirty seconds to go, Hornung kicked a twenty-six yard field goal to win the game, 9-7.

Karras was livid. On the Lions sideline, he stomped his right foot and then ripped his helmet off and forcefully threw it in Plum's direc-tion. I could see him cussing and screaming. I wish I could have heard what he was saying above the applause and cheers of the crowd.

It was a great win. I was jubilant. Dad and I hugged.

All the Packers were smiling and congratulating one another after the final whistle and McGee was shaking the coach's hand when Kar-ras, retrieved helmet in hand, his big almost-professorial face red, abso-lutely shaking with anger, stormed over and, from about seven feet away, pointed at Lombardi. "Ya fat wop bag o' PUS!" he screamed. "We're gonna see your ugly dago face in Detroit on Thanksgiving. And you, McGee, you stink! You're a worthless piece of washed-up *monkey* shit. I hope to hell Train knocks your ass out cold before you get a chance to eat your goddamn Thanksgiving turkey!" Turning back to the Old Man, he lowered his voice and said, more calmly, "Hey, Lombardi, did your big ol' homely wife bring her *flask* to the game today? *Did she? Huh?*"

Just then I lost it. Just then something came over me. "Fuck YOU!" I yelled at Karras. "Fuck you, you fat four-eyed Greek *cock-sucker*, you greasy piece of souvlaki! Hey, kiss my rosy red ass, you big ugly *lamb* fucker!" He looked at me askance for just a moment, his brow furrowed, but then just scratched his head and walked away.

Hornung and McGee and Thurston, a few feet away, were laughing uproariously. *"Souvlaki!"* Hornung guffawed. *"Lamb fucker!"* Taylor was laughing too, tears running down his cheeks. Skoronski and Jordan, shaking hands, were smiling.

I noticed that the Old Man was just staring at me, his face blank. I stared back for a few moments. "Coach," I said after a bit, "can I talk with you?" He nodded. "Listen, sir," I said, our faces close. "I'm not going to rat on my friends to you any more. That's over. Never again, sir. I can't do that." I paused. "I hope you understand."

He glared at me for a moment, his eyes hard, face dark, and jaw muscles working. I thought he'd commence yelling. I thought he might even hit me. I didn't care. Maybe I'd see Marie again some time at Proski's on a Friday night. That great coleslaw. I noticed that Dad, standing next to the ebullient pair of Kramers, Ron and Jerry, was staring at me. I didn't know what he was thinking. But after a moment Lombardi just nodded. "Okay, Percy," he said. "Just remember what I told you about certain women, son. Remember who you work for, who you represent."

Turning from me, he clapped McGee on the back and then turned to Hornung and embraced him and smiled, that gap-toothed grin. "Hell of a game today, Paulie," he intoned in that deep baritone voice. *"Hell* of a game!"

The Golden Boy looked directly at me from over Lombardi's shoulder, his blue eyes bright. His high forehead was shiny with sweat but his wavy blond hair was fairly unruffled. He nodded his big head and winked.

)

A Research Assistant for Meyer Lansky

I WORKED AS A RESEARCH ASSISTANT for Meyer Lansky, the reputed "financial wizard of the Mob," during his twilight years in Miami Beach. I was, when I met that lovely man, a gangly Jewish *pisher* living in Florida with my mother but originally from Brooklyn. My beloved Brooklyn. I had a beautiful head of straight black hair that was my pride and a huge hooked shnoz that wasn't. My mother, Sylvie, had wearied of winters in the north and, as soon as I graduated from Erasmus Hall High School, shlepped us to Miami hoping to land herself a rich retired widower—preferably Jewish—so she could sit on her *toochis* and wear fancy clothes and expensive jewelry and not have to scrape by for every miserable shekel for the rest of her life.

But, alas, such fortune had thus far eluded her and in mid-1975 she was working the late morning shift at Wolfie's Deli at 21st and Collins, pink palace of overstuffed sandwiches, where she'd quickly gained a reputation as the most abrupt and impatient and biggest-mouthed waitress among a sizable crew of transplanted female New Yorkers with similar job duties and personal traits. I loved her dearly and felt protective of her, particularly considering that I was an only child and it had always been just her and me. I'd never known my father, and my mother would never tell me who he was. Oh, there'd been vague references to someone she'd been seriously involved with before my birth, but try as I might I never could get her to tell me more. When I pressed too hard, she invariably got right in my face and informed me in no uncertain terms that further questioning was unwelcome. "Look, Solly," she'd say, "I told you that I don't want you asking me about certain things. *Drai mir nit kain kop.* Do not bother my head any more on this matter."

It was at Wolfie's that I met Meyer Lansky. He and his brother, Jake, and three or four other elderly Jewish guys—*alter kockers*, as they called themselves—met there for brunch most days and always sat at the same table: a large semi-circular one in a corner not far from the kitchen but not visible from the windows on either Collins Avenue or 21st Street. Mr. Lansky always sat at the far left corner and Jake at the opposite corner. The other regulars who sat between the brothers included Benny Sigelbaum, Yiddy Bloom, Harry Stromberg, and often Abe Lazar—all short, bald or balding, paunchy, neatly dressed men in their mid-seventies or older. They were well-off retirees who, as my mother informed me, had not all precisely earned their gelt through endeavors of which the U.S. Department of Justice officially approved.

My mother'd finagled a busboy job for me a few months after she'd started working at Wolfie's, and I'd subsequently contrived to usually work the same shift as she so that I'd be aware of and could punish any customers who failed to treat her with a requisite level of respect.

Although I occasionally cleared tables, my specialty was, when people were seated, greeting them and setting a bowl of fat kosher pickles and a plate of hard-crusted rye bread with caraway seeds on the table and then bringing coffee. It wasn't a complicated job, but it had its drawbacks—primarily the pickles. More than anything in the world, I detested the sight and sound of someone holding a big ugly pickle to his mouth and loudly biting off a piece and chewing it. *Argh!* The crunchiness, the pickle juice dribbling down a chin—oh, the horror!

I was one of the few Jewish busboys—most being stone-faced Cubans who spoke little English—and Wolfie Cohen, the owner, liked for me to kibitz with the customers. "Good morning, young ladies," I'd say to a table of stooped-over blue-hairs whose pancake makeup was starting to crack a bit from the late morning heat. "Do all of you have your prom dresses chosen yet? Oh, your first kisses will be *so* exciting! Coffee for you girls?"

"Nu?" one of them would say. "A nice polite young boy, and so tall. First kisses? Ach, who can remember? So maybe, young man, you'd like to meet my granddaughter. A *shaineh maidel* she is, such a nice girl. And *talented?* Don't ask!"

Mr. Lansky—I could never bring myself to call him anything but that—was the shortest, maybe five-four, and quietest of his brunch group and the most ... well, intimidating. In appearance he was unremarkable: graying hair combed straight back and parted razor-sharp high on the left; neatly dressed, usually in light-gray trousers and a pale

-blue short-sleeved shirt that he never tucked in, perhaps to de-emphasize his mild paunch; and, like his companions, the tanned, leathery, liver-spotted face, neck and hands common to elderly Floridians. It was his eyes that scared me. They were dark-brown, almost black, and cold. The first time I met Mr. Lansky, while I was putting the pickles and bread on their table, I tried my usual shtick with his little group. "Well," I said, "I see the Boy Scouts convention is in town. How are we all today, fellas? Feeling terrific?"

"Ah," Yiddy Bloom replied. "So tell me, *boytchik*, how should we feel? I looked in the *Herald* first thing this morning and didn't see my name in the obits, so it's a good day, yes? Now if I could just take a real crap I'd donate a thousand dollars to Beth Israel, they should light an everlasting candle in my name."

All the men laughed, except Mr. Lansky. He just stared at me, looking directly into my eyes, as though sizing me up. His look wasn't exactly disdainful or disapproving, just intense and studious. Our eyes met for just a moment, and in that moment I immediately questioned myself: Was my smart-ass remark out-of-line, even patronizing? Had I not shown proper deference? Did this old man somehow know of my almost-daily self-gratification habit just from looking at my face? Or were the pickles perhaps just not up to his standards? Yet he said nothing. I smiled weakly at him and he may have smiled back, I'm not sure; if so, it was subtle. "Well," I said, feeling flushed, "I'll be back with your coffee in a minute."

When I returned, Mr. Lansky nodded his head and quietly thanked me and then asked a question. "Tell me, young man," he said, "do you know who was the president just before Woodrow Wilson?"

"Why," I answered, a bit flustered, "no, sir, I don't. That is, I should, but ... "

"Meyer," Benny Sigelbaum said, "forget that. Ask him if he knows what Clemenza promised the Rosato brothers."

"*That* I know," I said. "Three territories in the Bronx."

"Right!" Yiddy Bloom exclaimed, raising his arms high like a referee signaling a touchdown. He picked two pink packets of Sweet'N Low from a small glass bowl, looked at them closely, and put them in the inside pocket of his green sport jacket. "That's what I said. But you, Harry, you're such a smarty, you said he promised them to knock off

Frank Pentangeli. You should excuse my bluntness, but when it comes to this movie, Stromberg, you know for nothing."

Harry Stromberg shrugged his shoulders. "So, what's the deal? You've seen it ... what? ... three times? ... four? So now you're a big *expert*? Me, I went once with my wife and I could hardly sit through it; my hemorrhoids, you'll pardon me, caused me such *tsoris*. So maybe, Bloom, you should call up this fat wop director, Coppola, and tell him how smart you now are—all of you, on this *farshtinkener* movie. Ach, you make me sick." Turning to me, he added, "So, young man, you too are a professor on this saga? Then tell me, you're so learned, how does Michael Corleone find out it was his putz brother, this Fredo, who betrayed him?"

They all looked at me and I felt embarrassed. "Well," I said, looking at my feet, "it was in Havana. Michael mentions to Fredo that Johnny Ola's in town and Fredo says he never met him before. Then a little later when they're in the nightclub where they see the Superman act, Senator Geary asks Fredo how he knew about the place and he says that Johnny Ola took him there, that 'old Johnny knows these places like the back of his hand.' He inadvertently lets on that he knew Ola, who works for Hyman Roth, before. That's when Michael knows that Fredo was lying and that he was the traitor."

Abe Lazar stood up and clapped and then shook my hand. "Bravo!" he said. "You passed Stromberg's silly test, boytchik. You're a *mensch*. So tell me this, what did you think of this Hyman Roth? A very nice man, no?"

I knew at once this was a set-up question. I knew that the Roth character in *The Godfather Part II* was based on Meyer Lansky. I even knew that the actor who played Roth, Lee Strasberg, had asked to meet with Mr. Lansky, to study him for the part, but that Mr. Lansky had declined. I, too, had seen the film—which had opened the previous December—three times, and the original four times. "Oh, yes," I said, looking at Mr. Lansky. "A very nice man. Quite intelligent. It was just a shame things didn't work out in Cuba."

Mr. Lansky smiled, just a bit, and I knew that he understood. "Sure," he agreed, "a fine fellow. But back to the president before Wilson. Would you be interested in going across the street to the public library, when you have a chance, to check this out? I would appreciate it. You see, we now and again play a sort of game, trivia questions—facts about history, politics, whatever. Sometimes we don't know the answer, we go to the library. You have young legs, so maybe you'll help us out?"

"Good idea, Meyer," Harry Stromberg said. "So you'll do it, young man? You'll help some poor old and tired farts, senior citizens, members in good standing of the American Association of Retired Persons, who can hardly walk anymore, who can barely butter their own bagels?"

Mr. Lansky gave Harry a look—a look I hoped I would never be the recipient of. "Harry," he said, "give it a rest already. Good God!" Then, turning back to me, he reached into his pocket and pulled out a small wad of bills. "Here," he said, handing me a ten spot, "this is in advance for your efforts."

I was about to thank him and accept his offer when my mother's loud, shrill voice pierced the air. "*Yeah*, yeah," I heard her say. "Hold your horses. I heard you the *first* time and I'll bring your damn check as soon as I can. I'm running around here like a crazy chicken with its head cut off, can't you see? My God, the entire population of Dade County's here today. So just give me a minute, *okay?*"

"So okay, already," I heard a deep, slow male voice answer. "Take your time. Whatta we got to do anyway? We'll just sit here and admire the pink decor, right, honey? My God, what a touchy broad."

I leaned over to see who'd said that, and immediately trotted over to his table. "Excuse me, sir," I said to the man—a tall, jowly, dumb-looking guy wearing a yellow polo shirt with *I Luv Cleveland* on it and green Bermuda shorts. "Is everything okay?"

"Well, the service here ain't exactly breakin' no speed records, kid. Other than that, things are, ya know, okay. Course, the corned beef, it's … what can I tell ya? It ain't like what we get at Corky and Lenny's back home."

"Oh, I'm *so* sorry to hear that, sir. Here, sir, let me clear some of this away. Oh, I'm so *sorry*, sir, I didn't mean to spill that water on your shirt. Are you okay? Let me get you a towel. God, I'm sorry! I am *so* clumsy."

"Awright, awright. It's okay. Jesus Christ! C'mon, Doris, let's get the hell out of here."

And don't come back, you rude ugly moron, I thought.

When I returned, my mother was taking orders from the old men. "The usual today?" she asked Jake.

He shook his big head. "Naw. I think today I'll have some matzo ball soup and a piece of honey cake. A *big* piece. You got maybe some *farfel* for the soup?"

My mother gave him a look. "*Christ*, Jake," she said sharply, "you've asked me that twenty times this month alone. Yes, we have farfel. Of *course* we have farfel. This is a freakin' Jewish deli, for Chrissake! What the hell kind of Jewish deli doesn't have farfel?"

"So excuse me for living, okay Sylvie? Forget the farfel anyway. I changed my mind." He took a pickle from the bowl and chomped off a third of it in one bite, causing me to shudder.

"Don't drai mir kop, Jake," my mother said. "I'll bring your farfel on the side—you eat it, fine; you don't, also fine. I'm sure the goddamn sun'll still come up tomorrow either way."

"So Sylvie," Harry Stromberg said, "you'll bring me some smoked whitefish and a bagel, lightly toasted? Cream cheese on the side. You got maybe a nice onion bagel today?"

"Yeah, yeah. Onion. Sure."

"And you'll bring my friend Hyman here"—gesturing toward Mr. Lansky—"a nice tongue sandwich on rye and some hot tea? Right, Meyer? That's a good girl. So, listen, you don't burn my bagel too bad, there'll be a nice tip for you."

"You're a *comedian*, Harry," my mother said, looking down her nose at him. "What're you wasting your time hanging around here every day? You oughta be doing a shtick in the Catskills. Grossingers. I'm sure there's hundreds of nice old Jewish women up there just shaking their heads, going, 'Oy, *mein Gott*, that Harry Stromberg, so talented he is, so funny! And what he's doing with his life? He's rotting away in Miami Beach with a bunch of dried-out has-beens, clogging his arteries with cream cheese, when he could be putting on a great show for us, letting the world see what a comic genius he is. Such a shame, a man like that!'"

They all laughed, even Mr. Lansky. "Sylvie," Bennie Sigelbaum said, "let me ask you something. If my Belle kicks the bucket, you'll maybe come live with me?"

"Sure, Ben," she answered. "Absolutely. I can't wait to feel your skinny arms around me at night and listen to you snoring and farting. I can't wait to hear you call out to me each morning: 'Sylvie, you've seen my teeth?' Oh, *bliss!"*

Again they laughed. My mother looked at Mr. Lansky. "That right, Meyer?" she asked, more respectfully than she'd spoken to the others. "Tongue on rye?"

"Yes, please," he said. "A middle slice. And some hot lemon tea, if you have, with a *bisel* honey. Thank you."

"Sure. Nice to see that *one* person here has some manners." Then, turning her head to the left, she yelled to someone at a table nearby. "Yeah, yeah, I'll be there in a minute already. Stop *kvetching* and be patient, for God's sake!"

"Sir," I said quietly to Mr. Lansky, "I should be able to go across the street in just a few minutes, on my break."

As I started to walk away, my mother grabbed my elbow. "C'mere," she said, leading me into the kitchen. "Listen, I saw Lansky give you a ten. Why?"

"He asked me to go to the library and look up something for him. What's your problem?"

Her face was tight and threatening. "Don't talk smart," she said. "And listen to me. Library, okay, but do not get involved with these guys. And if I ever catch you placing bets, I'll wring your scrawny little neck till your eyes pop out. Do you hear me?"

"Mom," I said, "what the hell's the matter with you? I'm just gonna look up something about a president, for Chrissake. What are you worried about?"

"Never mind. Just remember what I said." I didn't answer, and looked away. My mother grabbed my chin and forced me to look at her face. *"Hey!"* she said. "Listen to me here. These guys, they're bright, they're charming, they're funny, yeah sure, but let me tell you something, Solly—they're *crooks!* I like Meyer and Jake and all of them, but they're not exactly role models here. I've told you about these people; I know about them from the old days in New York. Lansky, he ran with Luciano, Bugsy Siegel, Costello. Do you remember me telling you that? Crooks, Solly, and not small-time hoods either. Believe me, I know these guys!" I still didn't respond, so she reached up and slapped the back of my head. "HEY!" she said. "*Farshtaist*? Understand me?"

Across the street, I sought the help of the young librarian at the Information Desk. Her name was Lisa, and she was both competent and marvelously cute: tight white shorts that did justice, pert little boobelahs, and the face of a young Talia Shire—putting me in mind of Connie Corleone at her wedding in the first *Godfather*, gazing adoringly at Johnny Fontane singing "O Marenariello" to her— "*I have but one heart ... this heart I bring you ...* " She was, I suspected, either Jewish or Italian, and either way I was interested.

When I returned, the men had finished their brunch and were sipping coffee and were back on *Godfather II*. As I learned, this was one of their main topics of conversation—that and their trivia questions; current politics; their various ailments, a significant number of which focused on their bowel or bladder difficulties; and their wives' Bal Harbour spending habits. As to the movie, their main focus was on aspects of it that, to them, were unclear or didn't make sense. Loose ends. Why, for example, did the young Vito Corleone bother to give Fannuci a hundred dollar payoff when he's going to shoot him a few minutes later? Was it Fredo whom we are to assume opened the drapes in Michael's bedroom in Lake Tahoe just prior to the assassination attempt? Who killed the two New York hit men who tried to murder Michael? Who, exactly, authorized the garroting of Frank Pentangeli by the Rosatos at their bar in Brooklyn? Was it Hyman Roth, or could it have been Michael? How did Roth know that Fredo brought the two million to Havana? Why didn't Michael knock off Willy Cicci after Willy testified in the Kefauver-style organized crime Senate hearings? Why was Pentangeli still a protected witness after he'd double-crossed the feds during those hearings? And so on. Usually, it was either Yiddy Bloom or Benny Sigelbaum who raised these questions; they'd gone together three times to matinee showings and planned to go again, hoping to become more enlightened as to these and other puzzlements. It was Yiddy's contention that the film would have been clearer and better if an hour, or even two, longer. Jake was also interested in these questions, though his ideas never made much sense. "Let me tell you something," I overheard him saying shortly after I returned, "it was Tom Hagen who killed them two hit men. I never trusted that fuckin' mick. He was a bad *consigliere*, like Sonny said."

"Hagen?" Benny Sigelbaum said. "Jake, you don't know what the hell you're talking about. You're *farmisht*. Just eat your honey cake and don't display your ignorance."

Mr. Lansky rarely took part in these discussions. Even though one of the main characters in the movie had been based on him, he was seemingly uninterested. The others never pressed him, other than to tease him a bit now and again, mostly by quoting Hyman Roth. "'Michael,'" Yiddy Bloom might say to Abe Lazar, "'we're bigger than U.S. Steel.'"

"That's right," Lazar would reply. "'But good health, the most important thing—more than success, more than money, more than power!'"

When I reported the results of my research to Mr. Lansky—it was that tub of lard William Howard Taft who'd preceded Wilson—he thanked me politely and asked if I'd be willing to help out again. "Yes sir," I said. "It would be my sincere pleasure to go to the library for you again."

THE NEXT day when I approached their table, I decided to lose my smart-ass shtick, not wishing to risk being again the object of Mr. Lansky's cold-eyed scrutiny. "Good morning, Solly," he said right away, before I could say anything. "How are you today?"

"Fine, sir," I answered. "Do you need me to look up anything for you today?"

"We'll see. Probably. We appreciate your help."

"So, boytchik," Abe Lazar said. "A question has come up. Two questions, really. First, this *meshugenner* Estes Kefauver, did he have a middle name? Second, Bloom wants to know if you know Vito Corleone's birthday."

"As to the first, I don't know but I'll find out. As to the second, it was December 7th—the day Michael dropped out of college and joined the Marines in 1941, Pearl Harbor Day."

"Good boy," Mr. Lansky said. "So, Solly, tell me about yourself. You're going to school, or what?"

But before I could answer, my mother whisked over to take their orders and I could tell from looking that she wasn't in a good mood. "Jesus Christ!" she exclaimed. "My tootsies are *killing* me. I need to soak in a hot bath for a month and never look at another damned bowl of borscht. I never could stand that crap. What'll it be, boys?"

"Borscht sounds good, Sylvie," Jake said. "Hot cabbage, not that cold beet *chazerai*. You got?"

"You're killing me, Jake," she said, giving him her look. "You're gonna be the death of me yet. *Borscht*, he wants. I suppose you want farfel in it too, huh? Honest to God, if I ... " I looked at her to see why her shrill voice had suddenly silenced and saw her staring at a tall, handsome, dark-complected, silver-haired man with bright-blue eyes standing next to Mr. Lansky, shaking his hand. He had a large curved nose with a small straight vertical scar on the bridge. My mother's jaw was hanging open a bit and her face had turned two shades paler.

"Hey, look," Yiddy Bloom said, "it's Hyman Roth's Sicilian messenger boy, Johnny Ola. Vinnie, *vee geyts*? How ya doin'?"

"Good, Yiddy," the man said. "Jake, how's it going?" Then, looking directly into my mother's eyes, his face softened. "Sylvie," he said gently, touching her cheek softly with just the backs of the fingers of his right hand. "Good to see you. How've you been?"

Still looking surprised and still staring at the man, she shrugged. "What can I tell you, Vinnie?" she said, almost whispering. "The years crawl by."

"Solly," Mr. Lansky said, standing up and touching my arm. "This is Mr. Alo, my friend and business partner."

"Proud to make your acquaintance, young man," he said to me, offering a large hand and looking directly into my eyes. "Any friend of Meyer's is a friend of mine." He was the best-looking man I'd ever seen and, except perhaps for Mr. Lansky, the most self-possessed. Looking into his face, I saw something that felt familiar but didn't know what.

"Solly," Benny Sigelbaum said, "did you know that this man here was the—how do you say?—the *prototype* for Mr. Johnny Ola in *God-father*? Some smart-aleck scriptwriter had the idea to steal his name and mix up the letters, reverse the vowels. Cute, no? Unfortunately, poor

Mr. Ola gets choked with a coat hanger in Cuba. Right, Vinnie? Oh, what a shame!"

"Garroted," I said.

My mother jammed her elbow into my ribs. "Don't you have work to do?" she asked, apparently recovered and back to her bitchy self. "Go and clear table eight. Wolfie's not paying you to sit and listen to this *cockamamie* gangster crap. C'mon, *scram!*"

I looked directly at Mr. Lansky and he nodded once, almost imperceptibly. "Nice to meet you, Mr. Alo," I said.

"Sure," he said. "You too, Sally. Take it easy, kid," and offered his hand again. I grasped it, and it enveloped mine. He squeezed as we shook, just once, and again I felt a strange sense of ... connection.

"It's Solly, sir," I said. "Not Sally."

His brow furrowed and he looked at me. "Oh," he said, "but I thought ... I mean ... well, son, whatever your handle, you can count on me."

I cleared table eight and then refilled the coffee cups of a sad and bored-looking middle-aged goyim couple at table nine who'd both ordered Wolfie's famous cheesecake, huge slices, and hadn't spoken one word to each other since they'd sat down and, I don't think, had even made eye contact with each other and now were just sipping coffee and chain-smoking unfiltered Pall Malls. The woman murmured a nearly inaudible thanks when I refilled her cup, but the man said nothing and didn't even look at me. I felt glad not to be them. From Mr. Lansky's table, I heard loud laughter and overheard Yiddy Bloom practically shouting. "Nu, Vinnie," he said. "Garroted! So finally you regret hooking up with this Hyman Roth character? Maybe better you should have stayed a *capo* with Genovese. Am I right, Meyer?"

Then two considerably overweight men sat down at table twelve and, after I'd put the pickles and bread at their table and was about to pour their coffee, I saw the fatter of the two gesturing toward my mother, who was taking orders at another table. "That Sylvie," he said. "What a *zaftik* plum! The toochis on that broad, huh? I tell ya, I wouldn't mind *shtupping* her sometime. I bet she'd do it too."

The other man nodded. "Yeah," he said. "I wouldn't be surprised. So offer her fifty, see what she says."

"*Fifty?* I'll give her twenty, she'll be grateful. She ain't exactly a bloomin' rose no more."

I felt my face flush and my throat constricting. I was still holding the coffee carafe and was about to either crack him over the head with it or pour the entire contents in his lap and then, rather than offer my wonted disingenuous apology, tell him that I hoped it would burn off his tiny miserable *schwantz* and then, with the assistance of a couple of the bigger Cubans, kick his disgusting fat ass out of Wolfie's forever. But before I could do anything I felt a hand on my elbow and turned around to see Mr. Lansky and Mr. Alo behind me, the latter grinning slightly.

"Solly," Mr. Lansky said, holding onto my arm, "think before you do something silly. When you act out of anger, later you usually regret. There are better ways."

"Meyer's right, son," Mr. Alo said. "Here, let me." He walked over to the two slobs and, from behind, put his arm gently around the fatter one's shoulder and leaned down and, smiling beautifully, whispered something in the man's ear. The man tried to turn to look into Mr. Alo's face, but couldn't because of the pressure on his shoulder. In a few moments his face blanched and he nodded, his jowls quivering. "Good," Mr. Alo said to the man, standing straight. "I appreciate that very much." Then, turning back to me, he playfully rubbed the back of my head. "See," he said, "peaceful is better. *Capisce?*"

Mr. Lansky touched my elbow again. "Solly," he said, "I'd like to talk with you a little bit. This afternoon, later, I walk my dog. You can join me?"

"Sure, sir. Is there a problem?"

He shrugged. "No problem. Just some thoughts. In the meantime, you can go to the library for us? We need to know this *schnorrer* hypocrite Kefauver's middle name, like Abe said." His face darkened. "That putz!" he went on. "He grandstanded about gambling—oh, how *despicable* it all is—and meanwhile he's out playing the dogs and ponies every chance he gets. Ach! And also another question we discussed. History, Solly, is so interesting, don't you think? We want to know when exactly did the Warsaw uprising start, and how long did it last, and how many goddamn Nazis did we kill?"

How many did *we* kill? I liked that.

That juicy Lisa was at the library again and mentioned that there was an information researcher job open. She looked up at me, her pretty brown Talia eyes opened wide. "Are you interested?" she asked softly.

After work, I went home, whacked off, took a shower, and read for a while. At the library, I'd found a book about Charlie "Lucky" Luciano, now dead, who, as my mother had mentioned, had been another of Mr. Lansky's business partners. They'd grown up together in New York. Lucky, I learned, was a stone-cold gangster.

Also at the library, after checking out Warsaw and Kefauver—it turned out that Estes was his middle name, his first being *Carey*—I'd looked up other things about Mr. Lansky in newspaper files. I'd known a little about him, but not his recent history. I didn't know, for example, that just a few years ago he'd tried to stay in Israel as a returned Jew, to avoid federal prosecution, but that the High Court had rejected him, and that other countries—Brazil, Argentina, Panama—wouldn't accept him either even though he'd allegedly offered them big bucks. There'd been a brief reference to that in *Godfather II*, but I'd forgotten. I didn't know that just two years ago he'd been indicted on several federal charges, including income tax evasion, but had beaten the rap when a former low -rank mobster turned informer, Vincent "Fat Vinnie" Teresa, had been shown to be lying when he asserted that he'd personally paid Mr. Lansky a percentage of illegal gambling profits. Trial testimony had revealed that Mr. Lansky had been recovering from a hernia operation in Boston at the time that Teresa had claimed they'd been together in Miami. Fat Vinnie's explanation: "He musta had a double."

Then it occurred to me that my mother wasn't home yet. Where was she? She always came right home from work to take a steaming bubble bath and smoke Virginia Slims and drink a few glasses of Chablis to unwind, but not today. Seeing Mr. Alo had unnerved her for some reason—God knows why—but why wasn't she home? I found myself getting a headache from the intrigues of the day; too much was going on that I didn't understand.

She still wasn't home by the time I left.

Mr. Lansky was waiting for me on the corner of 17th and Collins with his dog, Bruzzer. "He's a Shih Tzu," he explained. "I got him for Teddy, my wife, but now I take care of him more. Every afternoon, we walk. Sometimes we go to South Point Park or we drive on the Causeway over to Hibiscus Island and walk there. It's nice, Solly. My doctor tells me to get exercise for my heart, so this is what I do."

We walked quietly for four or five blocks, just making small talk. He asked me about myself, and seemed genuinely interested in what I had to say. *My God!* I thought. Here I am, a *nebish* nobody from Brooklyn and I'm walking down Collins Avenue in Miami Beach with one of the most famous—or infamous—men in the country, and he's asking me personal questions and paying me to look up facts in the public library.

"Solly," he said after a while, "I want to talk to you about what happened this morning. I saw how yesterday you poured water on that man in the restaurant and then today you were angry and God knows what you were going to do with those two schmucks who talked nasty about your mother."

I nodded. "I wasn't sure what I was going to do, sir. I wanted to kill that fat slob."

"I know. I've felt the same way, many times. But you've got to think. Number one, you can't protect your mother all the time. She's a big girl, and with a mouth on her too. Let me tell you, if that man had said anything to her, *vey iz mir!*, she'd have shriveled him with her tongue. I would've felt sorry for him. But number two, Solly, you got to consider better ways of dealing with problems. You pour water, make it seem like an accident, apologize, that's not what a man does. Or just strike out when you're angry. You can't fight every fight, you got to let some things go. And if you need to make a point, you do it straightforward. Like Vince did with that man."

"What did he say to him, Mr. Lansky?"

He looked at me and shrugged. "I don't know for sure. Vince, he's not a man to trifle with. He's a man you can learn from. But what he said isn't important. What's important is to be direct with people. That's how you become a mensch, Solly, a person."

We walked some more in silence. I felt a bit awkward, towering over him by almost a foot. I noticed that people we passed on the street, many of them, recognized Mr. Lansky. Some nodded to him, and he always acknowledged them. Now and again older Jewish women would stop and talk for a minute or two, and he was invariably polite and interested. Once, Bruzzer raised a rear leg and peed on the tire of a big

Lincoln Town Car that a scary Italian-looking man—a more benign Luca Brasi—had just parked. The man, coming around the front of the car, saw it and scowled at the dog and then at Mr. Lansky. "Bruzzer," Mr. Lansky scolded, wagging his right index finger, "that was very wrong. You must show respect." Then he looked directly at the man, his face devoid of emotion, and held his gaze. The scary-looking guy met Mr. Lansky's eyes for a moment and then shrugged his shoulders and walked away, muttering to himself.

At the corner of 11th Street and Washington Avenue, he paused for a moment and took a deep breath and then held onto my elbow as we crossed the street. I noticed that he looked a bit frailer. "Mr. Lansky," I said, "are you tired? Do you want to sit down for a while?"

He nodded, and I led him to a bus stop bench nearby, under a huge palm tree. "Ach, Solly," he said, wiping his brow with his handkerchief, "enjoy being young. Old age, let me tell you, it's no picnic." We were quiet then for a while, enjoying the shade and the mild breeze. Bruzzer fell asleep under the bench and commenced snoring and wheezing.

"Solly," he said to me after a bit, "something's on your mind, I can tell. Want to talk about it?"

I looked at him, saw his dark hard eyes looking directly into mine but not at all threatening. "Well," I said, "maybe this is silly, I don't know. It's just that, well, I never knew my father, Mr. Lansky, not at all. And my mother, she won't tell me anything about him. So I wonder about that, a lot. Then today in the restaurant, I had a silly thought when … oh, it's too *dumb* to even mention. But … well ... " I couldn't go on.

Mr. Lansky waited politely to see if I would continue and then, when I didn't, nodded and touched my arm lightly. "I understand, Solly," he said. "I know how this must eat at you. I don't know who your father was, and I don't think your mother's going to tell you. She must have her reasons. So you must accept this, and just go on with your life. Maybe some day you'll know, but maybe not." He paused and looked down at Bruzzer, who was still sleeping. "There are different kinds of fathers, Solly."

I wanted to ask what he meant, but before I could he yawned and stood up. "Bruzzer and I have to get back," he said. "I'm taking my wife tonight to the Fontainebleau, some cockamamie charity event. Me, at night I like just to stay home and watch TV, read. Spinoza, I've been reading lately. But Teddy, she likes to go to these fancy-shmancy parties, so sometimes I go. Jake'll be there too."

As we walked back, he again took my arm as we crossed the first street. "You know," he said, "every life, Solly, has its ups, its downs. Me, I've had some success, made some money, but I have a son with a tragedy, cerebral palsy; I've got a bad ticker; constant aggravation from the goddamn government. And I tell you this confidentially, the biggest sadness of my life was I couldn't prevent the death of the best friend I ever had, Ben Siegel. Him and Jake and me, we grew up together on the Lower East Side. Vinnie too, and Yiddy. I loved that man, and I think of him every day. So all of us, we have both *nachas* and *tsoris* in our lives, just different things. So you too, Solly. You never had a father, that's a sadness. But your mother loves you, you have your health, you're smart, you got a future. Do you understand what I'm saying?"

I nodded.

"Good," he said. "So here we are. I'll see you tomorrow, yes? *Zei gezunt,* Solly."

THE NEXT DAY at Wolfie's, the alter kockers were harping on President Ford. I noticed that Mr. Lansky looked better, more color to his face. I'd hoped that Mr. Alo would be there because I wanted to study him, maybe talk with him. But he wasn't, and I never saw him again.

"This guy," Abe Lazar was saying, "he's dumber even than my Uncle Mordecai, God rest his soul, and he was the dumbest guy in the five boroughs. Nixon, at least, he was smart. A fucking crook, but smart."

"Ach," said Yiddy Bloom, "Nixon wasn't that smart. If he was, he wouldn't have hired those two Nazis, Haldeman and the other one, that fat bald putz, who screwed everything up. What were those two—advertising guys in California, right? Or one of them was. So they come to Washington and start giving a mouth to Congress and thinking they got power, and you see what happened. Nixon, he should never have hired those *schlemiels*. Or at least he shoulda kicked their arrogant asses out the first year."

"At least Ford kept Kissinger," Jake said. "A short pudgy Jew, with a seven-foot-tall blond *shikse* wife. And don't be talkin' about fat bald putzes, Bloom. You hurt my feelings."

They all laughed. Mr. Lansky caught my eye and gestured me over to him. "Solly," he said, "I want to thank you for walking with Bruzzer and me yesterday. We enjoyed it."

"Me too," I said. "Thank you for … I mean … "

He waved his hand dismissively. "We'll maybe do it again some time?"

I nodded.

"Hey, boytchik," Benny Sigelbaum said. "We got a question. What business were Hyman and Vito Corleone in together in the old days, during Prohibition?"

Before I could answer, my mother came over to bring their food. I'd been asleep when she'd finally come home and then had left for work before her, so we hadn't had a chance to talk. She looked exhausted, and I noticed that the blue eyeshadow over her left eye, carelessly applied, was a bit streaked. "Here you are, guys," she said in a barely audible monotone. "Your orders. Hope everything's okay." I saw Mr. Lansky looking at her, studying her. But he said nothing.

"Thanks, Sylvie," Benny Sigelbaum said. "Hey, you okay?"

"Yeah, yeah. Fine. Peachy keen." Turning to me, she quietly said, "When you're done here, bring some more pickles to table ten. They gobbled them down like pigs, and they're squealing for more. Go on."

At table ten, two nicely tanned couples were shlurping coffee and giggling. The women, both stiff-haired bleached blondes with multiple chins, scowled at me disapprovingly as I set a second bowl of pickles on their table. As soon as I did, one of them snatched up the biggest one and loudly crunched off the end. "Well," she said, chewing and talking with her mouth full of pickle, "it took long enough."

"Yeah," said one of the men, "we're practically starving here. That waitress with the attitude, she said she'd be right back. What's the problem?"

"No problem, sir," I replied tersely. "Here're your pickles. I'm sure your orders will be up shortly." I looked at each of them in turn, directly, holding my gaze with each person for a moment. "Anything else?"

"Yes," the same man said, looking put out. "Tell that slow waitress to come back here. I wanna change my order. I don't want that stupid lox plate. Say, where the hell is she anyway? She said she was comin' right back and then she disappears to God-knows-where. Plus, I couldn't hardly hear her. I ask her what you get with the lox plate and she mumbles something, I don't know *what* the hell she said. The *last* time we were here, she broke my damn eardrums, I'm telling ya. I don't know what the hell's wrong with her."

I stared at him. "*Nothing* is wrong with her, sir. She's *fine!*" I moved over a step, bent down, and, from behind him, put my arm around his shoulders and whispered something in his ear. I probably shouldn't have said what I said, but I did and afterward never regretted it. The man's face turned red and he tried to turn around to look at me but I kept pressure on his shoulder.

Finally, I let go and he stood up, his face now almost purple, and began screaming at me. "Why, you little COCKSUCKER! Who the *hell* you think you're talking to? Who the *fuck* you think you are, threatening me? So she's your mother! How the hell am *I* supposed to know that? Why I've got half a mind to ... "

"What's wrong here? What's the *problem?*" It was Wolfie, looking upset. "What's going on here, Solly?"

My mother, followed by Mr. Lansky and Jake and Harry Stromberg, hurried over. My mother gave me one of her looks and I was glad to see her animated again, at least a little. My eyes met Mr. Lansky's, but I couldn't tell what he was thinking. Jake, on the other hand, was chuckling openly. "Cohen," he intoned, "what the hell kind of establishment are you running here? Can't a man eat a pastrami sandwich in peace without meshugeners yelling obscenities at busboys for no good reason? Damn good busboy, too. I'm shocked! *Really*, mister," he added, turning to stare menacingly at the seated man and raising his voice considerably, "you oughta show respect."

Wolfie ignored him. "What happened here?" he asked the couples. They all started talking at once, both blondes righteously indignant, their droopy faces unusually ugly in their choler. "*Sha!*" Wolfie yelled. "You're hurting my ears. One person at a time, for God's sake! You," looking at the man who'd screamed at me, "talk." The man told him what I'd said and Wolfie glared at me harshly and then at my mother, who—thank God!—was smiling at me. "Awright," he said, "sit down and eat. It's on me. Solly, c'mere."

I followed Wolfie into the kitchen. He put his hand on my shoulder and shook his head. "Look, kid," he said, "I gotta let you go. I hate to do it, but this guy's a big macher out at Hialeah. He's tight with the mayor and that money crowd. Oh, big bucks! You can't go around calling a guy like that names, even if he's a prick. I'm sorry."

"It's okay, Mr. Cohen."

"Maybe if you apologize, though, he'd ... "

"No!" I said. "Absolutely *not!*"

He sighed. "Okay, Solly, I understand. But you must understand too, I got no choice."

I nodded. "It's okay," I repeated.

As I left the kitchen, my mother was waiting for me. "Listen," she said, "what you did was dumb, and you know that, but I love you for it. Tonight we'll go out for Chinese, okay? You can get that moo-shu crap that you like. Okay, I gotta get back to work. The high rollers at table ten are gonna waste away to Treblinka survivors unless they stuff their stupid faces immediately."

I figured I'd go across the street to the library to see if the information researcher job was still available. Hopefully, that little Lisa would be there, hopefully in her tight white shorts. I'd need to start working on a shtick to seriously charm her.

Mr. Lansky caught my eye as I neared his table and gestured me over. "Solly," he said, looking directly into my eyes, "what's up?" I told him what had happened and told him my plans and he nodded approvingly. "Listen, you want me to talk to Cohen, see if he'll let you keep your job?"

I shook my head. "No thanks, Mr. Lansky. But maybe you'll keep an eye on my mother for me? Maybe keep the wolves and other asswipes away?"

He smiled and patted my arm. "Sure, son," he said. "The wolves and asswipes. And how about we call you over at that library once in a while, have you look up things for us. You can do that?"

I nodded. "Yes," I said. "Please do."

"Good," he said. "So here's a twenty, Solly, in advance for your help."

"So, boytchik," Yiddy Bloom said, pocketing three Sweet'N Low packets. "What are we going to do now when we need to know the number of the amendment that ended Prohibition?"

"I'm your man," I answered. "And," turning to Benny Sigelbaum, "it was *molasses*. Hyman Roth and Don Corleone, their business together in Prohibition was smuggling molasses between Havana and Canada, to make rum."

"You're okay, young man," Benny said. "See, Yiddy: 'Hyman Roth, he always makes money for his partners.'"

"Listen, kid," Jake said, "come over to the Eden Roc some afternoon. A few of us play gin rummy on the veranda out back. Sometimes it's windy, we have to hold the cards down with rubber bands on the table corners. So you'll come, we'll *nosh* on some chips, drink some … root beer or cream soda—I like that Dr. Brown's stuff—and we'll talk about the world. Whaddya say?"

I looked at Mr. Lansky. He shrugged his shoulders, just a bit. "Thanks," I said to Jake. "I might like that."

I decided not to worry any more about my paternity. Maybe Mr. Alo was my father, maybe not. Mr. Lansky had been right: my mother had her reasons—God knows what—and I'd just have to let it go. But she was wrong, most likely, about the alter kockers; maybe they'd been big-time baddies in the past, but now they were just a group of harmless old farts living out their days in Miami Beach, and I'd learn what I could from them—particularly Mr. Lansky—about how to be a mensch. The Eden Roc sounded fine. Maybe Jake or Yiddy could even give me an idea or two about how to impress little Lisa.

My mother came over to refill their coffee. "Sylvie, my love," Harry Stromberg said, "when you get a chance you'll maybe bring me some hot noodle kugel with sour cream? And some more tea for Hyman here. With honey. Right, Meyer?"

"AGAIN with the Hyman Roth *mishegas?*" she shrilled. "Give me a *break*, will ya, Harry? Enough is enough already, for God's sake! When are you guys gonna grow up and stop playing kid games? It's *very* irritating. Christ, I'm surprised you *shleppers* don't sit around dissecting Saturday morning cartoons."

They all laughed.

She turned to me and gave me one of her looks. "And *you!*" she said. "Get the hell out of here and get on with your little life."

About the Author

Ten Nobodies (and their somebodies) is Martin Drapkin's second work of fiction, following *Now and at the Hour*. His third is *The Cat Tender*. *Poor Tom*, a novel published by HenschelHAUS in 2023, is his latest work of fiction. He's also a photographer, specializing in black-and-white street photographs and portraits of mothers and daughters. He and his wife, Erica, live in rural Cross Plains, Wisconsin, with several mildly neurotic rescue dogs.

For more information, please visit Marty's website, www.drapkinbooks.com

www.ingramcontent.com/pod-product-compliance
Lightning Source LLC
Chambersburg PA
CBHW071200260626
47162CB00003B/1114